Back to Me

Back to Me

Wanda B. Campbell

www.urbanchristianonline.com

Urban Books, LLC
97 N18th Street
Wyandanch, NY 11798

ISBN 13: 978-1-60162-679-0
ISBN 10: 1-60162-679-7

First Trade Paperback Printing November 2014
Printed in the United States of America

10 9 8 7 6 5 4 3 2 1

Distributed by Kensington Corp.
Submit Wholesale Orders to:
Kensington Publishing Corp.
C/O Penguin Group (USA) Inc.
Attention: Order Processing
405 Murray Hill Parkway
East Rutherford, NJ 07073-2316
Phone: 1-800-526-0275
Fax: 1-800-227-9604

Come now, and let us reason together, saith the Lord:
though your sins be as scarlet, they shall be
as white as snow; though they be red
like crimson, they shall be as wool.

Isaiah 1:18 (King James Version)

Acknowledgments

First and always, I give thanks to my Lord and Savior, Jesus Christ, for empowering me with the gift to write novels that not only entertain but also change lives. I wouldn't be on this journey without His favor and grace.

On May 14, 2014, I celebrated twenty-five years of marriage to my friend Craig Campbell, Sr. We have enjoyed the perfect marriage, one filled with joy and happiness, heartache and pain, triumphs and failures, broken promises and forgiveness. Through every twist and turn we've held on to our commitment, and I'm a better person for having you in my life.

Chantel, Jon, and Craig Jr., most days I sacrifice my comfort and desires to ensure that you have every possible opportunity to succeed, and not once have I regretted it. Often I don't agree with your choices and methods, but at the end of the day, after I finish fussing, Mama's got your back.

As always, I send much love to my Alameda Health Systems–Highland Campus family: Mary Wong, Alaina, Denise, Camilla, and Amy. You ladies are the best. Rhonda Roberts, Shenette Jones, Cassandra Maxwell, and Tyora Moody, thank you for taking the time. A special thanks goes to Wanda B. Campbell Readers & Supporters Facebook Group and Denise Langston. It's your dedication and unwavering support that motivate me to keep writing. And readers and book clubs everywhere, thank you for investing your time and resources in my novels.

Acknowledgments

I never close out without giving special thanks to Israel Houghton. Once again your music ministry has carried me through. Jesus is definitely at the center of it all, and He is *more than enough*.

Prologue

Paige placed the lighted vanilla-scented pillar candle on her nightstand. She stared at the flame momentarily, then opened the drawer and removed the envelope. When she purchased it, the envelope had a glossy finish. Thirteen years of tears and sweat had rendered the surface dull and the corners cracked. It wasn't much, but the photo inside was the only memento she had to commemorate the day that forever changed her life. Before her trembling fingers could untuck the flap, a steady stream of tears flowed down her cheeks and gathered under her chin.

Under the weight of the memory of that fateful day, Paige dropped to the floor beside her bed with the worn envelope in hand. The pain from her knees slamming against the hardwood floor was nothing compared to the piercing ache in her heart. If she could turn back the hands of time and do things differently, she would. She would do so many things differently if she could just go back and use the knowledge she now had in her old situations. No matter how hard she willed it, Paige couldn't go back and right her wrong. She had conceded long ago that the hole in her heart would remain there until the day she died. During this time of the year, Paige wished that day would come sooner rather than later.

She reached for the terry bath towel she'd placed on the bed, and wiped her face. She had learned long ago that the strongest tissue was too weak to handle her heavy tears. After partially drying her face, Paige summoned the strength to look at the one and only picture she had of her baby boy. It wasn't a good picture. The once white edges had yellowed with time, and the fuzzy black-and-white image was recognizable only by a trained professional eye. Still, Paige was grateful to have the sonographic image, considering the sonographer had gone against the clinic's protocol by giving it to her. The older woman had hoped to change Paige's mind but had failed. Thirteen years later the image was all Paige had left of the baby fetus she'd once carried. Although the baby's sex couldn't be determined at ten weeks' gestation, instinct had told Paige that the baby was a boy with her espresso skin and the father's hazel eyes. She'd secretly named him Jonathan.

"Why didn't I keep you?" she groaned, cradling the worn picture. "I am so sorry. I really did want you. I was just so selfish." As it did twelve years prior, the apology turned into sobs, which then transformed into a prayer of repentance. "God, I am so sorry for destroying the gift you gave me. Father, please forgive me and give me another chance. I promise I won't place my will above yours again. Just one more chance, and I promise to be a better person. I'll help everyone I can. I'll feed the hungry and help the homeless. I'll be faithful to church. I'll pay my tithes. . . ." Paige bargained with God until no words were left and only her sobs communicated the depth of her despair.

Chapter 1

Paige McDaniels unlocked the door to her North Oakland real estate office on Monday, at precisely 7:00 a.m. After stepping inside and flipping on the light switch, she set her briefcase on the reception desk and raced to deactivate the alarm system within the allotted time. As her fingers punched in the numeric code on the keypad, the previous night's tears threatened to return. No one in the office but Paige knew that the alarm code she'd chosen was her baby's due date. Although the office was empty and would remain that way for two more hours, before the arrival of her staff, Paige refused to shed more tears today. She had already lost a full night's rest and was depending on the double espresso she'd picked up from Starbucks on her way in to get her through the morning.

She swallowed the lump in her throat and relocked the office door. Before retrieving her briefcase, Paige surveyed the three-thousand-square-foot office space, which she owned the title to. "Father, I don't deserve this, but I do thank you. You've definitely ordered my steps."

When Paige graduated with a master's degree in business marketing from Stanford ten years ago, she'd no idea she would one day own the most prestigious and profitable independent real estate company in the Bay Area. She'd big plans to work for a Fortune 500 company, like Coca-Cola or Procter & Gamble. That changed when her parents listed their home for sale with a national real estate franchise and received less than satisfactory results.

After months of excuses from the Realtor, her parents ended up selling the house for less than it was worth and had to scale down their retirement plans.

The ordeal sparked a desire in Paige to learn as much as she could about real estate. Eventually, she stopped sending out her résumé for other positions and started studying for the state broker's exam. She passed on the first try and planned to use the license to keep family and close friends from experiencing the stress her parents had when they sold their home. One day, while stopped at a red light on her way to the post office to mail off a batch of résumés for positions open in real estate, a real estate office sign caught Paige's attention. To this day, she still couldn't explain what had attracted her to the stucco building, but once she stepped inside, Paige knew that was where she belonged. An extensive conversation with the owner served as confirmation.

The owner, a broker named Mr. Carrington, ran the business with his wife, but he was planning on retiring the following year and was looking for someone to take over the business since his children had moved to the East Coast. That day Paige stopped seeking a job with a Fortune 500 company and went to work at the real estate office. For twelve months Paige worked long days and weekends, soaking up everything she could about the business from Mr. Carrington. He complimented her often on her work, yet when he presented her with an offer to sell her the business, Paige was awestruck. The business was worth more than he was asking for it and included the building. With her family's encouragement and Mr. Carrington's creative and lenient financing terms, Paige took a chance and dove into the Bay Area's competitive and oftentimes cutthroat real estate world.

Through the years, Paige watched new offices sprout up overnight around Oakland and in the surrounding cities, especially during the real estate boom of the early 2000s. She then watched those same businesses close just as fast when the housing market fell. Her business, Highpoint Real Estate, wasn't unscathed by the bust, but the company managed to reinvent itself to adjust to the real estate climate. After a barrage of foreclosures and short sales, both Highpoint's assets and clientele increased, and the company added a property management division. Paige's personal assets also increased. Thanks to upside-down mortgages and short sales, she acquired two single-family homes and a fourplex. Paige appreciated God's favor on her life but would trade the material blessings for a chance to go back and right the wrong she committed thirteen years ago.

She walked past the eight workstations and thanked God that each of them was occupied by an honest and reliable agent. Not all of them were Christians, but they all had integrity and good morals. Only once in ten years had a complaint been filed against Highpoint with the CalBRE, and that case was dismissed without prejudice. Once inside her spacious office, she switched on the light and, with slow, deliberate steps, trudged into the room in which she spent more hours than she did in her bedroom.

Ten–hour workdays were the norm for Paige on most days. In addition to running her business, Paige taught a junior entrepreneur night class at the local high school on Monday evenings. She also attended Wednesday night Bible study, Thursday night choir rehearsal, and Friday night intercessory prayer clinic. Between attending to clients on Saturdays, Paige volunteered at the local food bank, where she created food packages. Sunday, which she considered her day of rest, included singing on praise and worship in all three worship services and visiting the sick and shut-ins in the afternoon with the home care ministry. Although she enjoyed working and serving, Paige often wondered if she was doing enough.

She booted her computer and waited for the strong brown liquid to work its magic while she checked her e-mail. Halfway through the double espresso and before 7:45 a.m., she finished returning e-mails and went over the agenda for the next junior entrepreneur class. She was just about to review the company's trust account when her cell phone rang. She hesitated briefly after reading the caller ID.

"I didn't expect to hear from you today," Paige stated without offering the caller a greeting. It was Tyson Stokes, her good friend and the man who had fathered her baby all those years ago.

"Why not?" Tyson asked, as if he found the statement absurd. "We're friends, and I remember what today is just as well as you do. I know this time of year is hard on you. I just wanted to check on you."

"How does your wife feel about you checking on me?" Paige didn't mean to sound bitter, because she really wasn't. When the unwanted pregnancy occurred, she and Tyson discovered they made much better friends than lovers. They made the decision together to end the pregnancy. He supported her through the ordeal, and like Paige, he spent years regretting that decision. Through the years they would encourage one another, but now Tyson had others to lean on and to fill the empty space. When he recently married and celebrated the birth of his daughter, Paige shared in his joy by attending both the wedding and the baby shower. God had given her friend a second chance, but not Paige.

"Come on, Paige. You know Reyna's not like that. In fact, she's sitting right here, nursing Destiny. I explained everything to her, and she understands."

"Hi, Paige," she heard her former employee say in the background and regretted the misplaced hostility.

"Tell Reyna I said hello." Paige paused. "I didn't mean anything by that comment. I'm really happy for you, I just wish . . . well, you know."

"Trust me, I do know. I just completely released the guilt last year. Hold on. It will get better."

Paige had heard those words so much in the past, she wasn't sure she believed them anymore, but she needed something to hold on to, especially today.

"I know. I just have to keep working and believing."

"That's good. Stay positive and do something nice for yourself today," Tyson suggested.

"I am. I'm working," she said with a slight sigh. She heard the baby crying in the background. "Thanks for checking on me, but you better go. I think your spoiled daughter wants your attention."

"Spoiled she is," Tyson said proudly. "Oh, one more thing before you go. Kev said to tell you he referred a colleague to you."

Another client was just what Paige needed in her already jam-packed schedule to keep her mind occupied. "Thanks. Now get back to your family." She hung up the phone without waiting for a reply and then gulped the now lukewarm espresso.

"The most important thing is to create a product our schoolmates will like," suggested Jasmine, a twelfth grader with green synthetic braids pulled back into a ponytail.

"We have to consider quality and value first," Seniyah countered.

Jasmine's lips twisted, and her neck rolled. "Who cares about quality and value? Our target market is high school students, and everybody knows high school kids don't care nothing about quality and value. If it's popular, we'll buy it."

"It could be toast on a stick," another girl added, "but if the right football player endorses it, the entire student body will walk around eating burnt toast attached to toothpicks and will swear up and down how cool it is."

"That may be," Seniyah pleaded, "but our business can't give validity to every stereotype about us. We should want our business to make a difference."

"We will make a difference." Jasmine paused for dramatic effect. "All the way to the bank," she hollered, then gave one of the girls a high five and laughed.

To keep from laughing along with the high-strung teenager, Paige shifted her stance, leaning against the podium, and glanced down at her watch.

"Everything isn't about money," Seniyah said, pouting.

"When you don't have any, it is." Jasmine's face twisted as she scanned up and down Seniyah's thick frame. "Based on those Goodwill specials you have on, your every thought should be about money. You should wake up in the middle of the night, screaming, 'Lawd, where is my money!'"

Seniyah sulked in the chair, while the other seven girls laughed.

"Let's focus." Paige regained control of the junior entrepreneur class before the lively discussion got out of hand. "Although they have different philosophies, Jasmine and Seniyah are both correct in their approach to business. The key, which can sometimes be difficult but is possible, is to balance quality and value with demand. Do you get my point?"

All the girls nodded except for Seniyah, who hung her head. Paige felt sorry for her. She couldn't admit it openly, but Seniyah was her favorite in the group. For a teenager, she had great business insight and was a 4.0 student with a sixteen hundred SAT score. In four months Seniyah would graduate from high school at the top of her class, and then she would be off to Stanford on a full scholarship. Not bad for a girl from the roughest and most violent neighborhood in Oakland, a place known as the "killing ground." She was the youngest of six children and would be the first sibling to graduate high school.

Jasmine's home life wasn't much better, but thanks to her older brother, who specialized in street pharmaceuticals, Jasmine could afford the latest fashion trends and had a car. The green and yellow hair would make one think she wasn't too bright and didn't have any goals that didn't include acrylic nails and extensions. Paige thought that very thing until Jasmine approached her after the first class session and shared her five-year and ten-year plans. If Jasmine reached her goals, she'd own a chain of salon–child-care centers by the time she was thirty.

Paige walked over to Jasmine. "Let me explain further," she said, pointing at Jasmine's green hair. "Colored hair is in high demand. I've seen adults, as well as teenagers, with every color of the rainbow on their heads. The demand is there. The challenge is to produce a high-quality product that looks natural—something that doesn't make your hair frizz and that's easy to manage. Maybe a grade you can curl and not just braid."

"I get it." Jasmine looked perplexed, like she was in deep thought.

Seniyah finally looked up. "That's what I was trying to say."

"Well, you didn't say it right," Jasmine snapped.

Paige spoke up before more insults flew. "Now that we have an understanding, let's create our product."

Forty-five minutes and two interventions later, Paige jumped up from the small school desk, grinning like a proud mother instead of the community volunteer she was. After brainstorming and debating, the ladies had agreed unanimously on a business name and had decided to create and sell a product that would not only make their business profitable but would help others as well. DWAP, or Divas with a Plan, would make and sell beaded necklaces. A percentage from each sale would go into a fund to purchase blankets for the local shelter to distribute.

"Praise God! I am so proud of you all." Paige raised her arms and looked toward the ceiling. "And I know He is proud too. This venture can't help but be blessed. All we need is a little faith and hard work and DWAP will be—"

"Uh, Miss Paige," Jasmine interrupted, "have you forgotten that rule about keeping religion out of public schools? You can't be talkin' about God up in here. A teacher or an assistant principal might hear you and shut the program down. I believe in God like you do, but you need to wait till Sunday to catch the spirit. I need this program to help me learn the basics for my future hair and child-care franchises."

Paige's jaw fell.

"Isn't Jesus the same yesterday, today, and forever?" Jasmine stated more than questioned.

Paige nodded, still trying to find the words to address the fact that Jasmine had squelched her praise.

"Then He'll receive your praise on Sunday at church."

The others, including Seniyah, laughed at Jasmine's rebuke.

"I guess you're right," Paige answered, more embarrassed than offended. She walked to the blackboard and picked up some chalk and moved on to the next subject. "Let's identify our suppliers."

"That's right. Let's keep it moving. I have to stop by the beauty supply store after this," Jasmine announced.

Paige swallowed the smart comeback she had for the young lady with green hair. Paige was used to being in control. She directed conversations and instructed others and assigned tasks. Jasmine might have the body of a grown woman, but she wasn't an adult. Paige was the adult/mentor, and it was her responsibility to act like one. *Father, show me how to handle your child,* she prayed inwardly.

She was still praying twenty minutes later, when the session ended, and resisted the urge to ask the girls to join hands in a circle for a closing prayer. She settled on humming as she packed her materials away and walked to her car. She increased the volume on the satellite radio station and sang the words to the number one gospel song in the nation as she exited the faculty parking lot. The words to the chorus hung in the air once she spotted Seniyah walking down the street alone. Normally, her star student caught the bus.

She pulled alongside the curb and stopped. "Seniyah," Paige called before the power window fully descended. "What are you doing?" When Seniyah didn't answer, Paige shifted the gear into the park position and leaned toward the passenger window. "I said, 'What are you doing?'" This time she yelled the question.

Seniyah shook her head and pointed at her ears, indicating that the music was too loud.

"Oh," Paige mouthed and then adjusted the volume using the controls on the steering wheel and rephrased the original question. "It's starting to get dark. Why are you walking and not taking the bus?"

Seniyah repositioned her backpack strap on her shoulder. "I felt like walking. It's not too far."

"But it's late," Paige began, then stopped. For the first time she really studied the young lady she'd grown so fond of. Seniyah was about five feet, six inches tall. Her thick, wavy brown hair, which was pulled back and held together by a brown clip, matched the freckles sprinkled on her vanilla latte-colored face. Seniyah wasn't what her peers would consider pretty. She wasn't thin, and her clothing didn't complement her thick size, but Seniyah's determination to succeed reminded Paige of herself back in the day.

Chances were that Seniyah didn't have enough change to cover the bus fare, but Paige didn't want to crush her pride by asking.

"Get in, and I'll drive you. I'm going that way." *Father, forgive me,* she thought, repenting for the half-truth she'd just told. Paige had planned on driving through Seniyah's neighborhood on the way to the food bank on Saturday morning, but not tonight.

Seniyah's head jerked from left to right. She turned and leaned around, as if looking for someone, until her eyes settled on something across the street.

"No thank you, Miss Paige. I h-have to go," Seniyah stammered, then took off in the opposite direction.

By the time Paige repositioned herself in the driver's seat and looked across the street, whatever or whoever had captivated Seniyah's attention was gone.

Chapter 2

On Tuesday morning Paige dragged herself into the office, more tired than the day before. This morning her overfatigued body required a venti double espresso from Starbucks. Over the years Paige had patronized the coffee chain so much that the company had issued her a gold gift card with her name engraved on it. For an additional stimulant, Paige cashed in her reward points for a chocolate brownie.

She'd every intention of going straight home after the junior entrepreneur class last night and catching up on some much-needed rest, but the demons from her past had manifested themselves in her dreams and had robbed her of tranquility. In times past, the days leading up to the procedure's anniversary date were torture. Once the day was over, Paige's life returned to what she considered normal—endless hours of serving the Lord and her community. Along with the cries of her aborted fetus, last night's nightmares had included a new face—Seniyah's. Paige attributed the intrusion to the teenager's uncharacteristic behavior after class, and to nothing more.

She dropped her leather briefcase beside her desk and then flopped into the leather chair she loved so much and sipped her venti espresso. The clock on the wall read 7:30 a.m.—thirty minutes later than her usual arrival time, and yet she still had ninety minutes of solace left before the agents would began trickling in. She booted her computer and viewed her calendar. With only four listing appointments scheduled, Paige could plan to end the workday at five o'clock and head straight home. Tuesdays were her only free night, and she planned to take full advantage this evening by catching up on the sleep the past had stolen from her last night.

Two hours later, enjoying songs of worship through the computer speakers, Paige was still buzzing from the dark liquid and the brownie. Fatigue was long forgotten as she balanced the company's trust account and then reviewed the presentation folders for the potential listing clients. She didn't doubt for a second that she'd get each home owner to sign on the dotted line. She already had eager and qualified buyers ready to purchase a home in each of the neighborhoods. Thanks to the Bay Area's high home values, the 6 percent commission from the transactions would garner her enough income to cover household expenses and contribute to her savings for at least a year.

"Thank you, Jesus," she whispered. "You always take good care of me. If you would just give me . . ." The Sister Sledge "We Are Family" ringtone ended her plea.

"Hey, Ma," Paige sang into the phone. "How was the trip?"

Paige had shared her success by sending her parents on a thirteen-day Alaska and Canada cruise for their thirty-fifth wedding anniversary. Or what her mother referred to as their fortieth anniversary, since she had lived with Paige's father for five years and had birthed two children before he finally popped the question. In her father's version, he had to get married after Paige's mother—pregnant with their third child—showed up at his job with his clothes stuffed into garbage bags, demanding that he either make an honest woman out of her or move out. Since he didn't have anywhere to go, he took the remainder of the day off and went down to the county courthouse and married his sweetie pie. Thirty-five years later, Paige's father still referred to her mother by that endearing term. Paige prayed endlessly to one day experience half the love her parents shared.

"The cruise was wonderful! Thank you so much. You are such a good daughter. Alaska was beautiful, and your father and I played around like we did before y'all were born." Her mother giggled. "After all this time, that man is still a hot mess."

Paige joined in her mother's joy. "I'm so glad you had a good time. You and Daddy deserve it after all the sacrifices you made for us through the years." Her parents had worked for thirty years to maintain a stable home in the suburbs and to put Paige, her older brother, and her younger sister through college.

"Did you bring me something back?" Paige asked to sidetrack her mother and prevent her from showering her with more accolades. Humility was a quality that Paige practiced daily, believing that if she humbled herself, God would exalt her, or at least give her the desires of her heart.

"Of course, I got T-shirts and magnets and key chains for everyone I know. If I could have stuffed one into my suitcase and got through the security checkpoint, I would have brought you back one of them Alaskan men." Her mother's laughter filled her ear. "There sure are some fine men up there, and you can use something or someone to occupy your time."

"Mama!" Paige exclaimed. "How can you say that? You know I'm saved."

Her mother smirked. "I know the Lord too, but I'm smart enough to know Jesus and that real estate office won't keep you warm at night or make you sweat out a new hairdo."

"Ma, I'm getting off the phone now. Kiss Daddy for me." Paige disconnected the call before her mother went into her "When are you going to get a man?" speech. She'd heard that mantra enough over the years, especially since her younger sister married and had two children.

Although her parents professed salvation, from Paige's viewpoint they were too "worldly." Whereas Paige attended church practically every time the doors opened, her parents limited their attendance to the 8 a.m. service on Sunday. They danced and listened to R & B music and didn't see anything wrong with a glass of wine with dinner. Paige attributed their casual approach to Christianity to the fact that they were new converts, having joined the church just two years prior. Her parents just didn't understand that she was totally committed to the church and to doing the work of the Lord. She had to be; it was her only chance to right her wrong.

Paige stood and walked the length of her mahogany desk. After sitting for two hours, a good stretch was in order. She was no longer sleepy, but her muscles remained stiff. With her door only slightly ajar, she enjoyed enough privacy to do some of the stretches she'd learned back in her high school and college track days. As a symbol of modesty, Paige routinely wore her relaxed, past-shoulder-length hair pulled back into a bun or a ponytail and held it in place with a gold clip. Freedom from flowing hair allowed her to drop easily onto the carpeted floor and into a cat stretch.

While on her hands and knees, Paige closed her eyes, slowly let her back and abdomen sag toward the floor, and then arched her back, as if she were trying to pull her abdomen toward the ceiling.

"Excuse me, miss," a deep voice interrupted before she could return her body to the starting position.

Paige lost her concentration and collapsed facedown on the floor.

"Sorry, miss. I didn't mean to startle you." The gentleman stepped over her leg and reached down to help her up. "But I didn't see anyone out front. I heard music coming from this direction and—"

"How did you get in here?" she snapped and slapped his hand away.

The man stepped back and folded his arms. "Through the front door," he answered, and Paige didn't miss the smug expression or the sarcasm.

After maneuvering herself upright, Paige used her hands to smooth her skirt and blouse and prayed the stranger wasn't a future client. That way she wouldn't have to see him again and be reminded that he'd caught her in an awkward position.

"I repeat, how did you get in here?" Paige asked, planting her fist against her waist. "The office doesn't open for another"—she paused and looked up at the wall clock—"fifteen minutes."

"That may be, but the front door is unlocked and the lights are on. In western civilization that usually means an establishment is open for business."

"Western etiquette also dictates that one should announce oneself when entering a place of business and then wait to be invited into the confines of my office," Paige snapped back, which was completely out of character for her, but she was embarrassed. Normally, it was her smile that greeted people, not her rear end.

"This is *your* office?"

Paige folded her arms and stuck her chin out proudly, "Yes. This is *my* office and *my* building." She glared at the intruder as he unfolded his arms and leaned around her and read the gold-trimmed nameplate on the desk. That was when she noticed the chiseled biceps and pectorals outlined in the Under Armour long-sleeved crewneck shirt. The slightly hairy, bulging quadriceps weren't bad, either.

"You're Paige McDaniels?" he asked incredulously.

"Are you hard of hearing as well?" she asked after a silent rebuke for admiring the stranger's body.

"Wow," he said, facing her again. "You're Paige Mc-Daniels," he repeated, this time rubbing his chin.

The brief but thorough visual inspection made Paige uncomfortable, causing her to second-guess her modest attire.

"Now that you know my name, would you mind telling me who you are and what you're doing in my office so early in the morning? Uninvited, I might add."

The stranger offered her a full smile and in a firm tone said, "I am a man who's particular about where I spend my money, and I chose not to patronize a place of business whose owner is rude and insulting. Even if she's beautiful and has a nice rear end."

Paige gasped.

"Have a good day, Miss McDaniels."

Paige's mouth gaped as the stranger disappeared down the hall and then walked out of the building. What had just happened? She had never lost a potential client due to a bad attitude, and under no circumstance would she insult someone she'd never met before. Somehow she managed to do both while listening to worship music. "I'll have to fast an extra day for this one," she mumbled on the way back to her seat.

Chapter 3

Paige paused long enough to wipe perspiration from her forehead, using the back of her hand. Normally, while bagging food, she didn't exert so much energy, but with the bad economy and the high unemployment rate, the food bank was experiencing an increase in clients. The longer lines caused Paige to move twice as fast to keep up with the demand. Too busy to slip a printed invite to her church inside each bag, Paige said a quick prayer over each bag before placing it in the rotation for handing out.

Praying the strangers in need would be able to stretch the food bags until their next pay cycle had to gain Paige some atonement for her attitude the past three days. She'd prayed, fasted, and read the Bible every day, but none of that had yielded her a peaceful night's rest. Wednesday night Bible study and the all-night intercessory prayer hadn't removed the guilt she felt over uncharacteristically snapping at everyone in her office for things as minor as forgetting to turn off the conference room light. This morning, as she'd done every day since receiving salvation, Paige promised God she wouldn't do anything to bring shame to the kingdom.

"I tell you, these lines get longer every week," the lady working next to Paige stated as they removed the packaging from a case of pasta sauce. "If it weren't for God's grace, I'd be standing on the other side."

Paige read the name tag on the left side of the woman's chest. "Loraine, isn't that the truth." Paige paused momentarily to observe those on the opposite side of the partition, who were waiting for food. Nowadays, the "needy" weren't so easy to spot. With the bad economy, need no longer equated to dirty, smelly clothing, matted hair, and worn-down shoes. A good portion of those in line appeared to be working-class people who just so happened to come up short at the end of every month.

Her eyes zeroed in on two people who she assumed were a mother and her teenage son, and for a split second, jealousy gripped her. The mother appeared to be scolding her son, who seemed embarrassed to be there. She would trade in all her success for a chance to stand in any line with her son, to argue with him about homework and expensive tennis shoes, or even about cleaning his room.

Loraine's tap on her shoulder brought Paige's focus back to the task at hand. "We'd better move faster. This line is multiplying."

Paige shook her head to clear it. She had to stay focused if she wanted to keep from being trampled. The people in line looked as if they would pounce on her any second for the bag of groceries. With renewed energy, she grabbed two five-pound bags of potatoes and stuffed them inside two empty bags. Several bags later, Paige became distracted again.

"Hello, Miss Paige."

She knew that voice. After stuffing cabbage and a bag of rice inside a bag, Paige turned around and looked into the eyes of her prized student.

"Seniyah? What are you doing here?" As soon as the words left her mouth, Paige regretted them. Given her home dynamics, if anyone needed free groceries, it was Seniyah. Paige felt the young girl's embarrassment when her shoulders slumped and her head dropped. "I'm so sorry. I didn't mean to embarrass you. I'm surprised to see you, that's all."

"My mother couldn't make it today, so I had to come." Seniyah used her arms to close her worn jacket with the missing buttons but didn't raise her head.

Paige's heart went out to the young girl. More than likely, Seniyah needed the groceries to keep from starving next week. As hard as she tried to understand Seniyah's hardship, Paige couldn't fully comprehend it. Her father had made sure their family never went without. Paige wiped sweat beads from her forehead, mentally tuned out the chaos around her, and studied the young woman. Something wasn't right. Seniyah's wavy hair was more unkempt than normal, and her eyes appeared glossy.

"Are you feeling all right?" Paige asked while gently placing an arm around the girl's shoulders.

Seniyah lifted her head, but her eyes were focused on the volunteers behind Paige. "I'm just tired. It's been a long morning."

"Don't I know it." Paige patted her shoulder and then went to select a bag for her. Before handing Seniyah the bag, she added an additional bag of rice and a box of cereal.

"Thank you," Seniyah said, balancing the bag against her hip and finally making eye contact.

"Anytime." Paige smiled as an idea formed in her mind. She would try to minister to Seniyah. "If you can stick around for about forty-five minutes, we can go and have lunch, and then I'll drive you home."

Seniyah's head shook almost violently. "No, thank you, Miss Paige. I can walk. It's not that far. I have a lot of work to do around the house. Plus, I have homework. And I still have to do a marketing plan for DWAP before Monday's session." Her words ran together, and Paige assumed Seniyah was too embarrassed about her appearance to hang out.

"Well, maybe next time," Paige said, acquiescing, although she was disappointed. She would have loved to spend some uninterrupted time mentoring Seniyah. There were so many things she could teach her to prepare her for college. "Keeping those grades up is your number one priority. Stanford is waiting." Paige beamed with pride.

Loraine cleared her throat.

"I have to get back to work. I'll see you on Monday," Paige told Seniyah.

"Sure," Seniyah answered hurriedly and then rushed away.

"Call me if you need my help," Paige called after her, but Seniyah had disappeared in the sea of the less fortunate. She shrugged off the quick dismissal and dove back into her work.

Fifteen minutes later, when the next person she recognized approached, Paige nearly dropped a sack of potatoes on her foot.

"Let me help you with that," the gentleman offered and at the same time bent down and picked up the potatoes. "I need two bags please," he announced once he was upright.

Paige's mouth hung open as she fixated on the stranger who had barged into her office four days ago and had left her feeling like an idiot. She hadn't noticed the goatee and the square chin at their first meeting. He couldn't have been wearing that citrus-scented fragrance, either; surely she would have noticed that. He looked right through Paige as if she wasn't there.

"Where would you like me to set these?" he asked, holding up the sack of potatoes.

"Since you need two bags, you can keep those," Loraine said when Paige didn't respond readily.

"Thank you, miss."

Paige stood back and watched Loraine blush and pat her hair and then straighten her clothing. In a matter of seconds the man with the light brown skin and black, wavy hair had Loraine acting like a teenager. Paige shook her head in disgust.

"What are you doing here?" Paige failed to hide the irritation in her tone. Certainly this man with the perfect set of ultra-white, straight teeth and the designer jeans, not to mention the leather jacket, wasn't in need of free groceries.

The man offered a smirk instead of a smile. "Miss McDaniels, we meet again. You're not a morning or an afternoon person. Let's plan our next chance meeting at night. Maybe your manners will kick in by then."

"Ouch!" Loraine said and then resumed stuffing bags.

Paige refused to allow someone who was taking from those who really needed assistance to insult her. "Don't worry about my manners. At least I don't steal from the needy." She felt a healthy dose of satisfaction when the smile fell from his face.

He gestured for the guy behind him to go in front of him. "So you think I'm a thief because I asked for two bags?"

Paige placed a completed bag on the table in front of him. "The fact that you're in this line at all is sinful. Your jeans cost more than most of the people in this neighborhood make in a month. A few days ago you waltz into my business, claiming to have money to burn. And now you're in the free food line?" Paige folded her arms and cocked her head to the side. "Sounds like stealing from the poor to me."

"You are a real piece of work." He shook his head. "And just think, you do all this in the name of the Lord. I hate to think how you would act if you didn't know Jesus."

Paige paused, then placed the second bag on the table. "What is that supposed to mean?"

He balanced both bags in his arms before answering. "It's simple. When you pick up that big Bible I know you have at home, try reading Matthew chapter seven, verse one, while listening to that worship music. Then get a good dictionary to break down the words for you. Then maybe you can *live* the Word and not just read it."

Paige's cheeks burned with anger. "Just what do you know about the Word?" she barked, forgetting she was in a building filled with people she was supposed to be helping.

"Obviously, a lot more than you."

As she watched the stranger walk away, Paige's mouth hung open for the second time that day.

Chapter 4

Ever since she joined the praise and worship ministry, Sunday had been Paige's favorite day of the week. She began the day with early morning prayers and then meditation. This morning her prayer list included not only her family and close acquaintances, but also Seniyah. Once again, the young girl had invaded her dreams, but Paige had been able to get six hours of uninterrupted rest. Paige took that as a sign for her to help the girl, and before tomorrow's meeting with DWAP, she was going to buy her a new coat. She reasoned that that was what Jesus wanted her to do, since she had the means to do it.

The harsh words that the stranger/thief had spoken to Paige still irked her. How dare he accuse her of being a hearer of the Word and not a doer? Her comprehension was just fine. That was why she was handing out food to the poor in the first place. She'd never understand why sinners liked to throw the Word around when they're caught doing wrong. She prayed for nearly everyone she knew, but not for him.

She arrived at Restoration Ministries in time to join in with the intercessory prayer ministry before the start of the 8:00 a.m. service. As she walked through the parking lot, Paige once again thanked God for sending her to a wonderful church. Her previous church had had a lot of ideas on paper, but there had not been much action when it came to outreach and spreading the good news of the kingdom. Restoration Ministries had multiple active outreach ministries and a pastor who was gifted and able to teach the gospel to the young and the old, to the rich and the poor, and to the educated and the uneducated. Not once did she feel the need to question whether her tithe was being put to good use.

She hurried down the long aisle and dropped her jacket and purse on the pew nearest the front. Before she dropped to her knees, she glimpsed Mother Scott giving her a disapproving glare. Paige shrugged it off for now, knowing she'd get to the motive behind it later. Mother Scott was well known for voicing her opinions.

At the conclusion of intercessory prayer, Paige rushed back to the music room and secured her purse and jacket in the one of the lockers. Once again, she prayed, this time with the music ministry, for the Lord to anoint her voice to destroy every yoke and to lift every heavy burden. Then she walked onto the platform, totally depending on God's power to perform miracles in the life of everyone in attendance. Paige closed her eyes and listened for her cue, and then, with the passion she kept reserved for her Savior, she belted out the words to her favorite worship song. Jesus was definitely the lover of her soul. For sure He had taken her from the miry clay and had set her feet upon a rock. She loved Jesus, and she was doing all she could so that He would love her enough to grant her the family she desperately wanted. She needed Him to look beyond her faults and fulfill her needs.

Tears dripped from her chin as the words to the last stanza flowed a cappella in her alto voice. Paige took advantage of the praise that followed by dropping to her knees on the platform and worshipping with raised hands. By the time she composed herself, the praise and worship ministry had moved on to an uplifting song about the joy of the Lord. She swayed and sang, all the while wishing she possessed the joy she sang about.

No sooner had Pastor Drake finished the benediction for the first service than Mother Scott and First Lady Drake accosted her.

"Paige, didn't I—," Mother Scott began, but First Lady Drake butted in.

"You go easy on her, Scott. She's new at this."

"Oh, Lord, what did I do now?" Paige grumbled and then watched Mother Scott's facial expression change from annoyance to compassion. The petite woman even placed her bony arm around Paige's shoulder.

"Paige, sweetheart, did you forget our little conversation the other night?"

She knew Mother Scott well enough to know the pleasantries were a prelude to a tongue-lashing. Paige, in fact, had forgotten her and the first lady's rebuke at the all-night intercessory prayer session, because she considered the warning nonsense. What Christian would tell a single woman that she spent too much time at church? The concept seemed ludicrous to Paige.

"No, Mother, I didn't forget," she answered while reaching for her Bible. "I just don't agree." She offered a smile to soften her words.

Mothers Scott's eyebrows furrowed, and her arm slipped from Paige's shoulder. "So, you think we don't know what we're talking about?" She pointed toward the first lady.

Paige frantically scanned the now half-empty sanctuary for someone to come to her rescue and found no one. She had learned from watching others that the best way to oppose the praying duo was not to.

"That's not what I'm saying." Paige struggled to come up with an answer that wasn't a lie or that wouldn't come across as disrespectful. "I just—"

"Then please explain," First Lady Drake said, jumping in.

After clearing her throat, Paige continued. "Mothers, I know you mean well, but I have to follow what the scripture says and not yield to what others think I should be doing."

"Excuse me?" Mother Scott replied.

Paige almost lost her courage when Mother Scott's neck rolled. "Jesus himself said we must work while it is day, because when night comes, no one can work."

The mothers cocked their heads and stared at one another and then turned back to Paige.

"Baby," First Lady Drake began, "if you're going to quote scripture, take the time to learn the context in which it is given."

"And, sweetheart, I know you think you're super saved and all, but you ain't Jesus," Mother Scott added. "Even He knew when to rest. You spend more time in this church than the janitor. Just in case you haven't read the scripture yet, you can't make it to heaven by working yourself to death in the church."

Paige's cheeks burned as if she'd been slapped, but she had learned from Tyson that it was useless to disagree with them.

"Like we told you Friday night," First Lady Drake continued, "you need to pray and ask God what it is that He wants you to do in the kingdom. Every good work is not a God work, if it's not what He has planned for your life. If you're not careful, you're going to burn yourself out and become resentful."

"And another thing . . ." Mother Scott wagged a finger in Paige's face. "You need to check your motives for all this kingdom work you call yourself doing."

"What do y-you mean?" Paige stuttered, glad they were now alone in the sanctuary. After she led the congregation in worship, no one needed to see her lose her temper when confronting two old women whom she considered nosy. "I'm saved. I'm supposed to work in the church and help the less fortunate."

Both mothers shook their heads.

"You have so much to learn," Mother Scott said, and the first lady nodded in agreement. "We'll be praying for you, but in the meantime, you need to seek the Lord for His will for your life."

The prayer warriors fell to their knees and began the intercessory prayer for the next service, while Paige stormed from the sanctuary and took refuge in the confines of a bathroom stall, where she cried her eyes out.

Tyson and his best friend, Kevin, had assured her that despite their abrasiveness, the mothers were sincere and harmless, but right now Paige didn't agree with their assessment. She'd heard how they'd help Reyna and Kevin's wife, Marlissa, overcome their issues, but she considered herself on a different level than they were. Reyna and Marlissa had both struggled with alcoholism and traumatic childhoods, but she had not. Paige was doing everything she could think of to stay holy before God. How could God not be pleased with her efforts?

And why for the second consecutive day had her understanding of the scriptures been questioned? Neither the supposedly saintly mothers nor the arrogant stranger in designer jeans knew how many hours she'd spent reading scriptures and commentaries to learn about God. No one but God knew all the tears she'd cried, especially during the past week. How dare anyone judge her? How did a day that had started so well go so wrong? It wasn't even noon yet.

The sound of the bathroom door opening ended Paige's pity party. In record speed Paige grabbed tissue from the dispenser and wiped her face, then blew her nose and flushed the paper down the toilet. With her palms, she smoothed her hair and her skirt. Before opening the stall door, she leaned against the frame. *Lord, please help me. I can't continue like this.*

"Good morning, Sister Paige. How are you today?" a congregant greeted her at the sink.

"Blessed and highly favored," she responded with a smile and then headed back to the sanctuary to prepare for the next service.

Chapter 5

Paige slammed on the brakes to keep from hitting two students who were walking leisurely through the school's parking lot. Thanks to long lines and too few cashiers at the national coat retailer chain, she had only ten minutes before the start of the DWAP meeting.

"Sorry," she yelled out the car window and then gasped when the girl with the manicured nails made an offensive gesture. "Father, forgive her," she whispered, then pulled into a parking spot at an appropriate speed.

Paige liked to arrive early and spiritually prepare for the girls. After a typical Monday of writing offers and counterproposals, signings at the title company, and imbibing two espressos, Paige needed at least a few minutes to wind down before meeting the rambunctious group. A respite was not in the cards for Paige today.

Paige opened the door to the classroom and found the girls already there. Under Jasmine's direction, the girls had an assembly line going. Beads of every color in the rainbow sat in clear plastic bowls that lined the table. Rolls of stretch cord were stacked at one end of the table. They even had scissors and pliers ready for use. Paige stood in the doorway with her mouth open and her arms filled with bags of the supplies she'd purchased.

"Oh, hey, Miss Paige," Jasmine greeted her over the shoulder when she finally noticed her. "We already got started. The craft store had a clearance sale this weekend, so I had my brother give me some money to buy start-up supplies." Jasmine gestured toward the mound of empty plastic bags and boxes. "We all watched YouTube and learned how to make the necklaces." Her eyes traveled to Paige's bags. "We can use what you bought when we run out."

Paige stepped completely inside the room and smiled to conceal her disappointment. "Sure." She had thought she'd show the girls how to bargain shop and organize production. Turned out the girls didn't need her help.

Jasmine took the supplies from her without waiting for Paige to offer them. "Why don't you review our marketing plans while we work?"

Jasmine's suggestion sounded more like an order. Paige considered reminding Jasmine that she was in charge of the group, not her, but then she remembered her roles of volunteer and mentor. Her job was to guide them, not baby them.

"Sounds good," Paige conceded and sat down at a table in the back of the room.

Before Paige could settle in, Jasmine dropped a mini stack of file folders on the table in front of her. One by one, Paige reviewed and made comments on each girl's strategy. Every so often, she'd glance up to see the girls' process. By the time she finished reviewing the girls' marketing plans, DWAP had enough inventory to start taking orders. She restacked the folders and noticed there were seven instead of eight. That was when she looked up and realized her star student wasn't present.

"Where's Seniyah?" she asked, posing the question to no one in particular.

Jasmine smacked her lips at the same time her neck rolled. "She's late, and if she doesn't show up soon, we're going to vote her out of the group. She missed the shopping trip this weekend and the YouTube training class, and now she's late."

"I'm sure she has a good reason for not showing up," Paige replied, intent on calming Jasmine down.

"I don't care what the reason is. We all have issues and problems," Jasmine said. "It's not fair for us to do all the work. She's the one riding off to Stanford. She's supposed to be the smart one, anyway."

Several girls grunted in agreement.

"You're all smart," Paige said, correcting her. "You're just traveling in different directions." She looked at Jasmine, who was counting beads. "There is nothing wrong with starting out at a community college."

Although it shouldn't have, Jasmine's lack of compassion surprised Paige. Why couldn't Jasmine understand that not everyone had a brother with a thriving street pharmaceutical business to solve their problems?

"I know ain't nothing wrong with it, and the financial aid check ain't bad, either. I know because my brother gets one every semester."

Paige's head snapped up from admiring a necklace.

Jasmine went on to explain. "With that money, I can buy hair dryers."

"Your brother receives financial aid?" Paige asked incredulously. "Why? He's not in school."

True to form, Jasmine rolled her eyes and smacked her lips. "Of course he does. We ain't rich. And he does enroll every semester and does go to class." She paused. "Until the check comes."

Paige placed the necklace back in the pile for final inspection. "I didn't mean to imply you're rich," she said, fumbling for words. "It's just that your brother doesn't strike me as the school type. I didn't think he'd be interested in school."

Jasmine's face relaxed. "Why not?"

"Well, because, he . . ." Paige let the words hang when she noticed that seven sets of eyes had zeroed in on her mouth. How could she answer truthfully without offending not only Jasmine, but also everyone else in the room?

"You mean because he sells on the street?" Jasmine asked, finishing her sentence for her.

"Well, I—I heard . . ." Paige replied, stumbling. She fell silent when Jasmine laughed in her face.

"Your mouth is too holy to say *drug dealer* or *street pharmacist*."

The other girls joined in Jasmine's laughter.

"Well, that's what he is," Jasmine asserted. "Everybody knows it. But he did go to school to learn about business. That's how he started dealing in the first place. He saw how much money his classmates were making by selling to professors and other students, and he decided he could make money being a lifetime student with a hustle on the side and not have to pay taxes."

Paige's jaw dropped.

"Now he stays in school because that's his main customer base. And he's learning how to manage his money." Jasmine stepped closer to Paige, rolling her neck as she spoke. "See, Miss Paige, book knowledge isn't the only thing you can learn up at the college." Jasmine's lips smacked at the same time that she pivoted her feet and whirled around Paige. She headed toward the assembly line, where she exchanged high fives with the other girls.

Paige attempted to collapse into the seat in front of a student desk, but the small furniture couldn't accommodate her long frame. She settled for walking around the perimeter of the room and rubbing her forehead. Hearing about using school as an excuse to sell illegal substances was enough to give her a fresh migraine. And Jasmine had made it sound so normal.

"Miss Paige, are you all right?"

Paige, along with the other girls, looked in the direction of the voice. Seniyah stood in the doorway, wearing jeans and a baggy shirt.

Instantly, Paige's headache began to subside. Her favorite student had arrived. It didn't matter that she was nearly half an hour late or that grease stains decorated her sweatshirt. At least the girl had common sense and was on the right path.

"It's about time you got here," Jasmine responded before Paige could answer. "I hope you don't think we're going to do all the work while you do nothing." With rolling eyes, she circled Seniyah. "And where is your backpack? I know you don't have your marketing plan tucked under that greasy shirt."

At the snickers, Seniyah's head dropped. "I didn't get to finish. I had something to take care of."

"What?" Paige and Jasmine asked almost simultaneously, but Jasmine also snapped her neck and rolled her eyes.

"I don't understand," Paige said while rubbing her forehead. The migraine was back. "You said you were going home to work on it when I saw you on Saturday."

"Oh, so now y'all hangin' out? I know she's your favorite and all, but we could all use some help. We all tryin' to get out the hood." Jasmine shook her head and then stomped over to the other girls, whose facial expressions bore just as much attitude as Jasmine exhibited.

"You d-don't understand. It's n-not what you think." Paige found herself stuttering once again. She couldn't reveal that she'd seen Seniyah in the free food line. She couldn't have the girls thinking she favored one over the other, either, even if that were the case. "We weren't hanging out. I ran into her while I was working," she explained.

Jasmine smirked, and the girls cosigned with "Uh-huh."

"That's all it was," Seniyah said, trying to reassure them. "I was taking care of business for my mother when

I bumped into her. I didn't receive any special treatment. Miss Paige treats us all the same."

"That's right. I'm equally invested in each of you. I want to see all of you succeed," Paige lied, trying to figure out a way to explain the wool coat she had for Seniyah in the trunk of her car. She walked to the front of the room and stood next to the chalkboard. "Come on, ladies," she said, attempting to finally gain control of the class before things got further out of hand. "Let's take a break from production and decide on a marketing strategy."

The girls didn't object verbally, but each one eyed Seniyah with distain.

"First, I want to commend each of you on completing a marketing plan." She paused and turned to Seniyah. "You have my business card. You can e-mail me yours tomorrow morning," she said, more to pacify the other girls than to rebuke Seniyah. "All of you have great ideas that can take DWAP beyond this twelve-week class. With some guidance, I can see a sustainable business in the near future."

Paige noted that all the girls, except Seniyah, cheered and exchanged high fives, but she didn't comment. Her favoritism had caused enough friction for one night.

Forty-five minutes later, the class ended. While she was running through the parking lot, Paige yelled, "Seniyah, wait." The short sprint would have been easy if she weren't wearing boots with three-inch heels. Seniyah stopped and spun around. Even under the dim lights in the parking lot, Paige could see the weariness on the teenager's face. "I have something to say to you," she said between huffs.

Seniyah cowered, as if she expected to be reprimanded for not completing her assignment. "What did I do now?"

Once again, Paige's heart ached for the young girl. She was obviously accustomed to negative treatment. "Nothing. Follow me to my car. I want to give you something you need." With a smile Paige assured her everything was fine and then nudged Seniyah in the opposite direction.

With every step toward her car, Paige prayed for Seniyah—for everything from her basic needs to her self-confidence. If she was going to succeed at Stanford, she needed to believe she belonged there just as much as the students from rich families. She also needed to speak with Seniyah about her appearance and effective communication skills, but tonight wasn't the time for that.

Seniyah reached the car just as Paige pulled the designer black wool coat from the trunk. She thrust it at her. "What do you think?" As always when she did the Lord's work, Paige's expectations were great. The style wasn't what teenagers in the inner city favored, and the wool didn't exactly go with sweats, but the coat would keep her warm. "Well?" Paige said when Seniyah didn't respond with the enthusiasm Paige had expected.

Seniyah glanced over her shoulder before saying, "It's nice, Miss Paige, but you didn't have to buy me a coat. I have a jacket."

Paige heard the embarrassment in her voice. Even though she was poor, Seniyah had her pride. "I know," she said, remembering the fleece sweat jacket she'd seen Seniyah wear in the past. "I just thought this would be a nice change for the colder days, and for next winter at Stanford," she added with a smile. "Besides, it was on sale," she lied again, glad she'd removed the price tag.

Seniyah's facial muscles relaxed, but she didn't smile. "Thank you," she said and took the coat from Paige, holding it against her body.

Paige pressed the electronic button to close the trunk. "You can thank me by completing your assignment and arriving to class on time." She started for the driver's door. "I'll be waiting for that e-mail."

"Yes, Miss Paige. First thing tomorrow." Seniyah started backing away. "See you next week. Thanks again for the coat."

"Take care."

Inside the car, Paige selected a praise tune and sang all the way home. She'd added another item to her list of good deeds, totally ignoring the fact that she had lied to do so.

Chapter 6

As Paige drove down Highway 13 after Sunday worship service, she considered how deceptive the Bay Area's weather could be. The bright sun and the cloud-free blue sky gave the appearance of a warm day. However, the thermostat in her car registered forty-eight degrees. To local residents, the low temperature was near freezing. A scarf, gloves, earmuffs, knee-length boots and her long wool coat kept her warm.

In many aspects her life mirrored the deceitful weather. From the outside, Paige's life appeared to be in order, but inner peace was beyond her reach. Regret and pain resided in her spirit daily, and she had occasional bouts of depression. Two weeks had passed since the anniversary of the abortion, and she was sleeping through the night again, but not restfully. Every morning tense muscles greeted her, accompanied by a headache, which would leave after her daily dose of Starbucks.

This morning, instead of drinking Starbucks, Paige prayed until the pressure subsided enough for her to prepare for church. Today wasn't her assigned Sunday on the praise and worship team, so she was able to arrive for the service an hour later. As fatigued as she was, Paige should have gone straight home after the service, but being a glutton for punishment, she found herself headed to Kevin's house for the celebratory dinner following the christening of Tyson's daughter.

Kevin and Tyson were best friends, so the fact that they were godparents to each other's children wasn't a surprise. What did surprise, and to some extent hurt, Paige was their insistence on including her in their happy lives. True, she had befriended both of them in college and had kept in touch over the years. They even attend the same church. She had handled both Kevin's and Tyson's real estate transactions. And yes, she was happy that Reyna, who was her former employee and was now Tyson's wife, had rededicated her life to the Lord, but they just didn't understand how miserable their happiness made her. Yet she couldn't bring herself to turn down the invitation. If she were truthful, she enjoyed the fellowship. Hanging with Jenningses and the Stokeses and their extended family was the extent of her social life outside of work, church, and community service.

As the Moraga Avenue exit approached, she considered going home, but something compelled her to continue on to Kevin's house. Once she had parked her car, her unexpected anticipation motivated her to practically skip to the front of Kevin's house. She rationalized that her excitement was due to the chance she had to spend time with little Destiny. She had observed the baby during the ceremony at church and thought she was adorable. Even from three rows back, she could see the hazel eyes the baby had inherited from her father, and had wondered if her baby would have had Tyson's eye color also.

"God, help me enjoy this day," she prayed before pressing the doorbell. "Help me to be happy without feeling pain."

"Hey, Paige." Kevin leaned in and, after a brief hug, stepped aside to allow her entrance. "I'm glad you could make it to see my beautiful goddaughter." He held out his arm. "Let me take your coat."

Before the coat had completely fallen from Paige's shoulders, Kevin's wife, Marlissa, joined them with their eighteen-month-old son on her hip. "Hi, girl. I hope you're hungry."

"Actually, I am." As a rule, Paige fasted until after service on Sundays. The two women left Kevin as he was hanging the coat.

"Good, because you know we always have too much food," Marlissa stated and steered Paige into the formal dining room, where a buffet covered the ten-foot mahogany table.

Paige's stomach growled, but before she satisfied her hunger, she looked around the room. Just as she expected, everyone was there—maternal and paternal grandparents, extended family, several church members, people she didn't know, and, of course, those bossy prayer warriors from the church. About fifty people were packed into Kevin's house.

"Hello, everyone," Paige said above the friendly chatter and then made her way to the guest of honor.

"Paige," Tyson said, standing with baby Destiny in his arms and Reyna by his side. "We're glad you made it."

Paige briefly studied her old friend and her former employee and coveted their genuine love, but only for a moment. "You know I wouldn't pass up a chance to hold this gorgeous baby," she said, looking down at Destiny. "Reyna, I swear all you were was an incubator. She looks just like her daddy."

Reyna smiled and conceded, "Well, at least she has my complexion."

"And your temperament," Tyson added. "And just like her mama, she has me wrapped around her finger."

"Seriously," Paige said once she stopped laughing, "I'm happy for you, and not just because of Destiny." She locked eyes with Reyna. "I'm proud of how you've turned your life around. How are your plans for school coming?"

Reyna leaned against Tyson and wrapped her arms around his waist. "Thanks to my wonderful husband providing me with a housekeeper and tuition, I start school in three weeks."

"Being married to a lawyer has its benefits," Paige teased.

"It sure does." Reyna got up on tiptoe and kissed Tyson's cheek, then grabbed Paige by the arm. "Let's get something to eat." She led Paige to an empty seat to hang her purse.

Paige's purse strap had barely draped the chair before Mother Scott's voice rang out. "How are you doing? And don't say, 'Blessed and highly favored,' and don't speak in tongues."

"We ain't in church now. You can talk normal," First Lady Drake added.

The room erupted in laughter.

Paige wasn't sure if she preferred to be accosted by the prayer warriors privately or to be embarrassed publicly. One thing was certain. It was useless to confront them, because although their delivery could be harsh, their assessment was correct.

"Besides hungry, I'm fine," Paige answered through a forced smile.

"There's plenty to eat," Mother Scott responded. "I'm just happy to see you someplace other than church. Make sure you get some of that potato salad. It's good. I know because I made it," she added as an afterthought.

"It ain't as good as it used to be," First Lady Drake said, butting in, "but it's all right."

"Ain't nothing you make half as good as it used to be. That's why you got that German chocolate cake from the bakery," Mother Scott shot back. "And you had the nerve to try to pass it off as homemade."

First Lady Drake's jaw fell. "What are you talking about?"

Mother Scott leaned back and wagged her index finger. "You had the nerve to remove the cake from its original box with the label on it and wrap it in foil, but you forgot to take the doily from underneath the cake. The bakery's logo is plain as day."

First Lady Drake rolled her eyes at her prayer partner. "So what? It must be pretty good, since you're wearing half of it on your hips."

Mother Scott smacked her lips and snarled at the first lady. "Well, at least I don't need a water hose to measure my hips."

Paige couldn't prevent her mouth from hanging open as she listened to the two women who were supposed to be holy prayer warriors. Their behavior was reprehensible. They had the nerve to complain about how much time she spent at church. Given their ungodly behavior, the prayer warriors needed to live inside the sanctuary.

"Lord, have mercy! I don't believe this—" Paige began, but the mothers cut her off.

"You don't believe what? That's it's possible to have fun and still be saved?" First Lady Drake questioned.

"You're too deep for me. Everybody knows Drake and I are the very best of friends and we poke fun at one another all the time." Mother Scott gestured around the room. "You see ain't nobody paying us any attention but you. Maybe you should stop praying for mercy and ask the Lord to help you relax."

"Yeah," the first lady added. "You gon' mess around and give yourself a stroke."

Paige couldn't believe it. In a matter of seconds the dynamic duo had gone from attacking each other to double-teaming her. She looked at Reyna for help, but the other woman just shrugged. Paige continued on to the buffet table without offering a rebuttal.

"I know they come across as harsh, but trust me, they got your back," Reyna offered once they were out of earshot. "Those sisters are some real ride-or-die chicks in both the spirit and in the natural. Trust me, I know."

"That's what Tyson keeps telling me," Paige replied dryly.

"You know lawyers don't lie, so you should believe him." The two shared a laugh. "Seriously," Reyna said, sobering, "just about everyone in this room has benefited from their fervent prayers and their rebukes. You remember how torn up I was, don't you?"

Paige surveyed the crowd once again. In the room were former alcoholics, drug users, manipulators, gamblers, and sex addicts, and those were just the ones Paige knew from church. All had testified about how the mothers had helped them find deliverance. Even Kevin's mother—a former pastor—credited the mothers for helping her see the light. That might be the case for them, but Paige thought the mothers could use a refresher Bible lesson on drawing in people with love and kindness.

"Of course I remember your rebellious days, but let's not talk about that now. I'm starved." Paige had had enough of the rude church folks.

Once she was at the buffet, Paige felt the magnitude of her hunger. The spread for the six-month-old baby's christening was a smorgasbord of her favorites. In record speed she was balancing one plate loaded with tiger prawns, barbecued ribs, and fried chicken wings and another plate piled high with salads, fruit, and macaroni and cheese.

"You really are hungry," Reyna teased and then filled a cup with punch for Paige.

"You know how it is when you have to fast until after service every Sunday to hear a word from the Lord," Paige answered matter-of-factly, as if every Christian abstained from food on Sunday mornings.

Reyna's face twisted before she started back to the table. "I thought pushing the plate back on Sunday was optional, not mandatory."

"Oh no. We're supposed to eat from the spiritual table first, then from the natural table. That's how we learn what God's will is for our life," Paige explained, but inwardly she admitted that the regimen hadn't cleared up her foggy life.

"Well, I usually just ask Him, and He directs me on what His will is for me. Since that's working, I'm going to stick with that for now," Reyna said after placing the punch on the table for Paige.

"You sound like my mother," Paige mumbled as Reyna walked away.

Casual Christianity was something she'd never get used to. Her hunger caused her to cut her usual three-minute grace down to one minute, and she vowed that she'd add the two missing minutes to her bedtime prayer routine. Within seconds, Paige had tuned everyone out and was gripping a barbecued rib in one hand and a tiger prawn in the other. Within five minutes the first plate was piled high with clean bones, and barbecue sauce dripped from her fingertips. She'd just finished wiping her hands with a wet towelette and popping a jumbo shrimp into her mouth when she heard a commotion behind her.

"If that's the only vacant seat, no thank you," a familiar voice said. "I'd rather stand."

Paige ceased chewing and snapped her head around. It couldn't be, but it was. Standing next to Kevin, in a dark brown tailored suit, a tan shirt with gold cuff links, and alligator shoes, was the stranger she'd come to detest. He was holding a loaded plate.

Kevin's head tilted toward his male guest. "You're kidding, right?"

"No. I'm not sitting next to that mean, judgmental, rude woman."

"Man, are you serious?" Kevin asked.

The man's presence and his assessment of her discombobulated Paige to the point where she forgot she'd just popped a jumbo shrimp into her mouth, and attempted to swallow. The shrimp got lodged in her throat, obstructing her airway. Instantly, her hands flew to her throat, and the gasping began. After several failed coughing attempts meant to dislodge the shrimp, frantically, she grabbed Kevin's arm.

A throbbing pressure in her head caused her eyes to slam shut at the same moment that she heard someone begin to pray in a tongue she didn't understand. She guessed that Kevin understood her dilemma, because almost instantaneously, rock-solid arms lifted her from the chair and spun her around. What felt like the heel of a hand struck her between her shoulder blades several times before the arms encircled her and then a fist pressed into her torso, just above her naval. After three powerful thrusts the shrimp became dislodged and landed on Kevin's shoe.

Partially bent over, Paige didn't wait to say a prayer of thanks. Between each labored breath she thanked God for sparing her life until her breathing returned to normal. When she finally opened her eyes, the brown alligators came into focus. It was then that she realized it was the stranger's arms that were wrapped around her and not Kevin's.

He released her at the same time that she stood upright. The clapping and praising from the crowd distracted Paige long enough for her to gather her thoughts before expressing her gratitude to the man in the brown suit. She turned to face him, only to discover that he had removed his suit coat and was eating, as if nothing life altering had just happened.

"Here. Drink this." Kevin had returned with a bottle of water and was now offering it to her. In the commotion she hadn't seen him walk off.

Moments later Reyna and Marlissa joined them.

"Are you sure you're all right?" Reyna asked, also handing Paige a bottle of water.

"I'm fine, thanks to . . ." Paige turned to the man, who was now devouring ribs and potato salad, and let the words hang.

"We've got to stop meeting like this," he said before she could swallow her pride and address him. "These dramatic moments are getting old."

"Huh? You two know each other already?" Marlissa asked.

"Of course, they do," Kevin answered. "I referred him to Paige for some investment property."

Paige gasped like she was choking again. "What?"

Kevin's face twisted. "Didn't Tyson tell you about Serg-X?"

"Who?" Paige wanted to know.

Kevin turned to his guest. "Man, I thought you said you met Paige?"

The guy took a swig of water before answering. "I did, but we didn't have a chance to discuss business. She was too busy worshipping and doing the Lord's work to give me the time of day. She doesn't even know my name."

"Well, let me formally introduce you," Kevin offered after he and the ladies shared a laugh at Paige's expense. "Serg-X, the woman whose life you just saved is Paige McDaniels, real estate broker extraordinaire. Paige, this is my colleague Dr. Sergio-Xavier Winston Simone, but he goes by Serg-X. He's the lead neurologist at Sutter."

Paige's cheeks burned with embarrassment. In their two previous encounters, she'd treated the man like a common criminal. Yet in her crisis he hadn't hesitated to come to her aid.

"Hi. Um, it's nice . . . Hello, Serg-X," she said, stumbling over her words until he stood and ended the awkwardness.

"My friends call me Serg-X. You can address me as Sergio-Xavier, Mr. Simone, or Dr. Simone. Or better yet, you don't have to address me at all."

"Ouch!" Marlissa said and then tiptoed away, with Reyna following.

For the third time, Paige watched his back retreat, and for the first time she wanted to chase after him.

Chapter 7

Sergio-Xavier dumped his half-eaten food in the trash on his way to a place that was still undetermined. He just knew he had to get away from Paige McDaniels. He had been to his colleague Kevin's house only once before and guessed that the French doors on the other side of the room led to a deck or a patio. His assumption proved correct. The doors not only led to a deck, but also afforded him views of the Bay Area's three major bridges and the San Francisco skyline.

The second he stepped through the doors, the dry coldness chilled him to the bone. He walked over to the wooden railing and stuffed his hands into his front pants pockets, all the while thinking the freezing temperature was warmer than Paige's attitude. The woman could freeze water with just a look.

In his thirty-five years, he'd never felt like disrespecting a woman, yet on three separate occasions her callous personality had caused him to do just that with ease. The men in his family would not be proud. His father, grandfather, and uncles prided themselves on rearing respectable men who held women in the highest regard. He wasn't proud of his behavior, but Paige McDaniels had a way of irritating him to the point where he disregarded everything he'd been taught.

The effect she had on him left him confused, and confusion was not something he was used to. As a physician, he functioned based on logic and data. She disregarded him, and her words insulted him. Her prejudices infuriated him. Yet, in her moment of distress, he didn't hesitate to come to her aid. Seconds before he'd been so disgusted with her, he'd refused to sit next to her, but her distress had ignited his compassion.

"That's just adhering to the oath," he mumbled to himself, referring to the Hippocratic oath, which he'd taken upon graduating from medical school. "I'd help anyone in need." Yet that didn't explain why he had practically snatched her from Kevin. As a trained surgeon, Kevin was more than capable of performing the Heimlich maneuver.

He rocked on his heels, trying to generate heat. When that didn't work, he paced the length of the deck. Common sense dictated that he retreat back inside the house and enjoy the fellowship and food, but he didn't want to see *her*. One more lap around the deck and he made up his mind. He'd go back inside, thank Kevin for inviting him, present the parents with a gift, and then excuse himself.

He turned on his heels, but before he made it to the double doors, Paige stepped through them, wearing her coat and gloves.

His shiver was more animated than necessary. "The temperature seems to have dipped ten degrees."

"I guess I deserve that, Dr. Simone," she responded with her chin out. "My behavior toward you hasn't exactly been professional or Christian."

He took a step backward. "Christian? I came to your office to hire you, and you in turn yelled at me. Then you accused me of being a thief without knowing anything about me. And today you can't even say thank you after I saved your life. You're speaking to me now only because you know I'm a doctor and that places me on your level."

"First of all, Mr. Simone, you didn't save my life. God equipped you with the knowledge to help me, but He saved my life."

Sergio-Xavier looked down at the wagging gloved finger and shook his head. Paige McDaniels was way too spiritual for him.

"Just because you're a doctor doesn't place you on my level. I came out here to thank you for allowing God to use you, but your ego is too big. You're already claiming God's glory."

Sergio-Xavier was no longer cold. The ebony beauty standing before him had managed to bring his anger to a level that frightened him. This woman had no idea to whom she was talking. The insult she'd just unleashed was far worse than all the others combined.

"Reverend Mother McDaniels," he sneered, "if I didn't already have a personal relationship with God, I wouldn't be inclined to get one after meeting you. Now I understand why people don't like Christians."

"What do you know about Christians?"

He thought the neck rolling and eye rolling juvenile but didn't address them. "I know enough to know that I'm not one—"

"That's what I thought," she interrupted, "so don't be judging me."

"Judging is not something I do, because scripture clearly tells us not to. Besides, you pass enough judgment for ten people." He stepped around her and reached for the doorknob. "For your information, I'm not a Christian, because the majority of Christians are like you—self-absorbed and self-righteous, and they are masters at judging everyone but themselves. What I am is a Christ follower, because I follow the teachings and actions of Jesus Christ." He opened the door, but just before stepping over the threshold, he added, "If you have another medical crisis, don't have it around me. I'm not so sure I would do what Jesus would do the next time." He remembered he was a guest in Kevin's home and avoided slamming the door just in the nick of time.

Attitude seeped from Paige, only to be replaced by shame. She hadn't meant to lash out at him. She'd actually come outside to thank him and to apologize for her previous behavior, but his insults had hurt her. How dare he imply she was stuck-up? She never looked down on people and didn't consider herself on a higher level than anyone else. The comment about her Christianity didn't help, either, although her behavior proved his point, though it was off base.

The cold wind further cooled her attitude. She needed to get back inside before her toes froze. "A little frostbite might be a small price to pay to avoid that man," she grumbled before turning the doorknob. With any luck, the good doctor would stay out of her space.

The second she stepped back inside, her wish was granted. Across the room, Sergio-Xavier had his suit jacket on and his coat hanging over his arm. After a brief conversation with Tyson and Reyna, he handed them a small gift box, then headed for the foyer, Kevin following behind.

"What am I doing?" she asked with each step she took toward them. Her feelings were hurt, and she still had her pride, but for some reason, Paige couldn't let him leave without thanking him. That was the Christian thing to do.

"Dr. Simone, may I speak to you for a minute?" she said in a timid voice that sounded foreign to her. From behind, she observed that his left arm was still midway through the left coat sleeve. His head shook before he resumed the motion of putting on his coat. "Please."

Both Kevin and Sergio-Xavier turned around just then.

"If you need some privacy, you can use my study," Kevin offered.

"That won't be necessary," Sergio-Xavier answered while continuing to button his coat. "Whatever Miss McDaniels has to say to me, she can say right here."

***

"All right." Kevin eyed Paige with uncertainty before walking away.

Paige almost lost her courage when Sergio-Xavier finally focused on her, but she had to continue so her prayers would be received. His dark eyes always appeared to be examining her soul.

"I'm sorry," she said without preliminaries. The sooner this conversation was over, the sooner he would leave her presence. "Thank you for helping me earlier."

"Is that all?" he said with more disdain than Paige thought necessary.

"What else should there be?"

He stuffed his hands into leather gloves. "Miss McDaniels, if you don't already have a clue, my explaining it to you won't help."

Once again frustration got the best of her. Paige was used to hardball negotiations, but this was ridiculous. Something more important than a million-dollar deal was on the table. Her self-preservation and pride were at stake. "Look, I'm trying to make amends with you, you know, call a truce, but you're impossible."

He raised an eyebrow. "*I'm* impossible?"

"All right, okay," she said, her hands waving in the air. "I was rude, and I said some things I shouldn't have. That day at my office, I didn't know you were Kevin's friend. And that day at the food bank, well, I'd had a rough week." She briefly looked away, thinking of the memory. "I was tired and sleep deprived—"

"What's your excuse today?" he interrupted.

Paige's mouth opened and closed, but she didn't have a comeback that wasn't a lie, and she wasn't ready to reveal that she just didn't like the man. "There is none," she finally conceded. "I don't have one today." Her head dropped. "Today I was just plain wrong."

"How about mean and nasty?"

Paige figuratively and literally swallowed what little pride she had left. "You're right. What I said was mean and nasty."

At the sound of his laughter, her head rose and she found a mouth with a set of straight ultra-white teeth smiling at her.

"What's so funny?" she wanted to know. Could he be callous enough to find this funny?

"You are." He was smiling, but Paige knew an insult was coming, and he didn't disappoint her. "I bet that took a lot out of you. You're an enigma, and I'm sure I never want to figure you out. In this case, I'm going to do a WWJD. I'm going to accept that pathetic apology, since it's the best you can do. And I'm going to add you to my prayer list." Then he was gone.

Paige stood there staring at the etched glass in the door, trying to understand how anyone could insult someone and then offer to pray for them. More importantly, why did the idea of Dr. Sergio-Xavier Winston Simone praying for her excite her? And why did he have so many names?

Chapter 8

On Monday morning Paige skipped into her office building, feeling more refreshed than she had in days without the aid of caffeine. For the first time in weeks, she had enjoyed a restful night of sleep. No tossing and turning and no disturbing dreams. She attributed the peace to last night's prayer time. During the two-hour session she had cried, repented, and thanked God repeatedly for sparing her life. As much as she loved shrimp, Paige doubted she would ever taste one again.

After deactivating the alarm and manually locking the door—something she'd been doing since being caught with her butt in the air—Paige trotted into her office and turned on her favorite worship music and sang along while she worked. Two hours later, when the receptionist and the agents arrived, Paige had her whole week planned out. She was in the middle of reviewing a counteroffer when the intercom sounded.

"You have a visitor," the voice announced.

Paige glanced down at her appointment schedule. The 9:30 a.m. slot was empty. *This could be a new client,* she reasoned, since over 30 percent of her clients started as walk-ins. "I'll be right out," she answered.

Before walking into the reception area, Paige smoothed her hair bun and refreshed her clear lip gloss. Paige felt so good, she opted to leave her suit jacket draped across her chair. Believing modesty was best, Paige almost never displayed her hourglass figure.

She rounded the corner and extended her hand. "Good morning. I'm . . ." The remaining words stuck in her throat now that she knew her visitor's identity.

Sergio-Xavier took her hand. "Good morning, Miss McDaniels. After further consideration, I've decided to give you another chance, since I caught you off guard the first time. I stopped by on my run to schedule an appointment with you."

She finally released the breath she'd been holding to keep from passing out. The man didn't believe in beating around the bush, but he did have a dedication to physical fitness. Only a fanatic would be out in fifty-degree weather in an Under Armour compression shirt and shorts. The bulges underneath the black fabric reminded her of what those arms felt like wrapped around her body, causing her to stare.

"Miss McDaniels?"

"Get behind me Satan."

"Excuse me?"

His raised voice snapped Paige away from her lustful thoughts. She hadn't meant to say the command out loud. Neither had she meant to hold on to his hand for so long.

"What I mean is, I'm free now," she said, clarifying the matter after releasing his hand. "That is, if you're available."

His eyes were doing it again, examining her like she was a microscopic specimen.

"Are you sure? I don't want to impose if you're busy."

"I'm sure. Follow me." She turned and started for her office. After several steps she looked over her shoulder to see if he was following her. He was, and she prayed the rest of the way. Today was a good day, and Paige was determined not to let him ruin it. No matter what he said, she would maintain her professionalism.

"Dr. Simone, please have a seat," she directed once they were in the confines of her office.

He hesitated, but only briefly, before taking a seat. "Thank you."

An uncomfortable silence followed. Paige stalled by looking at her computer, then straightening papers on her desk, all the while mentally reciting scriptures.

"Dr. Simone, I must admit, I'm surprised to see you this morning. When we parted yesterday, I wasn't sure if we had reached a truce or not," she finally said.

"If we hadn't, I wouldn't be here," he answered in the no-nonsense tone she was used to. She resisted the urge to roll her eyes. "I'm looking for some investment properties, preferably four fourplexes. Fixer-uppers are fine, as long as they're in good neighborhoods."

"And just how much are you prepared to spend, and how soon?" she asked while typing in the information on her computer screen.

"Soon as possible, and no more than three hundred thousand each, repairs included."

She continued typing. "Is it safe to assume you've already solidified financing?"

"This will be a cash transaction."

Her fingers slowed, but only momentarily. She was used to working with financially secure clients, but she had a feeling Sergio-Xavier was on another level. As they worked through the client intake form, Paige learned that Sergio-Xavier was single and lived within five miles of her office, near UC Berkeley.

"I have everything I need to get started," Paige said after printing a copy of the broker's agreement for him to sign. "Can you answer one question for me?"

"Sure," he said after reading the document and signing on the dotted line.

"Why do you have so many names? Two first names is kind of ghetto for someone of your caliber, don't you think?"

He leaned back, and the smirk on his face suggested that this might be the shortest client relationship of her career.

"Miss McDaniels, I was just beginning to think you're an intelligent woman, and then you open your mouth and say something stupid. Actually, I expected that, because you really can't help it. It's who you are."

The truce was officially over. Paige stood and pounded her desk with her palm. "Are you calling me stupid?"

He remained seated, totally unmoved by her animated behavior. "What I'm saying is, stop judging people by your measuring stick, because your vision is blurred."

Paige shook her head, in total confusion. "What?"

"Sit down and listen, and I'll explain it to you."

Paige huffed and puffed and rolled her eyes, but she sat down. She didn't want to listen, but she had a feeling she needed to. Then she would throw him out and tear up the contract.

"First of all, I wasn't born a doctor. I was born a regular human being, so my caliber, as you call, it is not important."

His humility surprised her, but she didn't show it.

"My paternal grandfather had five daughters and no sons. I was the first male in the family, and my mother wanted to name me after her Latino father, Sergio Xavier. My father wanted to name me after his childhood friend Winston, who died of sickle-cell anemia while in high school. The day I was born, my parents reached a compromise and honored them by giving me both of their names. Sergio-Xavier is my first name. Winston is my middle name. So you see? There is nothing ghetto about my name."

"Oh," Paige mouthed more than voiced. "So you're Latino?"

"Actually, my mother is Latino and African American, and my father is French and African American, but that's beside the point. Stop making assumptions about things you know nothing about."

"I don't do that," she retorted, defending herself. "At least not on purpose."

"Yes, you *do*," he answered emphatically. "You judge people with ease based on your self-imposed high standards."

His words cut so deep and quick that Paige didn't have a chance to brace herself. A tear escaped before she could get into self-preservation mode. She blinked rapidly and looked away. "If I'm such a bad person, then why did you come here today?"

If he noticed the tear, he didn't mention it. "Honestly, other than divine intervention, I don't know why I'm here today. When I left you yesterday, I had no intentions of seeing you again, but as I jogged down the hill, I felt compelled to stop here."

"Really?" Her voice was just above a whisper.

"Look, Paige," he said, leaning forward, "for the record, you're not a bad person. More than a little misguided, but not bad."

If you only knew what I did, she thought as another tear fell.

"And despite what I said a moment ago, you are intelligent and beautiful, with a nice rear end."

"What—"

"Hold on," he said when she stood up again. "Before you start throwing holy water on me, I'm not flirting or being lustful. Just stating facts."

Slowly, she returned to her seat.

"Gee whiz," he said, shaking his head. "Why do women always think a man wants them just because he compliments them?"

"Sorry."

He stood to his feet. "Look, let's try this from the beginning. Hello, Miss McDaniels. My name is Sergio-Xavier Winston Simone, but you can call me Serg-X."

Suppressing a grin, she stared at his extended hand a long time before accepting it. "Hello, Sergio-Xavier. You may call me Paige."

"I'm glad there's only one of you," he said after the handshake.

"I guess this means we're friends now?" she asked, with more anticipation than she thought necessary.

"No," he answered through that perfect smile. "But at least now we can have a cordial business relationship."

She observed him as he prepared to leave, and felt the need to say something to prolong the visit.

"Thank you for giving me another chance," she said and handed him her business card. "For the most part, I'll be contacting you, but just in case you ever need to reach me, all my numbers are on there."

He held the card in the palm of his hand. "I look forward to doing business with you, Paige."

This time, instead of watching his back, Paige walked beside him back to the reception area. With each step, she had a feeling her life was about to change. For better or worse, she didn't know.

Chapter 9

"Way to go, ladies! We are on our way!" Paige exclaimed with more excitement than she'd felt in years.

DWAP was officially up and running, and during its first week it had had enough sales to cover production expenses and to purchase more supplies, with a little profit left at the end. The marketing ploy of having the varsity football and basketball players wear the necklaces was ingenious. After one week nearly half of the student body was sporting DWAP originals, and according to the girls, even the geeks were wearing them. Although pleased, Paige wished the idea had been Seniyah's instead of Jasmine's.

"Check this out," Jasmine said, waving a handful of purple order slips. Another one of Jasmine's ideas. "Purple represents royalty, and DWAP ladies are definitely royals," she had said while trying to persuade the group to select that color. "I have orders for at least fifty more, and this doesn't include what everyone else has done."

"Very good, Jasmine. Now you need to work on increasing your orders every week," Paige told her. Paige wanted to encourage her, but she didn't want to give her a false sense of ease. Running a business was hard work.

Jasmine smacked her lips. "Whatever, Miss Paige."

Paige ignored the teenager's attitude. Jasmine was always angry about something. "Divas, let's hear your reports on how you're doing, and then we can start production and do inventory control."

For the next twenty minutes, Paige stood in the back of the room while the divas stepped up to the podium individually and reported on their progress and outlined their goals for the following week. Paige felt like a proud mother as she listened to them identify selling opportunities and cost-saving measures. They effectively applied the principles she'd taught them, but what made Paige feel like dancing in the spirit right there in the classroom was their appearance.

During the first meeting, Paige had emphasized how important it was to look professional in the business world. At the time she didn't think the girls were paying attention, but tonight's display proved otherwise. They weren't fans of long skirts and sleeves, but at least the tattoos and body piercings were covered. Most importantly, Jasmine's hair was one color, blue, and it was pulled back and held together by a clip.

Paige squeezed her long frame behind a student desk when her protégé took the podium. That way she wouldn't have to worry about hiding her excitement about Seniyah's brilliant ideas. She couldn't jump up from the small desk if she wanted to. She smiled as Seniyah opened her notebook and began her presentation. She looked confident in the wool coat Paige had given her, although Paige thought it fit more snugly than it should. She'd purchased a larger size purposely to accommodate Seniyah's fuller frame, or so she'd thought. Paige attributed the fit to the thick sweats the girl wore underneath, and then gave Seniyah her full attention. On her next shopping trip, she'd purchase Seniyah some dress slacks.

Within seconds, disappointment couldn't begin to describe how Paige felt. Seniyah spoke with confidence, but her ideas were mediocre at best. Her sales ranked at the bottom, and she didn't have any concrete ideas about how to turn them around. It was then that Paige remembered that Seniyah never did e-mail her that marketing plan from the previous session. Unlike with the rest of the girls, at the end of Seniyah's presentation, the only person clapping was Paige. As her mentor, she had to encourage her.

"Are there any questions or suggestions for Seniyah?" Paige asked the group in hopes of helping Seniyah gain a better grasp of what she was supposed to be doing.

"Ooh, ooh, I have a question," Jasmine said, waving her hands in the air.

Paige knew this wouldn't turn out well, but she had opened the door and couldn't close it now.

"How much longer do we have to carry her?" Jasmine asked. "It's obvious she don't have a clue about what she's doing."

"No one asked you to carry me," Seniyah shot back, uncharacteristically outspoken. "I know what I'm doing. I've just been too busy lately to focus on the project."

"It's not a project!" Jasmine yelled, silencing the murmuring among the other girls. "It's a business, our business. If we don't believe in it, no one else will. No one is waiting in line to hand us a free ride out of the ghetto like you have. I need this to work. This training and community college may be all I get."

Jasmine's passion surprised Paige, but she couldn't allow Jasmine to insult Seniyah. Sure, the girl needed to work harder, but Seniyah's family dynamics were quite complicated. "Jasmine, let's not be too hard on Seniyah, just because she applied herself and earned a scholarship," Paige said, maneuvering from behind the desk and walking to the front of the room. "At least she's trying."

"And just how do you know?" Jasmine snapped. "She hasn't participated in any of our production sessions on the weekends. And she comes here late and doesn't complete assignments. So unless you know something we don't, just how do you know she's *trying?*"

Paige's steps slowed as she neared the podium to stand next to Seniyah. She'd grown accustomed to dealing with Jasmine's outbursts. Usually they were misguided, but not this time. Paige had assumed Seniyah was now participating in the weekend production sessions, and although she'd arrived earlier than last time, tonight Seniyah was still late. For once Paige didn't have an answer to defend her favorite student. Neither did she like the unassuming expression Seniyah wore.

"Instead of attacking one another," Paige said, facing the group, "I think we need to come together as a team and work on our weaknesses." She intended to spend some one-on-one time with Seniyah before the next session.

"We've been doing that," Jasmine shot back, gesturing toward the rest of the girls. "She's the one who is not acting like a team player," she added, pointing at Seniyah.

Paige had to regain control before Jasmine convinced the group to vote Seniyah out. One of the rules governing the group was that everyone had to participate, or else they'd be asked to leave the group.

"In any business there are people who work harder than others. However, DWAP's goal is for every member to contribute to its success," Paige told the girls. "That being said, instead of the regular production session on Saturday, I'm willing to attend and provide training and team-building skills." She paused and turned to Seniyah. "Everyone must attend." She faced the group again. "If any issues remain after that, then we'll reevaluate and make any necessary changes as a group."

In the silence that followed, Paige prayed that Seniyah would get more involved and would lose the nonchalant attitude. She couldn't admit it out loud, but Jasmine was right. Everyone had problems.

"Fine," Jasmine finally said. "Where do you want to meet?"

Paige exhaled a sigh of relief. "We can meet at my office. I have a conference room. Let's say three o'clock? The address is—"

"We have your card," Jasmine said, cutting her off, then walked to the production table and started counting beads. The rest of the girls followed, including Seniyah, but at a slower pace.

Paige planned to speak with Seniyah after the other girls left, but as soon as the session ended, Seniyah darted out the door. Paige ran out to the parking lot in hopes of catching her, but the black wool coat was nowhere to be found.

Chapter 10

Paige sat in her usual third-row seat during Wednesday night Bible study and wondered if she was still saved. For the first time ever, she couldn't comprehend the words written on the pages of the borrowed book, which was supposed to bring her life. Pastor Drake was an excellent teacher, and the Word of God was powerful, so the problem had to lie within her. She'd allowed other things, namely, Seniyah, to distract her and weigh her down to the point where she couldn't focus on anything else.

Afraid that Jasmine's lack of compassion would diminish what little self-esteem Seniyah had and would cause her to quit DWAP and maybe give up on her dream of attending Stanford, after last night's session, Paige had gone home and had prayed nonstop for the young girl. She'd dozed off several times while on her knees, only to awaken and continue praying. Her body ached so much, she could barely move when her alarm clock sounded this morning. Her fast from caffeine was short-lived. This morning she'd finished off a double espresso in record speed.

Throughout the day, thoughts of Seniyah had distracted her to the point where she forgot to meet clients at the title company to sign the final documents for the purchase of their first home. When the anxious husband called her cell phone, she lied and said she was stuck in traffic. She repented as she left the office and got a speeding ticket en route to the title company. When she finally rushed into the title company, winded, the couple was so angry, they threatened to back out of the deal. It took Paige thirty minutes to calm them down and reassure them of the solid investment they were making. She even threw in a gift card to a home improvement store.

It wasn't until she sat down on the pew in church that she realized she'd left her Bible at home. She routinely kept her Bible inside her briefcase so she wouldn't forget it. Now she missed Pastor Drake's teaching on being an effective light to the world. She had checked out right after the topic appeared on the screen, because thoughts of how she was lighting the way for Seniyah's future had consumed her.

Without a doubt Paige knew it was her responsibility to give Seniyah a better life. She didn't believe in luck or happenstance. If it weren't God's will for her to help Seniyah, He wouldn't have placed the girl in her life the way he had. Seniyah needed what Paige had to offer: she could teach her how to present herself as a respectable young woman and how to succeed in school, and whenever the opportunity presented itself, Paige would teach her about the Lord. She had to dig deeper and discover what was going on with the girl. Seniyah was her assignment, and Paige would see to it that she didn't become another statistic.

When Pastor Drake asked the audience if they had any questions, Paige closed the Bible and placed it back on the pew in front of her and left before the benediction. Another first for her, but she needed to map out a plan and maybe get some sleep.

Paige sang and danced from room to room as she cleaned her house. It was indeed a day the Lord had made, and she was determined to be glad and rejoice. After two mentally and physically draining days, Paige had skipped the Friday all-night prayer session and had soothed her tired muscles in a hot bubble bath, then had collapsed onto her bed and fallen into a coma-like sleep. She'd slept so well, she didn't change positions until her alarm sounded at 8:00 a.m. She'd got up without pressing the snooze button, and after brewing a cup of Columbian coffee in her Keurig, she'd turned on the sound system and started her weekly chores. Living alone and being a neat freak made the task easy. By nine thirty the dust had been wiped away, the clothes had been washed and sorted for dry cleaning, and the Pergo floor had been dust mopped. She had just enough time left to shower and get to the food bank on time.

The clear blue sky didn't deceive her today. The thermostat inside her Lexus registered sixty-nine degrees, perfect for jeans and a scoop-neck tunic. Paige's wardrobe consisted of dark, conservative colors, like brown, black, and navy blue, and an abundance of white blouses. She was content in believing that dressing modestly was an outward sign of her inner commitment to God. As a result, Paige's skirts stopped mid-calf, and her sleeves hit near the wrist. Tank tops, shorts, and open-toe shoes were out of the question.

Her mother thought Paige would die an old maid because of her style, and she made a point to tell Paige that every chance she got. "It's a good thing I'm around. Otherwise, a man wouldn't be able to see what he's getting, since you cover everything up," she would say. "A man can tell how his woman will look in the future by how her mother looks." Her mother would then pose to display her full breasts, tiny waist, and voluptuous hips. "You better learn to use what your mama gave you before you get too old." If only her mother knew that using what her mama gave her was what had gotten Paige into trouble in the first place.

Paige had grown numb to her mother's musings, until today. For some reason, the black jeans and brown sweater didn't suffice. Maybe she should consider adding more style to her life, she thought. *But why?* she asked herself. Due to her past mistake, no viable suitors were on the horizon. More than likely her mother's prediction would come to pass—she'd die an old maid.

"No, I'm not going there today," she mumbled as she turned into the food bank's parking lot. "It's a beautiful day, and I will enjoy it, even if I am miserable." She started singing as she climbed out of her car and mechanically set out to perform her Christian duty.

"Good morning, Paige."

Her Nikes hadn't touched the pavement three times before the stimulating, and yet irritating, voice interrupted her singing. Sergio-Xavier. She hadn't seen him since the morning she took him on as a client, but they had an appointment for Tuesday afternoon. At that moment, she didn't want to see him, but she also didn't want to lose a client. With a manufactured smile, she turned in the direction of his voice.

"Hello . . ." She let the rest of the greeting hang while studying his physique, which she tried unsuccessfully to ignore. Sergio-Xavier was over six feet tall, and his body was well proportioned and toned. Although he wore a polo shirt and black jeans, she had visions of the biceps and quadriceps underneath.

"Too holy to speak this morning, are we?"

His cocky response snapped her from the trance. "I didn't expect to see you out here," she said, referring to him unloading the supply truck. "Actually, I didn't expect to see you at all today."

"Why not?"

She thought it was a rhetorical question until he set the box on the ground and folded his arms, as if waiting for an answer.

"Well, at the risk of saying something stupid, as you put it . . ." He arched an eyebrow but didn't rebut the dig. "I didn't think unloading an eighteen-wheeler was something a lead neurologist would have the time to do."

"I see you have thrown our last meeting here into the sea of forgetfulness." He bent down and retrieved the box. "You better alert the staff that I could be stealing this food." He chuckled and went to place the box on the conveyor belt.

"I thought we called a truce?" she said when he returned.

"We did," he answered and then flashed what she considered a deceitful smile. "But I couldn't help it. You're too predictable. I bet all kinds of ridiculous thoughts about why I chose to spend my time at the local food bank when I could be out on the golf course are running through your pretty little head."

"Predictable?" Paige started to argue the point but then figured, *Why?* The man had told the truth. She did want to know why he would spend his Saturday morning among common folks. He walked back to the truck, and she followed. "Well, are you going to tell me why you're here? I know it's not because you enjoy my company."

"Of course not," he smirked en route to the conveyor belt, carrying another box. "I get better conversation from the people in line. They're more genuine."

Paige shot daggers at him and stomped the pavement to keep from punching him in the face. How dare he make a comment like that?

After placing the box on the conveyor belt, he stood in front of her. She didn't like that he was standing so far into her personal space, but he smelled good.

"Let me explain before both your head and neck start rolling and your finger starts pointing," he said, as if dealing with angry African American women was something he did on a regular basis.

She huffed and puffed but didn't give him the tongue-lashing and animation he deserved.

"You want to know why I'm here not because you're concerned, but because you're nosy. You can't figure me out, because I don't fit into any of your preconceived notions of what someone on my level does. The problem is, you don't know what level I'm on. You only have assumptions based on outward appearance. Similar to how you embrace salvation."

"How dare you—"

He threw his hands up and cut her off. "Hold on. Let me finish, and then you can tell me off."

Her fists relaxed and tightened, but she bit her lip to keep from yelling.

"My family's nonprofit foundation is a major contributor to all five local food banks. We not only provide financial assistance, but also give of our time by serving the community. We rotate among the different sites, which is probably why we didn't meet before now, but I'm sure you've seen my family members around, doing everything from unloading trucks to handing out food. You just didn't know you were in the company of millionaires." He leaned in even closer, as if trying to get his point across. "So, the food you accused me of stealing is actually food I help provide."

Paige felt her jaw dropping, but she was too stunned to stop it.

"As for conversation, the people in line are real. They are here because they're in need. They're not too prideful to admit they need help. What I like most about the crowd is no one judges anyone. Out here I'm just another guy helping out, not Dr. Simone. You have the working and the unemployed, the young and the old in every color of the rainbow, but status means nothing here. They respect one another and share the common goal of survival. I'm simply humbled God has given me the means to help them. I meet fascinating people every time I serve. And for me, it's not an obligation, but an honor."

If it were possible, Paige would have become liquefied and flowed down the drainage pipe. Ashamed didn't begin to describe how low she felt for misjudging him, but the jealousy surprised her. Sergio-Xavier possessed the inner fulfillment she yearned for. If nothing else, Sergio-Xavier had been consistent in his attitude and insults since the day they met. He knew his mind and wasn't afraid to voice his opinion. He was rooted and grounded in his convictions.

The smug smile he wore made her almost hate him for the mere fact that he'd discovered his own identity and charted his own course. Paige, on the other hand, had no idea why she showed up at the food bank every Saturday, other than it was part of her Christian duty. She did have compassion for the needy, but giving of her time was one way she achieved atonement for her past sin. For Paige, serving was an obligation.

Paige blinked back the tears this realization had caused and prayed that her voice wouldn't betray her. "I don't know what to say. You're certainly not who I thought you were. Again, I'm sorry." She expected him to gloat, but he didn't. "I have to get inside," she said and then turned and walked away when she could no longer stand his intense stare.

"Paige, wait."

The feel of his hand on her body made her stop, but she didn't turn around. The warmth against her shoulder amazed her since he was wearing work gloves, and she a sweater.

"I hope you're not upset. I really wasn't trying to pick another fight."

She hoped the smile she pasted on before turning would be enough to convince Sergio-Xavier his words hadn't cut her to the core. "Sure you weren't, but it's all right. I deserved that." The self-preservation tactic worked. Those full lips parted into that deceiving smile.

"I assume you're working a two-hour shift today?"

She nodded.

"I'm free until evening. How about grabbing a bite to eat afterward?"

Paige shook her head as to clear it. Did he just slap me with the pitiful reality of what my life has become, and then ask me out? she thought. "Are you asking me out?"

"Of course not," he smirked. "I wouldn't date a nosy woman like you, but I would share a meal with a pretty face."

"Really?" Her pasted smile turned genuine at his compliment. "You must really think I'm pretty. You've said so twice in less than ten minutes."

His hand jerked away, as if he had just realized he was stilling touching her. "No, I don't." He let the rest of the sentence hang and abruptly turned away.

Paige remained glued in place, watching him stomp away, only to return and intrude into her personal space once again.

"You're much more than pretty," he said in a much softer tone than she had expected. "To me, you're drop-dead gorgeous. Any man, including myself, would be proud to be seen with you. That is, until you open your mouth."

His words soothed her earlier wounds, and the laughter that followed released the tension. "Is it possible for you to give a compliment without an insult?"

"It's about as possible as you going twenty-four hours without misjudging someone. Believe it or not, that happens only with you."

Paige playfully slapped his arm. "I'll work on my *slight* problem if you work on yours. And yes, I'll make you look good by sharing a meal with you. We can discuss the properties I selected for you."

He started back toward the truck. "Good. I'll see you at one o'clock. Now go inside and perform your saintly duty."

"Whatever," she said, rolling her eyes as she turned away. She went halfway down the walkway leading into the building and then retraced her steps. She couldn't have lunch with him. "I'm sorry, but I can't go. I forgot that I already have plans," she said as he moved from the truck to the conveyor belt. "But we're still on for Tuesday."

"No problem," he said after setting the box down. "Have fun."

"It's not a date." For some reason Paige felt the need to explain. "I have a special session scheduled with my young entrepreneur group at my office."

Her statement appeared to surprise him. "Are you serious?"

"Yes," she answered proudly. He wasn't the only one with a heart to give back. While working at the food bank was her duty, Paige had a passion for mentoring. "I mentor a group of high school girls on Monday evenings."

"I have to see this for myself," he teased. "Would you mind if I came along and watched you in action?"

Maybe to gloat or maybe to prove she wasn't a bad person, Paige welcomed the idea of Dr. Sergio-Xavier Simone observing her and the girls. DWAP was her pride and joy, one of the few things she'd done right. "Sure. I'll meet you at my office."

"I'll see you later, Sergeant." Sergio-Xavier offered a salute and then resumed working.

Chapter 11

"What the heck was I thinking?" Sergio-Xavier banged the steering wheel of his Chrysler 300 for the third time and still didn't have a logical answer to why he was parked outside of Paige's office with a picnic basket.

He hadn't meant to invite her to lunch, but the pain etched on her face had touched him in a place in which he didn't desire to be touched, at least not by her. True, he'd wanted her to eat crow for calling him a thief, but he hadn't expected the tears. She'd attempted to camouflage them, but he'd seen them. In an instant the hard exterior had crumbled, and what remained had shaken him to the core. Beneath the misguided religious fanatic shell rested a wounded soul crying out for help.

He looked upward. "Okay, Lord, I get it." He appreciated his spiritual gift of discernment, but this was one time when Sergio-Xavier wished he could turn the gift off. "Father, please show me quickly why our paths have crossed. I know it's much deeper than buying property." After the prayer, he sat there a while longer, waiting for an answer. When one didn't come, he collected the picnic basket and exited the vehicle. All the way to Paige's office building, he hoped she'd be pleased with his lunch selection.

Instead of greeting him, Paige pointed to the picnic basket and said," What's that?" when she opened the door. Since she was in the office alone, she waited for him in the receptionist area.

To keep the peace, Sergio-Xavier simply answered, "Lunch. I thought we'd have enough time to eat before your class." He noticed that she hesitated before stepping aside to allow him entrance. "Don't worry. I'm a doctor, remember? I took an oath not to murder anyone."

"Whatever. I'm not going to let you ruin my day twice." He expected the eye rolling, but the feel of her fingertips against his hand as she pulled him down the hall and into her office surprised him. "I didn't know you were picking up food, so I stopped at Subway."

"I see," he said, looking at the unwrapped sandwich on her desk. "I should have called. I'll just save this for dinner." He turned, intending to take the basket back to the car, but her hand moved up his bicep.

"No, you will not. I can eat Subway any day of the week, but I will not pass up a chance to enjoy a real meal at your expense."

Before he could devise with a comeback, Paige snatched the basket and in record speed unloaded the contents onto her desk. "What's in here? It smells delicious." She gasped. "How did you know I love soul food?" she asked and then bit into a piece of fried catfish before he could answer. "Kevin must have told you."

"Uh, actually, I haven't talked with Kevin in a couple of days."

She attacked the catfish again.

"Had I known you like catfish so much, I would have gotten you some."

She stopped chewing. "Huh?"

"The catfish *was* for me," he explained. "I got the fried chicken for you."

He watched Paige's eyes almost double in size. "There's fried chicken too?" she said, opening the remaining containers. "I don't eat like this often, because it's fattening, but I love fried chicken and catfish."

As he leaned against the wall, uncontrollable laughter poured out of Sergio-Xavier. This Paige was hilarious and quite adorable with a chicken leg in one hand and a forkful of collard greens in the other. She didn't even bother using the plates.

"I've got to get a picture of this," he said and pulled out his cell phone. "I never thought I'd see you on the verge of gluttony. Just don't choke. I can't perform the Heimlich and snap a picture at the same time."

The stoic Paige returned, but only for a brief moment. "I am not a glutton," she snarled, then dug into the yams. "If you want some, you better come on." She smiled and offered him a fork.

After snapping several pictures, Sergio-Xavier joined her at the desk and ate, all the while wondering what was happening to him. Paige's pleasure in the meal he had selected pleased him more than it should have, and he couldn't stop thinking about the feel of her hand on his body. How was it possible to dislike someone and enjoy being in their presence at the same time? When he looked up at the contentment resting on her ebony face, Sergio-Xavier knew the answer to that question was a long way off.

"Ms. McDaniels, I am truly impressed. You're awesome with those young ladies. DWAP can't help but be successful."

Paige didn't bother hiding the huge smile before turning around and acknowledging Sergio-Xavier's compliment. "Thank you," she answered humbly, but she felt like screaming. For two hours she had taught and mediated between eight high-strung teenagers. For once Seniyah had arrived on time, and Jasmine had kept the insults to a minimum and hadn't taken over the class, but the tension had remained. By the time they had finished the team-building activities and had redefined DWAP's goals and mission, the group was motivated to work harder and work together. Jasmine and Seniyah had even called a truce by shaking hands.

"I wish I could take all the credit for today's session, but I can't. I had a little help." She nodded at him. "Thank you for assisting me."

"What did I do?"

Paige thought the twisted facial expression was cute, and she said as much, in her own way. "Those young ladies are a handful, but with a handsome man in the room watching them, they were on their best behavior. I even caught some of them gawking at you. If it wasn't too much to ask, I'd invite you to every session."

"I doubt if my presence made a difference at all. Those young ladies are smart. With proper guidance, I can see them going far in the business world." He paused, as if he had remembered something. "Do you really think I'm handsome?"

Giggles Paige hadn't heard since she was a teenager poured from her. Without giving thought to her actions, Paige pinched his cheek and said, "You're more than handsome. You are fine, which is why I don't like you." His sudden move backward from her touch sobered her. "I totally agree with you. Those young ladies will go far, especially Seniyah," Paige added to save face.

"Seniyah?" he questioned, still beyond her reach.

"Yes. Seniyah is remarkable." Paige started collecting the used paper for the recycling bin to hide her embarrassment. "Oh, did I mention she has a full scholarship to Stanford and she's graduating at the top of her class?"

He walked around the table, straightening the chairs. "I was under the impression that your star student is Jasmine, the one with the blue hair."

Paige thought the idea absurd. "No way! Jasmine is ambitious, and with a lot of help she may actually leave the hood one day. She'd need to learn proper English first and settle on a normal hair color."

"True," he agreed. "But that's why she has you to teach her."

Satisfied the conference room was clean and ready for Monday morning, Paige turned out the light and started for her office. "I'll teach her what I can about business, but it wouldn't surprise me if Jasmine never left the hood. It's part of who she is." Paige stopped abruptly and turned around, causing him to walk into her. "Did I mention her brother is a street pharmacist and she plans to attend community college to collect financial aid? Isn't that crazy?"

He chuckled. "Crazy, but not unheard of. People do it every day. For some, it's taking advantage. For others, it's called survival."

She continued the trek to her office. "Call it what you want. At least Seniyah earned the money that will be given to her."

He entered her office but didn't sit down. "Seniyah, that's the one who sat on the end, in the black wool coat, right? The one who kept her head down and participated only when you directly asked her a question?"

"That's her," Paige said with resignation. "I know I have my work cut out for me."

"I'll say this at the risk of starting another argument, but make sure you're working with the right person for the right reasons."

He was right. She didn't like the implications of his words. "And just what do you mean by that?" she asked, standing behind her desk.

"Jasmine may be rough around the edges, but she is hungry and shows natural leadership ability. Based on what I've seen of the two young ladies, I'd place my money on the one with blue hair. That's just my opinion."

She sat down. "Really? It's a good thing you're not a gambler," she teased. "I'd take all of your money."

"I bet you'd try, in the name of the Lord, of course."

A comfortable silence filled the space. Paige straightened her desk and then checked her e-mail.

"It's been real, but it's time for me to go. Is there a garbage can out back?" Sergio-Xavier said a minute later, breaking the silence.

"Huh?" Paige looked up from the computer. She had been so engrossed in her e-mail, she hadn't noticed he had collected her garbage and was standing at the threshold.

He held up the tied bag. "I'll throw this out on my way out."

She looked down at the clock on the computer screen. It was almost six o'clock. She stood up and stretched. "It is getting late, and I should be going as well. Thanks for lunch."

"No problem, but next time I'll get you a double order of catfish. It won't be for a while." He patted his stomach. "I indulge in that many calories only once a month."

"And don't forget the German chocolate cake, either," she shamelessly added and then walked around the desk. "So what do you have planned for this evening? A hot date with your beautiful Latin girlfriend?"

His cocky smile returned, and for the first time, Paige noticed the right dimple. "You would think that."

"Well, am I right?"

He smirked. "Of course not. I don't have a Latin girlfriend, or one of any other nationality, for that matter. I am totally single."

Although the declaration surprised her, Paige was relieved to know he wasn't attached. "Are you serious?"

"If I had a girlfriend, do you think I'd spend my day with you?" His smile let her know he was only joking. "I do have an engagement tonight with an African American and Latin beauty. My six-year-old niece is preforming in her school's play, and I promised I'd be there."

"That's great." His sense of family touched her, but at the same time she didn't want him to leave. "Have fun." She retrieved her briefcase to conceal the emptiness that threatened to overwhelm her once again.

After Paige turned off the lights and locked her office door, Sergio-Xavier followed her, with the picnic basket in hand, down the hallway once again and outside to the parking lot.

"What are you doing tomorrow?" he asked after dumping the trash in the large receptacle. "That was a stupid question. Of course you're going to church. What I meant to ask was, would you like to attend service with me?"

"Do you actually attend a service, or do you watch a telecast?" she teased.

"You're laughing, but I know you're serious. Why don't you join me and see? With your distorted view of the Word, you need all the church you can get. You should get daily downloads on your smartphone."

Paige wanted to return the insult but couldn't think of anything, because she was actually receiving daily downloads already on her phone. "Maybe next time. I have to sing with praise and worship at the eight a.m. service."

"That's perfect. I attend the eleven o'clock service."

"Well, I . . ." She struggled to find an excuse. "I volunteer for the second service as well. And I go out with the home care ministry, and then there's the night service."

"You don't have to attend every service to be saved. Besides, you'll hear a solid Word at my church." He reached into his back pocket and pulled out a card. "Here's the address. I'll be waiting for you outside at ten forty-five."

He stuffed the card into her hand and then walked toward her car. She followed. "Now get inside," he ordered after taking her keys and unlocking the door.

Paige obeyed, but not without a protest. "Just how do you know I'll be there?"

He smirked. "That's easy. You're nosy, and you can't wait to judge if my relationship with the Lord is as strong as yours." The huffing and puffing that followed didn't move him. "I'll see you tomorrow." He closed the car door and walked away.

Paige glared at him through the rearview mirror, but she didn't say anything. Once again Sergio-Xavier had read her like a book. She would show up tomorrow, and then she'd gloat.

Two hours later, as Paige settled into her quiet bedroom, depression visited her once again. Her parents had each other. Kevin and Tyson had a wife and a child to keep them company. Even the nosy prayer warriors had friends. Paige had nothing but an old, faded image.

Just as she reached for the light on the nightstand, her cell phone alerted her of a text message. After wiping away tears, she read the message and then laughed out loud. Sergio-Xavier had sent her the photos he'd taken of her earlier, while devouring lunch.

Even with greasy lips your face is beautiful, was the message attached to the photo of her eating a fried chicken wing.

Dr. Simone will definitely see me tomorrow, she thought before she turned out the light and laughed herself to sleep.

Chapter 12

Paige didn't need the address of the church. She'd passed by True Worship Ministries on numerous occasions while traveling around the city, showing property. The church had the reputation of being a church for all people. According to her clients who attended the church, the senior pastors, Reginald and Julia Pennington, were practical teachers and were down to earth, teaching the gospel without imposing man-made regulations. The campus sat on two acres of land and housed a community center, which served Oakland's down-and-out and up-and-comers.

"Just what I thought," Paige mumbled once she turned into the parking lot.

The crowd walking into the building was wayward at best in her opinion. She didn't necessarily believe one had to wear rhinestone-decorated suits and pinstripes to attend church, but jeans, sneakers, and flip-flops? The shoes were a common sight even in cold weather, but not at church. On a Sunday morning? And uncovered tattoos? Her church, Restoration Ministries, didn't have an official dress code policy, but most congregants dressed conservatively of their own accord. These people couldn't be serious about walking with the Lord.

"No wonder they have such a large membership," she said to herself. "Anything and everything is allowed up in here. I bet the pastor wears jeans and a hoodie." She shook her head in disgust before focusing on looking for a parking space.

A waving fluorescent stick caught her attention and directed her to an empty space right next to Sergio-Xavier's car. *What are the odds of this happening?* she wondered. Her hand had barely touched the door handle before Sergio-Xavier opened the car door for her.

"I knew you would come with your saint-o-meter," he told her. "That's why I gave the attendants your car's make and model and had them save you a space."

She didn't bother asking why the attendants would honor his request. He was wearing not only a blue tailored suit, but also that cocky smile she hated, which was outlined by a neatly trimmed mustache. The woodsy scent emanating from him arrested her the second he opened the door. She caught herself just before she was about to yield to the urge to close her eyes and savor the fragrance. She was saved and sanctified. She couldn't be seen lusting in the church's parking lot with a client. She ignored his outstretched hand and stepped from the car.

"Look, I received a great Word this morning from Pastor Drake, and I am not going to allow the devil to spoil my day."

"Are you calling me the devil?"

"You're not the devil, but you could certainly get me into trouble."

He laughed in her face. "I doubt that," he said, then once again extended his hand. "Come on. Let's go inside. You need all the church you can get."

She sneered but accepted his hand. Paige was about to ask why his hands were so smooth, but then she remembered he was physician. As they neared the entrance, Paige slowed her pace. Compared to the casual attire most of the congregants wore, she was overdressed in a calf-length skirt and blazer. With her white-collared blouse buttoned to the top, the only skin Paige showed was her hands and face.

"Are you all right?" he asked with more concern than the situation warranted.

"I'm fine, but I feel out of place," she admitted.

"Why? Because you have on that 'Take me to the water' outfit?"

Paige gasped.

"Don't worry. No one will mistake you for a saint, because it's a known fact that a long skirt can come up just as fast as a miniskirt."

"How dare you say that to me!" She struggled to free her hand, but it was useless. The soft hand she had admired moments earlier now felt like a metal bracelet.

"Will you calm down?" he said, leaning into her ear. "You're causing a scene. I said that only to prove a point."

"And your point would be?" she snarled through clenched teeth.

"Stop judging the gift by the outer packaging. See what's inside first." Once again he left her speechless. "Now come on. You'll be fine as long as you don't open your mouth."

With each step, Paige repented, because she had actually considered punching him with her free hand. The joy she'd experienced from his compliment last night was long gone. Instead of eating greasy fried chicken, Paige felt like smearing Vaseline on her face and beating his fine butt right into the pavement.

"Let it go, Paige," he said, holding the church door open for her. "You know I told the truth. Your face has been clothed with disgust since you parked your car. You don't think these people know the Lord, because they're dressed differently."

Anger seeped out and embarrassment rushed in and Paige entered the lobby with her head down. She'd just left a place where she sang about Jesus's unconditional love, undeserving grace, and unlimited mercy, only to learn that she didn't have any of those characteristics.

"Come on. I'll show you to your seat." He always moved forward, like his words didn't hurt. She hated that about him, yet she followed.

The floor level of True Worship was nearly packed to capacity, and from what Paige could see by straining her neck, so was the balcony. Unlike her all African American church, the cultural diversity of True Worship mirrored the Bay Area's population.

"Why are we going to the front? It's already crowded," she asked when they were more than halfway down the middle aisle. "Let's sit in the back."

"I already have our seats reserved," he answered without slowing his pace. "We'll sit here."

Her eyes followed his pointed finger to two empty seats on the second row, next to a man who nearly made Paige's heart stop.

"Oh, my God!" Paige gripped his arm with strength she didn't know she had. "That's Marcus Simone. You didn't tell me he attends here. I love his music, and I have all his CDs." Paige's words ran together, and her pitch rose several notches, but she didn't care. The man whose music never failed to uplift her spirit was just a few feet away.

"So you're a fan of Marcus's music."

Her words tumbled out at record speed. "Are you kidding? His music has carried me through some really dark times. I don't like just his music. I like him. I like—"

"You do know he's married, don't you?" Sergio-Xavier interjected.

Paige smacked her lips. "Of course I do. I mean, I like the genuineness of his music. I know everything about him. I knew he lived in the Bay Area, but I didn't know he went here, of all places." She pointed in his direction. "That's his wife, Shannon, sitting next to him. They have three kids—Marcus Jr. and Mariah, who are fraternal twins, and Marlon—and they're expecting their fourth in July. He has six albums, two DVDs, and a book and is in the process of coproducing a movie. He also owns a successful computer business." Paige closed her eyes and finally took a breath.

Sergio-Xavier grinned and shook his head. "You amaze me. I never would have thought of you as a groupie." He gestured for her to enter the row. "Let's sit down."

Paige gasped and gripped his arm again. "I can't sit next to *him.*"

"Why not? It's just Marcus. He won't bite."

She still wouldn't budge. "So you know him, then?" Paige considered it rude for him to laugh in her face, but to bend over, holding his stomach, in the front of the sanctuary was downright humiliating. "What's so funny?" she sneered.

"You are," he said after resuming an upright position. "You don't have a neutral cell in your body. You're either over the top or off the deep end."

"Explain, and hurry up before you embarrass me further."

"You're doing a fabulous job of that all by yourself." He pointed down the aisle. "That's Marcus Simone." He then pointed at his chest. "My name is Sergio-Xavier Simone. Do I know him? Marcus and I are first cousins." When she didn't readily respond, he added, "Our fathers are brothers. Do you get it now?"

"Yes, I do," she mouthed more than spoke. She could blame not connecting the last names on excitement, but the word *mortification* wasn't strong enough to adequately describe her feelings. In a sanctuary full of people, Paige fully understood what Sergio-Xavier had tried to tell her at the food bank. From following Marcus's career, Paige knew he was from a large, wealthy family with deep Bay Area roots. Now that she'd been enlightened, the resemblance was obvious, only Marcus had a ponytail and Sergio-Xavier's wavy hair stopped at his neckline. Now she knew how he could afford to spend over a million dollars on investment property. In addition to being a physician, Sergio-Xavier Winston Simone was a multimillionaire.

"Good. Now, please sit down before service starts."

Without protesting, Paige started down the aisle behind him, but she didn't have a chance to sulk. Once the two cousins greeted each other with a hug and a choreographed handshake, and once she sat down next to Sergio-Xavier, people of all shades and sizes acknowledged her with a nod. No doubt they were other members of the Simone clan. When Marcus said hello and shook her hand, she had to bite her tongue to keep from blurting out a request for an autograph.

"Are you all right?" Sergio-Xavier whispered in her ear once he was seated. "I wouldn't want you to spontaneously combust, being this close to your idol."

Since she was in church, Paige withheld the eye rolling, but she still spoke her mind. "Pull your bottom lip over your forehead and swallow."

"I'm just saying, you've never been this giddy over me." The smug expression gave the impression the comment was legitimate, but she knew better.

"That's because I don't like you in the least bit."

"Stop lying in church," he said and then stood. "I'll be back after service starts. In the meantime, try not to jump on Marcus's lap. Shannon will beat you down in the sanctuary." Then he walked away.

Paige slammed her eyes shut to stop the red dots floating across her field of vision and covered her mouth with both hands. She hadn't used profanity in years, but at that moment nothing would give her more pleasure than cursing him out. "Lord, please hold my tongue and my fists," she prayed repeatedly—though it was more like pleading—with no relief.

"Praise the Lord, everybody!" The boisterous voice over the sound system interrupted her petitions.

Both collective and individual praises filled the sanctuary and charged the atmosphere. The red dots were gone when she opened her eyes and found the majority of the congregation standing. Not wanting to appear a novice at church and wanting to see what was going on, Paige stood too.

The praise and worship ministry took the stage along with the band. The lights dimmed, and colored floodlights illuminated the sanctuary. *What kind of circus is this?* she wondered.

She stood through three selections, but she didn't participate. She was too busy scoping out the scene. Everywhere she looked, she saw people singing the words on the wall screens and worshipping and praising. She knew the songs, some of which she sang at her church, yet Paige couldn't let go and join in. She had to be alert, just in case something went down that wasn't right. As the third song came to a slow close, a familiar voice bellowed over the microphone in prayer. The voice didn't move her, but the name written on the big screen knocked the wind out of her: Minister Sergio-Xavier Simone.

"Oh no! He's a minister?" she thundered before she could stop herself. Thankfully, the music and his voice were loud enough so that only those close to her heard her rant. She looked to the left, then to the right. At least six sets of eyes, including her idol's, were zeroing in on her. Paige couldn't read their expressions, but the unanimous "Shush" they offered was loud and clear.

Paige bowed her head and, instead of praying, wondered how someone as rude and harsh as Sergio-Xavier Simone could be a man of God. Had she been that wrong about him? After much deliberation, she decided she hadn't. Sure, he knew the right words to pray and he *looked* the part, but the spiritual fruit just wasn't there.

"Turn around and make your brothers and sisters feel at home," Sergio-Xavier instructed the audience at the close of the prayer.

The gesture was obviously a ritual, Paige determined when the entire congregation hugged or shook hands with those in close proximity. Since she'd already greeted the Simones, Paige stepped out into the aisle and half-heartedly shook a few hands, then returned to her seat.

Her foe rejoined her before she could cross her legs at the ankles. "How are you holding up?" he asked.

"What type of stupid question is that?" Paige wanted to yell, but instead she asked, "Why didn't you tell me you're a minister?"

"You were too busy condemning me to ask and too self-absorbed to care," he answered in that no-nonsense tone she hated. "Now, stop talking in church before you say something crazy."

The blows his words carried were becoming harder to withstand. From a few conversations with the man, she'd gained a deeper understanding of the phrase "the truth hurts." She didn't like the truths he brought to light, and she wondered how she'd fallen into such darkness in the first place. "I thought we got past that?" she said.

"No, we just moved on," he said, resting his arm on the back of her chair. "We can talk about that later, but just know I have forgiven you."

She abruptly turned her attention to the platform to hide how much those four words meant to her. She'd give anything to *feel* forgiven for the moral crime she'd committed. Knowing theology was one thing, but believing it was another. She'd read Romans chapter ten, verse nine, so many times, she knew the exact number of letters the salvation scripture contained. Salvation she could comprehend, but forgiveness remained beyond her reach.

I'm wrong again, she thought when Pastor Reggie took the podium. He wasn't wearing jeans and a hoodie, but a black cassock. "Is he related to you also?" she asked, since Pastor Reggie didn't resemble the Simones.

"He's my uncle. His wife and my father are siblings."

"Oh," she mouthed and directed her attention to Pastor Julia, who was sitting on the dais, and wondered why she didn't use the traditional first lady title.

Pastor Reggie opened his Bible and began preaching. His teaching-style preaching resembled Pastor Drake's, and Paige liked that. Both had the ability to break the Word down, and both provide practical examples of its application. Pastor Reggie closed his sermon by sharing his personal testimony of forgiveness. He shared how his past sins had caused him to lose seventeen years of his son's life. He found peace and moved forward only after he learned to forgive himself. Only then did God restore what he'd lost and add more.

"Why can't that happen for me?" Paige wanted to scream, but instead she lowered her head in her hands and cried. The tears were slow until Sergio-Xavier stuffed his handkerchief into her hands. She expected him to say something humiliating, but he didn't. His firm hand squeezing her shoulder and pulling her to him surprised her, but she didn't resist. At that moment she needed comfort and the prayer he whispered in her ear. The soft strokes on the head were nice too.

He waited until she had regained composure before asking, "Are you all right?"

She didn't want to lie in church, so she answered, "I'm better," and then sat up but didn't face him. He didn't pressure her, but his arm rested around her shoulder until the benediction.

After the service was over, he turned to her and whispered, "Come on. I'll walk you to your car." He gripped Paige's arm in hopes of steering her out of the sanctuary before they were bombarded with questions. Normally, he wouldn't mind this family's curiosity, but Paige was too vulnerable at the moment. He sensed the earlier emotional breakdown was minor compared to the release she needed. Her tight shoulder muscles exposed her heavy burden more than the tears, but it wasn't his place to pry about the source. Their broker-client relationship didn't give him that right.

"Thank you," she answered, fiddling with her purse strap.

Sergio-Xavier's plan failed—they were ambushed the second they stepped into the aisle. "Oh no," he groaned.

"Hello. I'm Staci," said a woman with curly hair.

Another woman, with hazel eyes and honey-blond hair, stepped in front of Sergio-Xavier. "And I'm Lashay."

Both women held babies in their arms, but that didn't interrupt their mission. They peppered Paige with questions.

"What's your name?"

"Where are you from?"

"How did you guys meet?"

"How long have you been dating?"

"Slow your roll," Sergio-Xavier said, holding up the universal time-out sign.

"Not until you introduce us to your girlfriend." The one with curly hair smirked.

Knowing the interrogation would only intensify if he didn't give the women what they wanted, without correcting their assumption that Paige was *his* girl, Sergio-Xavier placed his hand on Paige's back and made the formal introductions.

"This is my real estate broker, Paige McDaniels." He turned to Paige, whose eyes were glossy. "These are my nosy, pesky cousins. Staci is Marcus's little sister, and Lashay is my aunt Julia's daughter."

"Hi, Paige," the women said in unison.

Lashay switched her baby from one arm to the other. "So how long have you two been dating?"

"We're not dating," Paige answered, too quickly and with too much conviction for him. "I'm helping him look for property, that's all."

The women exchanged glances. "Uh-huh," they chorused.

"So what attracted you to my cousin?" Staci asked, pushing.

"Well, actually—," Paige began but didn't get to finish.

"I hope you enjoyed the service," Shannon said, squeezing in between the cousins. "I was confused also the first time I stepped into a church. Keep coming. You'll get the hang of it."

"This is not my first time at a church service. I have a church home," Paige answered without conveying how much she was involved in the church.

"Oh, I'm sorry," Shannon replied, apologizing. "By the way you were checking things out during the first part of service, I thought this was your first time."

Sergio-Xavier cleared his throat to keep from laughing at Shannon's assessment of Paige.

"So did I," Staci added.

Paige's arm trembled underneath his fingertips. Sergio-Xavier had to get her out of there before another emotional breakdown occurred. "Excuse me, ladies," he said, butting in, "but I know for a fact each of you has a husband and at least two kids. Go mind their business and stay out of mine for once. We have to go."

"Don't get beat down in church," Staci warned.

With her free hand, Lashay pinched his arm. "Wasn't nobody talking to you."

"Whatever. You're still nosy. Always have been and always will be," he shot back.

Lashay ignored his attitude. "Yeah, I love you too, cuz," she said and then directed her attention to Paige. "I don't know how you deal with him."

"It was nice meeting you, Paige." Shannon extended her hand. "We'll chat next time, and I'll have Marcus autograph a CD for you."

Paige blushed. "Thank you so much."

Sergio-Xavier's chest muscles constricted, but he refused to acknowledge that Paige's excitement over another man bothered him, even if it was his cousin. "Love you, guys," he said, addressing his family collectively, then led Paige out of the sanctuary.

The walk back to the car was totally different. Paige didn't stare at the congregants, and she didn't walk fast. She didn't talk, either. On this journey Paige held her head down, and her steps were slow and gingerly. Her slight tremors were probably undetected by the throngs of people, but Sergio-Xavier's trained eye saw them. When they arrived at her car, instead of unlocking the door, Paige stood there, looking lost. Her pain pulled his heartstrings, and his protective instincts took over.

"Come with me," he ordered. "I have something to show you." He expected resistance, and when Paige didn't offer any, he unlocked his car and opened the passenger door.

"Where are we going?" she asked once they were both settled inside his car.

"It's a surprise, but trust me, you'll like it."

Her lips remained sealed, but her eyes spoke volumes to him. She was tired and scared.

"Sure," she whispered finally and then leaned back against the headrest and closed her eyes.

Sergio-Xavier pulled out of the parking lot without a destination, but he was determined to make Paige feel better. He didn't know her likes and dislikes, her hobbies, or how much time she had. What he did know was that he was more involved in Paige's life than he wanted to be.

"We're here," he announced forty minutes later, after pulling into the parking lot of his favorite restaurant in Pacifica.

For the first time since entering the vehicle, Paige sat forward and took in her surroundings. "Where are we?" She nodded when he told her the restaurant's name and location. "I've heard good things about this place. I'd planned on coming here one day when . . ." She didn't finish the thought.

"I love this place. I come here often to clear my head, as well as for the food. The view of the ocean and the sound of the waves crashing against the rocks are very calming."

"Wow," she said after stepping from the car. "The view of the bay is beautiful from here. I can't tell where the sky begins and the ocean ends." The five-star restaurant, which sat on the beach, had both indoor and outdoor seating.

"If it's too cool for you, we can get a table inside," he offered.

She turned and faced the beach. "Out here is fine."

After securing a table facing the beach and perusing the menu, the two sat in silence, watching the waves roll in, until a waiter came to take their order.

"I see you're staying away from those prawns?" he said in reference to the sea scallops she'd ordered.

"I love them, but I'll probably never eat one again."

He finally got a half smile from her. "Tell me what else you enjoy besides prawns, church, mentoring, and real estate."

Her confused expression said she didn't understand the question. "What else is there? By the time I finish with all of that, there isn't time for anything else."

"Wow. Your schedule is packed more than mine," he commented after she ran down her weekly schedule. "What do you for fun?"

"Life is not about fun, at least not for me," she began, then cleared her throat. "At least not at this time. Life is about serving and giving to others. I have to work out my salvation."

He didn't agree with the statement but refrained from saying anything that might start a disagreement. "When do you relax, or do you?"

Her despair seeped out in dry laughter. "I don't know what that means anymore. Honestly, I don't know who I am anymore. Three weeks ago I thought I knew myself and my purpose, but then I met you. In that short period of time you have made me question my ability to make sound decisions." She waited until the waiter finished placing their drinks and warm sourdough rolls on the table before continuing. "I did enjoy service today. It was nothing like the fabrication I'd manufactured in my head. Pastor Pennington is a very solid teacher. I learned a lot about you today." She took a sip of iced tea. "Are your cousins always in your business?"

He grinned. "Of course, and honestly, I don't mind one bit. My male cousins and I did the exact same thing and worse to every one of their boyfriends. My family is very close and harmless. That is, until you hurt one of us."

She raised her glass to him. "I'll be sure not to do that. Why did they assume I was your *girl*?"

He buttered a roll and set it on her plate. "Probably because I introduced you as my guest. I've never had a female guest before, and I normally sit on the dais with the other ministers. Oh, and everyone is waiting for me to marry and have children." He couldn't be sure, but he thought he saw a flash of pain in her eyes. "What about you? Tell me about your family. Do you plan to slow down long enough to marry and raise a family?"

It was pain he'd seen, only now it was more intense, causing her eyes to blink rapidly. "I'm the middle child of three, and the only one without a spouse or significant other and children. As screwed up as I am, my eggs will probably dry up before the Lord sends someone my way."

She raised an eyebrow, as if waiting for him to say something to confirm her prediction, but Sergio-Xavier didn't bite. His goal was to make her feel better, not join her pity party.

"Oh," she said, as if suddenly remembering something. "Why did you sit next to me, instead of on the dais?"

Perfect timing, he thought when the waiter delivered her salad and his soup. Revealing to Paige that he'd sat beside her because he'd felt a divine unction that she would need him wasn't something he wanted to do.

"Ooh, this is so good, and just what I need to clean all that grease you fed me yesterday out of my system," she said of the spinach, dried cranberry, candied pecan, and feta cheese salad.

"Go ahead and blame me for clogging your arteries. At least you're smiling again," he said while adding cracked pepper to his clam chowder.

She offered him a full smile, but no words. They enjoyed the rest of the meal in a comfortable silence. The rhythmic sounds of the ocean filled the space with peace.

"I can't remember the last time I've been to a beach or walked in sand," Paige said, leaning back in the chair after savoring the last bite of cinnamon crème brûlée. "It's been at least five years." She looked contemplative. "I'll have to write it into my schedule."

He thought the idea absurd. "Why wait? I have time if you do. We can walk on the beach now."

"No, we can't." She kicked her foot out and pointed at the heeled boot. "Leather boots aren't made for sand, and neither are tailored suits and alligator shoes," she said, noting his attire.

He pushed the chair back and bent over. "Don't get deep on me now. Take off your boots. We can walk barefoot." Within seconds the alligator shoes were off, his socks tucked inside, and the tailored pant legs were rolled up.

"I see you've done this before," she said but still made no effort to join him.

"Sometimes I come here after a hard case and just walk for hours. Then, there are times I come to pray and mediate."

"Maybe next time," she said, shaking her head. "I'm not prepared today. I need a pedicure first and the right outfit and . . ."

"I figured this would shut you up," he said when she stopped talking after he lifted her left leg into his lap and unzipped her boot. "Relax and enjoy the moment. God placed this beauty here for us to enjoy."

"I know, but—"

"No buts. Just enjoy." He took more time than he should have removing her nylon socks, but he liked the feel of her soft skin and the contours of her muscles.

"Don't be trying to feel me up," she warned when his hands lingered.

"If I did try, I'd get lost in all this material." He laughed. "If you want to go sailing later, we can use your skirt as a sail."

She kicked his leg and then stood up. "Forget you."

He smirked. "I doubt that's possible. Wait here," he said, collecting their shoes and suit jackets. "I'll put these in the car, and then we'll walk."

"It's not like I have a choice."

Sergio-Xavier considered pointing out the obvious but recognized the self-preservation tactic and continued on to his vehicle. When he returned, the table was empty. Paige had started down the beach.

For a moment, Sergio-Xavier stood watching her hold her skirt up as she gingerly stepped in the sand. The sun glistened against her ebony skin, giving her calves a glow. Even on the beach, her body language was tense. Something was driving her to "work out her salvation," as she put it, but Sergio-Xavier wasn't sure he wanted to dig deep enough to learn what that was.

"Having fun yet?" he asked once he caught up with her.

"Maybe."

Her smile said what her mouth would not. She was having fun, all right, but she would never give him the satisfaction of knowing he'd given her any joy. Her arm interlocked with his, but he doubted she realized the two resembled a couple.

"How do you manage being a minister and a doctor and remaining so normal?"

He shrugged. "I don't know what you call normal, but I handle my vocation and my profession by keeping my role in perspective."

She stopped walking and looked up. "What do you mean?"

"My role is the same with both. I am not a healer or a savior. I am just one of the many vessels He uses to fulfill His plans. I have to totally rely on Him to do anything. I pray before I exam every patient, and I pray for everyone I counsel spiritually. I *try* to do only the things He tells me to and to refrain from things that are not His will. Do I always get it right? No, but that's where the blood of Jesus comes in."

Her eyes glossed over before she turned toward the ocean. She maintained that position the remainder of the walk, without talking. Sergio-Xavier didn't talk, either; he spent the mile walk in silent prayer for Paige.

Chapter 13

Blue streaks had already begun to break through the dark sky when Paige placed her coffee cup in the dish rack to dry on Monday morning. Normally by this time she'd be waiting in the drive-through line at Starbucks, but today she'd decided to enjoy an extra half hour of relaxation before starting her hectic week. Instead of racing to Starbucks for a caffeine fix, she had brewed a cup of herbal tea in the Keurig and had sipped it while reading a daily devotional.

Although the previous day's events had left her emotionally drained, stiff muscles and fatigue didn't plague her body this morning. After a hot bubble bath the night before, she'd slept like a baby. The realization that yesterday was the first Sunday she'd attended only two church services in three years hadn't come until her head touched the pillow. Even more surprising had been the absence of condemnation for hanging out on the beach on the Lord's day. "The church mothers would be proud," she'd moaned before drifting off to sleep.

Sergio-Xavier had been the perfect gentleman, not that she was looking for one, but the man had turned out to be everything she thought he wasn't. He'd sensed and fulfilled her needs without her having to articulate them. He'd known when to allow her to talk and when to be quiet and let the ocean's waves speak for her. Most importantly, he hadn't cracked jokes about the corns on her feet or her rough heels. She hadn't had a pedicure since the beginning of last spring, but she vowed to get one as soon as possible.

"I can't put this off any longer," she mumbled while drying her hands. She didn't want to make the call, but she had to for her own peace of mind. She picked up the landline and punched in the numbers. "Lord, please don't let me say something stupid." She finished the plea just before he answered.

"Dr. Simone speaking."

Paige's breath caught. They had talked on the phone before, but this morning Sergio-Xavier sounded different. His voice was deeper and, Lord help her, downright sexy.

"Hello? Is someone there?"

"It's me. Good morning," she managed to say after clearing her throat. "I was calling to remind you of our appointment tomorrow afternoon."

She heard his chuckle and envisioned those full lips parting into a mischievous grin.

"Let me guess. You misjudged your assistant, and she quit. Now you have to make reminder calls at seven a.m., right?"

She joined in his laughter. "Something like that. Is this too early for you? I assumed you'd be getting ready for work as well."

"You know what they say about assumptions. When you—"

"Watch yourself, Preacher."

"As long as I have you to keep me straight, I'll be fine." His laughter subsided, and Paige wished it hadn't. It was warm and soothing. "Actually, I'm already at the hospital, preparing for rounds."

"Well, I won't keep you, then—," she began, but he interrupted.

"What's the real reason you called?"

Why do you always have to be so direct? she wanted to scream but instead swallowed her pride. "Thank you for yesterday. Well, actually for the entire weekend. I had an emotionally draining weekend, and you helped me through the rough spots. Thanks for being patient and understanding. I really needed that. Every time I see a beach, I'll think of you." She envisioned him gloating during the long silence that followed. "You're the best client I've ever had, and I haven't sold you anything yet." Nervous giggles flowed uncontrollably from her.

"You're welcome." His staid tone threw her off balance. She'd expected laughter or a joke. "I have to go, but I will definitely keep our appointment tomorrow. I want to get this project off the ground before spring."

That was a nice dismissal, she thought but said, "Okay, well, have a good day."

"Paige," she heard him call just as she was about to disconnect the call.

"Yes, Dr. Simone?"

"Feel free to use this number in the afternoon and evening hours as well. If you need me, I'm just a phone call away. Have a good day and a great time with the divas tonight, sweetheart." Then the line went dead.

Paige replaced the cordless phone on the charger and then collected her briefcase and jacket from the closet and prepared to leave for work. She'd backed halfway out of the driveway before Sergio-Xavier's last words registered, causing her to slam on the brakes. "He called me sweetheart!"

"Divas!" Paige hollered uncharacteristically upon entering the classroom. She'd expected a few surprised expressions from the DWAP girls, but the looks of distain and disgust were uncalled for.

"Hi," the group chorused, greeting her collectively with the dryness of the Mojave Desert.

Jasmine, now with burgundy curls resting on her shoulders, stepped forward. Her twisted lip and scrunched nose made Paige second-guess her decision to wear the gray- and black-checkered, floor-length broomstick skirt and gray sweater instead of the usual black suit. "What's up with you?"

Totally deflated, Paige looked down and lifted the skirt to show off the new pair of gray leather boots she'd picked up after her last client. "What do you mean? This outfit is cute and modest."

The other girls snickered, but Jasmine outright laughed in Paige's face.

"I've got to work with you," Jasmine said and at the same time grabbed Paige by the hand and led her to a regular-size chair that had been placed in the middle of the room. Once Paige was seated, Jasmine added, "You'll never hook a man as fine as Dr. Simone, looking like this."

Paige bolted upright from the chair and stood toe-to-toe with the young girl. "What are you talking about? I'm not trying to hook a man, especially not him. I'm saved. I'm waiting on the Lord. I am—"

"You'll be waitin' awhile," one of the girls interrupted, "because won't no man be able to find you under all that fabric."

"I'm sure the good doctor knows how to feel his way, but at some point he's going to want to see what he's working with," another girl added.

Paige gripped the back of her chair. "Now wait a minute!" Paige was not about to let these unsaved, oversexed, and half-educated high school students insult her about her lack of sex appeal. "You are way out of line to discuss my personal life here. I am not one of your girlfriends. I am your instructor. I volunteer to train you, not to

discuss some imaginary relationship with Dr. Simone."
With every word, she shook more violently. "We will not
discuss my personal life!"

"We know, because you don't have one," someone
hollered.

Uncontrollable laughter filled the room, but Paige
stood her ground. Her chest heaved and her cheeks
burned, and she was on the verge of tears, because the
jesting words carried the truth. "That is none of your
business!"

"Wrong again," Jasmine said, correcting her. "You
made it our business when you made him part of our
training session. We saw how he was checking you out."

"That's not true. He was here only to observe," Paige
retorted, defending herself.

"He did. He checked you out, and we peeped him out.
He likes you, but you're going to have to step your game
up to get him."

What little professionalism and tolerance Paige had
left vanished. "I don't want him!" she screamed. "And I
do not want to discuss this any further. Now, get down to
business, or I'll cancel the session and quit this group."

Jasmine's lips smacked. "Whoa, Miss Paige. What
happened to all that professionalism you was teaching
us?"

"Little girl, how dare you turn this around on me?"
Paige screamed so loudly that her voice squeaked.

The room echoed with a collective "Shh!" from the
girls.

"Will you tone it down before an administrator comes
in here and shuts us down?" Jasmine pleaded with both
hands raised, and then stepped into Paige's personal
space. "For the record, I am not a little girl. I am eighteen
years old, which legally makes me an adult. I am the same
height as you, and my body is just as curvaceous as yours,

but tighter, considering your age." She pointed to the chair. "Now, sit down so we can get started."

"Started on what?" Paige snarled.

"Not *what*. Who."

"Who?"

"You, Miss Saved and Sanctified, and running over with a spirit and speaking in an unknown tongue that even you don't understand."

"I will not allow you to make mockery of—"

"Let me break it down for you this way," Jasmine interrupted. It was good that she butted, as Paige heard every curse word she knew floating though her head. Jasmine looked around the room. "Everyone who has more than black, brown, blue, and gray in their closet, owns at least one pair of open-toe shoes, and doesn't wear a bun, please slide back one step."

Everyone retreated but Paige, who remained planted where she was standing and seething with anger.

"Now do you get it?" Jasmine asked.

"I know what's in my closet, and I look in the mirror every morning. So I don't need for you to tell me what I look like," Paige snapped. "For the last time, let's get to work on this project before I leave."

"Ugh!" Jasmine frantically waved her hands in the air. "You still don't get it. DWAP's work is done. We met at my house yesterday, after church, and filled this week's orders, balanced our accounts, and restocked our inventory."

Now Paige was totally confused. "Why would you do that, knowing we would meet tonight?"

"So we could have the whole time to help a sista out." Jasmine pointed to the black case on the table. "We're giving you a makeover, and I'm going to show you some quick and easy hairstyles so you can get rid of that bun. We went online and determined your color palette and printed it out so you can take it with you when you shop. Seriously, we know you're not *tryin'* to get a man, but you can look good for yourself. I mean, you're pretty already, so you just need some enhancement."

Jasmine pointed to the chair again. "Now, sit down so we can get started. We promise not to have you looking like a fifty-dollar hussy. It's just that you've helped us so much, and this is our way of showing you some appreciation for taking time out of your schedule for us." Jasmine giggled and then added, "You better take this, 'cause we ain't got no money to raise you an offering."

Paige didn't realize she was falling until her bottom hit the seat of the chair. She hadn't seen this coming. Her purpose was to help forsaken inner-city youths, not the other way around. The idea of her learning something from them had never crossed her mind. Neither had she thought that any of them cared about anyone or anything other than themselves. She'd been wrong again.

She scanned the table more closely. The table contained not only make-up and color swatches and fashion magazines, but also a bowl of grapes and plastic cups, along with two bottles of store-brand apple cider. The girls' dead silence enabled her to hear the jazz music playing from someone's smartphone. They had planned what they considered a girls' night, and seeing the anticipation on each of their faces, she knew she couldn't disappoint them.

"Okay, let's get started," Paige said between fake coughs, meant to camouflage how much the grassroots effort touched her.

Cheers of "Great!" and "Let's get started" filled the room, but only momentarily. The ladies were on a mission and went right to work. Jasmine disassembled the bun and plugged in the curling iron.

"Have some of this," one girl said, handing Paige a cup of cider and a small bunch of grapes.

Another girl held up swatches of colors that would look good with Paige's skin tone. Paige nodded and tried to remember the fashion tips. "Don't worry if you can't remember it all. I made some note cards for you," the girl told her.

As soon as Paige finished the cider and grapes, two girls grabbed each of her hands and proceeded to give her a manicure.

"You have beautiful hair. I don't know why you insist on hiding it in that throwback bun," Jasmine said and then instructed someone to hold up the hairstyles that would do Paige's foot-long tresses justice.

A giggle slipped from Paige, and for once she didn't try to stifle it. She was actually having fun with the girls. The idea of her sitting motionless in a chair while these kids helped her look good was hilarious, and all because they thought Sergio-Xavier was interested.

While the curls cooled and rested, Jasmine started on Paige's make-up. "Now before you start speaking in tongues and rebuking the devil," Jasmine said, holding up the M•A•C color palette, "we didn't steal this. My cousin works at Macy's, and she gave me a deal, but don't ask me what kind of deal. Just trust me, it's legal. We know your whole body is saved, sanctified. Won't no stolen product adhere to your face. It would just slide right off."

Paige wanted to laugh along with the girls, but she couldn't move or talk. She settled on grunting to communicate that she got the dig, but made a decision not to complain later. They were only having fun, and to be honest, so was she.

"Get the mirror," Jasmine ordered with only twelve minutes of their scheduled time left. She tilted Paige's head upright after adding the finishing touches to her hair.

Paige opened her eyes to find the girls had packed the leftover snacks and had cleared everything away. Next to her briefcase were the note cards and the pictures they'd shown her earlier. A big square mirror was thrust in front of her face before she could finish surveying the room.

"Well, what do you think?" they all asked at once.

Paige almost didn't recognize herself. Since she'd joined church, her make-up kit, if she could call it that, had consisted of lip gloss and night cream. She now had a full face, but the colors looked natural and her skin glowed. She still went to the salon for a relaxer every six weeks, but she hadn't worn her hair down in over a year. Her plain, chipped nails were now shaped and smoothed and had a wine color that complemented her skin tone.

"Well?" the girls persisted. "Do you like it?"

Paige looked into seven pairs of expectant eyes and for a moment was disappointed. That was when she realized one girl was missing, Seniyah. Paige had been so caught up in the impromptu event that she hadn't noticed the girl's absence. She'd talk with Seniyah later, but she wouldn't disappoint those who were present.

"I love it!" she screamed.

"Shh!" the girls chorused. "You're going to get us in trouble."

"I love it," Paige whispered, then opened her arms for a group hug. "Give me a diva hug, but don't mess up my hair," she warned. "I look good."

The hug ended almost as soon as it had begun. Time was running out. The janitor's keys could be heard from down the hall.

"Thank you so much," Paige said. "You divas are the best. I can't promise I'll look like this every day, but I'll do my best . . . ," she began.

"And let God do the rest," the girls added, finishing the slogan Paige said at each session.

The girls gathered their belongings, and as they started for the door, Paige touched Jasmine's arm to get her attention.

"Yes, Miss Paige?" Jasmine asked.

The joy in the young woman's eyes almost made Paige lose courage. "I know you spearheaded this. Thank you. The gesture was nice, but you need to work on your presentation. This could have gone much smoother if you hadn't opened with insults."

Jasmine looked contemplative. "Okay. Well, then, add communication skills to this project. If you teach us, we will listen. We're not all hopeless heathens. Some of us just don't know any other way. We're products of our environment, but if people like you, who know better, teach us better, many of us will listen. Not all of us want our tombstone to say born, raised, and died in the hood." She gestured toward the girls, who were now milling about. "Why do you think we're here? We want better. Our generation approaches things differently than yours, but that doesn't mean you should count us out."

Paige nodded. That was exactly what Sergio-Xavier had said. "Okay, I'll remember that."

Jasmine gripped the door handle. "I'm serious. We may travel the hard road, but we do have goals. Take Seniyah, for example. She's at the top of the class and on her way to Stanford on a full-ride scholarship. She may go into labor while giving her valedictorian speech, and she may have to leave her baby with her mama while she's at college, but at least she'll be in school."

Paige's head ceased nodding and started shaking violently. "Whoa! What did you just say? What baby?"

Jasmine let go of the door handle and stepped back to allow the other girls to file out. "Aw, Miss Paige, don't tell me you didn't know your favorite student is five months' pregnant?"

"Oh, God, no." Paige's lips continued moving, but no sound came forth. She heard words of agony in her head but couldn't get them out.

"That's old news," Jasmine continued, talking like it was normal for a smart high school girl to end up pregnant in her senior year. Maybe it was normal. Child-care centers were as common as cafeterias in most inner-city high schools. "She's due a month after graduation. That gives her about six weeks to bond with her baby before heading out to Stanford. Good thing the school is not that far away."

"Oh, God." Paige's moans grew louder and faster. "What am I going to do?"

Jasmine flipped the light switch, then exited the room, and Paige followed her out into the hallway. "Right now you're going to get out of here before the janitor comes. Then I hope you make a trip to the mall and pick up somethin' cute, like in those pictures we showed you." Jasmine turned and started walking. "Oh, yeah. Tell Dr. Simone we said hello. He can thank us later," Jasmine yelled over her shoulder as she walked down the hallway.

Paige's feet stayed glued to the linoleum until dust from the janitor's broom sprayed her boots. Thirty minutes later, she pulled into her two-car garage without knowing how she'd made it home. She didn't remember the highway or the stoplights, as thoughts of Seniyah's pregnancy and how she'd missed it had dominated her brain. They'd had numerous discussions about her going away to school. Seniyah was happy, or so Paige had thought, but not once had she mentioned that she was not only sexually active, but pregnant also. Didn't the girl know how hard, if not impossible, it was going to be for her to manage classes and raise a child? And what about money? Seniyah was dirt poor.

As Paige moped through the house, hanging up her coat and storing her briefcase, so many things made sense to her now. Seniyah's inattentiveness, lack of enthusiasm, and body language all screamed pregnant in hindsight. "That's why the coat was tight," Paige grumbled and flopped facedown on her bed. Her Bluetooth chirped at her ear, denying her the chance to drown her sorrow on the comfortable bed. While still lying facedown and without bothering to check the caller ID, Paige pressed the button and answered the call.

"Paige McDaniels speaking," she greeted in her manu-factured business voice.

"Good evening, Paige. Is this a bad time?"

Paige turned on her back and then bolted upright. Sergio-Xavier's sonorous phone voice had that effect on her, and he was a good distraction from her current problem. "Hi. Please don't tell me you're canceling our appointment tomorrow."

"I gave you my word I'd be there, and I always keep my word. Please remember that."

"Good, because I put much effort into locating the perfect properties for you. By the way, you never told me what your plans are for the properties."

"We can discuss that tomorrow. I called to see how your meeting with DWAP went. I'm sure they kept you on your toes."

"You have no idea." She sighed and looked up into the wall mirror opposite her bed. The devastating news about Seniyah had overshadowed the special evening the girls had planned for her. The bouncy curls and flawless make-up in the mirror reminded her that the evening was about her. "Jasmine said you can thank them later."

"What exactly should I be thanking them for?"

The uncertainty in his voice made her giggle. "You'll see tomorrow," she said, standing and posing in the mirror. "Just know that it was all their idea. I had nothing to do with it."

"Well, in that case, I can't wait to see what those brilliant young ladies have come up with." He paused for a long moment. "Paige, what's bothering you?"

She plopped back down on the bed, wondering how he knew her world had been turned upside down once again. "Why do you ask that?"

The breath he blew into the phone came across as static through the Bluetooth. "I know we don't consider ourselves friends, but we've spent a considerable amount of time together lately. I think I know you well enough to tell when something is weighing you down. I can hear the sadness in your voice, and I bet your shoulders are slumped."

She looked into the mirror and then pounded the mattress with both fists. Her shoulders *were* slumped. She hated when he was right, and had to stop him from gloating. "Can you also tell when you're getting on my nerves?"

"Of course I can, but I don't care about your nerves. However, I am concerned about your emotional and spiritual well-being."

"Your concern is appreciated, Minister Simone, but I already have a pastor to watch over my soul," she snapped.

"True, but who watches over the rest of you?" He continued talking through her silence. "Everyone needs at least one human to safely vent to. Someone they can share their joy and sorrow with and not worry about judgment. I know *you* can't offer that unconditional acceptance, but I can."

She rolled her eyes, as if he could see her. "Are you applying for the job?"

"After enduring your crusty feet yesterday, I thought I filled the position."

His hearty laughter made her laugh and prevented the shame she'd expected to surface. "What can I say? Your girl's been too busy running a successful business to sit in a nail shop."

"Sweetheart, I get it. You're low maintenance. Now tell me what's wrong, so I can pray for you and go to bed. I have an early case in the morning."

"You're going to pray for me?" she asked, stalling.

"Will you stay focused and stop stalling? I'll pray for you just like I did yesterday."

"Okay, okay, I get it," she barked into the phone. She'd tell him anything to keep from thinking about how good his arm felt around her as he prayed. "Seniyah's pregnant," she blurted, rubbing her forehead.

"I know."

Her fingers ceased their movement at his nonchalant response. "What do you mean, you know? I just found out tonight."

"When I met her on Saturday, that was the first thing I noticed. Her stomach was more rounded than normal, and she had what some would call a pregnancy nose, meaning her nose has a spread appearance."

Her head shook in disbelief. "How did you notice all of that?"

"I've been around plenty of pregnant women in my family, and remember, I am a doctor."

"I didn't know until Jasmine told me tonight. I mean, I noticed Seniyah was getting thicker, but I didn't see her as pregnant. I must be a blind idiot," Paige said with resignation.

"I wouldn't call you an idiot, but you are blind to many realities."

She sucked in her breath to mask the pain those words inflicted. "What does that mean? I'm sure you're just dying to explain." He didn't disappoint.

"You have a tendency to see people only through your preconceived ideas and notions of how things should be, and you justify it with religion. I'm not sure why, but you have a strict set of salvation standards that you follow and think everyone else should. Those who don't heed to your line, you have little or no compassion for. The problem is, your measuring stick is flawed. This causes you to miss out on many opportunities and remarkable people. In the process of, as you say, 'working out your salvation,' you're too busy doing what you consider good things, and so you're missing the things and the people God has for you to help."

Her palms rubbed vigorously against the comforter, but she didn't cry. His words hurt and held some truth, but she couldn't stop working now. Recognition from God had to be close.

"Self-absorbed and judgmental," she whispered, recalling the adjectives he'd used to describe her.

"Don't sound so hopeless, sweetheart. You have a good heart, and your intentions are good. For example, what you're doing for DWAP is great. You're teaching those young ladies skills that will help them throughout adulthood. However, the way you judge Jasmine for using slang and wearing colored hair is wrong."

"You're right," she admitted, thinking back on how Jasmine and the girls had taken care of her, giving the best they had. "But I still don't like you."

"That's not going to stop me from praying for you."

The prayer began before she could offer a comeback. For what seemed like forever, Paige listened to her antagonist pray for every area in her life. He even prayed against mechanical failures in her vehicle. No one had done that before, and yet it felt natural to her.

She echoed his amen at the close of the prayer.

"Good night and sleep well. I'll see you tomorrow."

The earlier stress had dissipated, and peace captured her. "Good night, Minister Simone."

"Oh, and Paige?" he said before disconnecting. "I don't like you, either." Then the line went dead.

She fell back on the bed, pounding the mattress and kicking her feet in the air. "Ugh! I can't stand that man!" she screamed, while making the decision to make a quick run to the mall between clients tomorrow.

Chapter 14

Paige checked the mirror in the sun visor one last time to make sure she had "stepped up her game," as the girls put it. A phone call to a personal shopping assistant at Macy's allowed Paige to purchase five new outfits in colors from the swatches the divas had given her, two pairs of pumps—one sling-back—and a M•A•C color palette in less than an hour and thus make her scheduled appointments. The demonstration the make-up artist performed at the M•A•C counter almost mirrored the job the divas had done. *I still got it,* she thought, smiling at her reflection.

The clock on the console indicated she had five minutes before her most annoying client arrived. With finesse and anticipation, Paige excited the car and walked around to the trunk to retrieve her briefcase. As she leaned into the trunk, the slight breeze caused loose curls to fall into her face. With ease she tucked the hair behind her ear. Something she had to get used to again, along with feeling the air against her legs. She'd worn pants and long skirts for so long, even in silky Berkshire nylons her legs felt bare.

After placing the briefcase and security key on top of the trunk, Paige smoothed her red dress, which stopped just below the knee and had a sweetheart neckline. The colors swatches and magazine photos the girls had selected worked. The color and style highlighted her skin tone and body perfectly, and the dress was appropriate for both work and church.

Just as she rounded the car and stepped up onto the sidewalk, Sergio-Xavier pulled into the parking lot. She waited for him while updating her electronic key.

"Good afternoon," he said as he walked past her and continued up the walkway.

She whirled around. "And just where do you think you're going without me?" With a fist planted on her waist and a wide grin on her face, she watched Sergio-Xavier retrace his steps, joy filling her.

At first he just gaped at her, and then he smiled. "Paige?"

"Of course it's me. Who else would it be?" For reasons she'd deal with later, the look of sheer delight on his face made her feel good and empowered. She took full advantage of the situation. "Were you expecting someone else? Are you cheating on me with another broker?" She stepped into his personal space and then wished she hadn't. The man smelled too good. "You better not be cheating. I have your signature on the dotted line, and I will sue you."

"I don't doubt that you will," he said, relieving her of the briefcase. "What's going on with you today?"

"Actually . . ." She turned around and struck several poses. "This is what you can thank the divas for. Last night they gave me a makeover," she said, leaving out the motive behind it. Sergio-Xavier didn't need to know that the girls assumed the two of them were dating, and she didn't want to give him any ideas.

"Thank them? Sweetheart, I'm going to pay their college tuition."

"You don't have to do all that!" Paige snapped as laughter poured from him. "I didn't look that bad."

"No, you didn't, but this is better." Before she could brace herself, he pulled her into an embrace. "You were beautiful before, but now you're fine and . . ." He didn't finish the sentence, but his hand stroked her hair and rested in the center of her back. "You're very attractive, and guess what?"

"What?" she panted. She'd been in the middle of inhaling his cologne when he asked the question.

He lifted her chin, forcing her to look at him. "You're still saved. God still loves you."

"Why is he staring at my lips?" she wanted to ask, but instead she said, "Thank you. I needed that." She stepped out of the embrace. "We'd better get started. We have four properties to see, and I have Bible study tonight."

He seemed to force his grin, but Paige couldn't dwell on that. She was too busy rebuking the desire to kiss those full lips.

"So what are your thoughts?"

Paige had asked him that same question at the three other properties, and like the other times before, Sergio-Xavier doubted Paige could handle the thoughts floating through his mind. He barely could tolerate them.

For the past two hours he'd followed Paige around, half listening to her presentation on the pros and cons of each property. He'd heard the important points, like the price, the size, and the condition of the properties, but the rest was a boggled mess. She'd walked him through units and rooms, but visions of Paige's hips and shapely legs had blocked his concentration. The way she kept flinging her hair wasn't bad, either. Although he didn't care for her judgmental attitude, he'd considered her attractive before the makeover, but now she appealed to him on a deeper level, and he didn't like that.

"Well, what do you think?" Paige asked again.

"It's doable," was his manufactured answer.

Paige looked perplexed. "What does that mean? You never did tell me what your plans are for these properties."

"I plan to use the properties to house low- to moderate-income families. I want to offer hardworking families a decent place to live outside of the hood, with the amenities of a gated community. I'm targeting working-class families with children."

"You really have a heart for people."

Her smile, which showed her approval of his plan, pleased him. He didn't like that, either. "I try to give back and empower people as much as I can."

"Great. So are you ready to go back to my office and empower me with a big commission check?"

He chuckled to relieve the tension in his body. "Let's do it, or would you like to catch an early dinner?"

"The office is fine," she said, placing the property profile back into her briefcase. "I have too much on my mind to eat. To be honest, I haven't had much of an appetite since learning of Seniyah's pregnancy. I just can't figure out what to do about it."

He took the briefcase. "Why do you have to do anything? Did she ask you for help?"

"Well, no, but I can't sit back and allow her to ruin her life. This baby cannot prevent her from receiving an education. She has too much potential, and I have invested too much time making phone calls and calling in favors to make sure she has everything she needs."

"So this is about you?" he asked, risking an argument.

"No, this is my Christian duty. I'm empowering her, just like you're going to empower the families you plan to house."

On second thought, an argument would be good to keep things in perspective and bring his hormones back under control. "You're comparing oranges to apples. The people I plan to help are seeking assistance. Not only has Seniyah not asked you for help, but she also didn't even inform you of her pregnancy. If you're providing everything she needs for school, what are you leaving for her to do? How is she invested in her future? I think you have Christian duty twisted with the need to feel good about yourself." The second the words left his mouth, he regretted them. Not that he didn't believe them to be true, but his motive for saying them at that time and in that manner wasn't pure.

Paige didn't say anything in retaliation, and for once Sergio-Xavier wished she would grace him with one of her off-the-wall comments. Even an insult would be nice. Anything to erase the pain etched across her face. She snatched the briefcase from him and left him standing in the empty building.

He paced the room, berating his actions until he remembered they had driven over in Paige's car. By the time he ran outside, Paige's tires were screeching out of the parking lot. During the time it took to hail a cab back to his vehicle and drive to Paige's office, his conscience forced him into a truth he did not want to face but had to acknowledge.

"Thank you, God," he uttered when he saw her car in the parking lot. He parked and walked into the building, past the receptionist, and straight into Paige's office and closed the door behind him.

She looked up, startled, but recovered quickly. "I was going to send this certified mail, but since you're here, take it." She threw the document at him and continued working.

He didn't bother looking at the paper, knowing it was a cancellation of their agreement. "Paige, I am so sorry. I didn't mean to hurt your feelings."

"Do you get some kind of sick enjoyment from saying hurtful things to me?"

Her scowl made him flinch, but he walked over and stood beside her chair, anyway. "Honestly, today was the first time I purposefully set out to hurt you with my words. For that, I am ashamed."

"Why did you do it? Why did you ruin my day? I know we're not friends, but why couldn't you just listen and for once not judge me? Like that day at the beach. You were so caring last night, how could you be such a jerk today?"

He hunched next to her chair. This was not a conversation he wanted to have with her, but he couldn't require more of her than he was willing to give. "I wasn't prepared for what I saw today—"

"What are you talking about?" she interrupted. "You knew we would be looking at property today."

He took her hand. "Please don't talk. Just listen. When I'm done, if you want to curse me out, then fine."

"I already did that in car on the way over," she admitted. "I'll repent after I hear what you have to say."

He shook his head before continuing. "Today your appearance threw me off balance. I wasn't prepared to see you in this light. I liked the presentation more than I wanted to, and I didn't know how to handle that, so I tried to pick a fight with you."

"So, you really didn't mean what you said about me?"

He exhaled, relieved his attraction to Paige had gone over her head. "I shouldn't have expressed it in that manner, and not at that time. I believe in your heart, you mean well." He watched her expression change, but couldn't read her thoughts. "Please forgive me. I promise not to take my frustrations out on you again."

She snatched her hand away. "I don't know what's going on here, but we need to get some things straight."

"Okay," he agreed contemplatively.

"First of all, we need to define our relationship. Officially, you're my client, but you're more involved in my life than my few friends and family. For some strange reason your intrusion seems normal. I admit, you've had a positive impact on my life, but it's hard to like you."

"I feel the same way about you," he concurred. "However, I think there's more to like than dislike about you."

"So, are we friends now? Before you answer, being my friend doesn't give you the right to treat me like crap."

"Sweetheart, it's never my intention to treat you with anything but respect," he said, reclaiming her hand. "We can be friends as long as you keep an open mind about life and people in general."

"I'll try," she said and half smiled. "And for the record, I don't mind you expressing your opinion, but presentation is everything. I may not like what you say, but I'd be more apt to receive it."

"That's fair." He stood up and extended his hand. "Forgive me, friend?"

Although her eyes rolled, Sergio-Xavier knew he'd won her over the second her lips curled. "Whatever, Serg-X."

He pulled her upright and embraced her. "Only my friends and family can call me that, so I guess it's official. We're friends." He stepped away before yielding to the temptation to kiss her forehead. Instead he pointed to the paper on her desk. "So are you going to rip that up?"

A knock on the door distracted her from answering. "That must be our food," he announced and went to open the door.

"What food?" Paige wanted to know, but he made her wait.

"You can set it over there," he told the deliveryman, while pointing at Paige's desk. After handing the man some bills and dismissing him, Sergio-Xavier turned back to Paige. "I called in an order on my way over. I figured after we made up, we could have dinner together before you run off to Bible study."

"You just knew I'd forgive your sorry butt, didn't you?"

He ducked the pen she threw at him. "Don't knock a man for trying to keep hope alive."

She opened the box on her desk. "It's not about hope. You seem to know more about me than I find necessary. Like this." She pointed at the deep-dish chicken and spinach pizza. "How did you know I love this pizza?"

Sergio-Xavier didn't know how to answer the question without sounding mystical or deeply spiritual. He couldn't admit he'd become so tuned in, he sensed her desires, so he sidestepped the question. "Who doesn't like Zachary's? It's the best in the Bay Area."

"You're right about that," she said, closing the box and pushing it aside. "Before we dig into that, let's write up the offers. It'll take only a few minutes."

He agreed and allowed Paige to take control. He trusted her completely with the transactions, accepting her suggestions about the offering prices and other terms and conditions. After signing on the dotted lines, he handed her a check in the amount requested.

"I'll deposit this into my trust account," she said, enclosing the check in a bank deposit pouch. "Now let's eat, so I can get out of here. I have to be on time for the Lord." In an unexpected move, Paige walked around the desk and sat in the chair beside him.

"Wouldn't want you to keep the Lord waiting." He chuckled and reached for a paper plate at the same time she did. Their hands briefly touched, but he ignored the warm sensation and grabbed a pizza slice.

"Since we're friends now, I can ask you a personal question." Paige leaned back in the chair and crossed her legs at the knee. Something he preferred she wouldn't do.

"Go ahead. I'll try to answer."

"With your deep pockets, why do you live in a loft?"

This he could handle. "Since I'm single, I don't see the point in living in a big house with empty rooms. I'd rather wait until I have a family to fill the rooms, instead of coming home to an empty space. I already have the land and the blueprints drawn up for when the time comes."

She held the slice of pizza just beyond her lips. "I'm confused. If you want a family, then why aren't you at least dating someone?"

He swallowed before answering. "As a minister, I can't date every and any woman I find attractive. For me, dating has to be for the purpose of marriage, not for a lust fest between the sheets. Basically, I'm waiting for the right woman."

She ceased chewing, and he thought the way her brows knit was cute. "Wow, so you've never been with a woman. At your age, that's remarkable. You deserve sainthood."

"Whoa! Hold up." He set the plate on the desk. "I didn't say all that. I'm nowhere near the status of sainthood. I've made plenty of mistakes, and yes, I have been with a woman. In fact, I was engaged once. However, now I choose to remain celibate until marriage." He paused, then added, "If that ever happens." The reality that he might not ever enjoy a family of his own was a sore spot he usually kept hidden.

Paige scooted the chair closer to him. "Now that we're friends, I can be a little nosy. What happened? Why didn't you get married? Let me guess. Your award-winning personality ran her off? Please tell me. I can't wait to hear this."

Paige bubbled with laughter, but he didn't join her. The woman had no idea how much the indiscretion had cost him.

"Okay, friend, I'll tell you, but promise me you won't use the information to pass judgment on me."

She grabbed another pizza slice and then leaned back in the chair again with her legs crossed at the knee. "I promise to keep an open mind," she said, swinging her left leg.

Sharing this part of his life with Paige would definitely put them on a deeper level, but maybe it would also prove to her that God loved people with flaws.

"In my last year of medical school, I met this beautiful woman at a church revival service. We both ended up going out to eat with a group after service, and we immediately hit it off. Nicole didn't mind that I was a minister, and I loved the fact that she was a PK—preacher's kid. We both shared a solid Christian foundation and had many shared interest, and she was *fine*. I thought we would be great together. We started dating and within no time became inseparable."

Paige's leg stopped swinging. "Sounds like the perfect match to me."

"That was on the surface. The second I introduced Nicole to my parents, my mother told me in Spanish that the woman wasn't right for me. 'Something is wrong with her,' my mother said, standing right in front of her. Of course I didn't listen. I was head over heels in love with her beauty. What my parents didn't know was that this goddess was my first. We started having sex within weeks of meeting and continued on a regular basis. What I thought at the time was love had me so intoxicated, I couldn't resist what she freely offered. I had to have her, even if that meant walking away from the ministry. I did just that. Two weeks before my ordination, I denounced the call and left the church."

"Oh, my." Paige shifted positions and leaned forward but continued chewing. "What happened next?"

"Well, after I stopped attending church, I was free to sin openly, so I moved her into my apartment. Within weeks she suggested we get married and stop living in sin, and of course, I agreed. My family pleaded with me not to get married, but my ears were closed and my heart was encased by lust. Finally, my family stopped talking and started holding prayer sessions on my behalf. My family was praying, and Nicole was busy planning a wedding with her best friend. And I was busy funding my love's every desire."

He stopped and gulped lemonade. Paige kicked his leg for him to continue.

"About a month before the wedding, I was yearning to see her so badly. I skipped lab and came home early." He paused. After all this time the details of Nicole's betrayal were still hard to share. He swallowed and pressed forward. "Nicole and her best friend were there in our bed, having sex. Turns out their definition of *best friend* was different from mine. I couldn't see it before then, but the two had been 'besties' since freshman year."

Paige scooted to the edge of her seat. "Your fiancée was bisexual, and you didn't know it?"

He shook his head. "No, I didn't. The two attended church together, shopped, and just hung out. When Nicole wasn't with me, she was with her. I didn't see anything odd about it, because my sister and cousins did the same things with their female friends. Besides, we enjoyed a very active sex life. Turns out Nicole isn't bisexual. She's a lesbian, has been since high school. When I demanded she end the relationship with her girlfriend, she refused, saying she loved the woman but needed to marry me to keep her secret hidden from her family and the church. Oh, did I mention that Nicole was a seminary student?"

"No, you didn't." He heard sadness in her voice but didn't think it was for him.

"After I flatly refused to marry her and keep their secret, Nicole and her girlfriend packed up her belongings and left my apartment that night. Before slamming my door, Nicole explained why our sex life had been so great. She had been fantasizing about her girlfriend while with me. So basically, I walked away from God for a woman who had never loved me. Looking back, I don't think Nicole even cared about me. I was just a means to an end, and I was too stupid to see it. It took a long time to get over that, but I have, and I'll never place myself in that position again. I went through a period of not trusting myself and people, but with God's help and a loving family, I have overcome. I learned my lesson. I'll never again engage my heart with someone or give my body to someone other than the person God has for me."

The warmth from Paige's hand stroking his soothed him, and for once he didn't resist the comfort.

"The reason your judgmental attitude irritates me so is that I've been the fallen one. We sing the words to just get back up again, but sometimes a person can fall so far, they lose confidence that they can get back up. One can fall so low that the curb can look like a skyscraper. When a person is down, they don't need theological rhetoric. What they need, what I needed, was love and compassion. What I have on and how many hours a day I spend in church are irrelevant. And outer appearance speaks nothing of character."

"I get it," Paige said just above a whisper. "Really, I do."

Chapter 15

Paige's car came to a screeching halt once she pulled into a parking stall in the last row of the parking lot. Normally, she arrived thirty minutes early to pray with the intercessory prayer team, but tonight she had only five minutes to run across the parking lot, find a seat near the front, and say a quick prayer before Pastor Drake started the lesson. She grabbed her Bible and, after electronically locking the car, sprinted through the parking lot. Pastor Drake stepped up to the podium the exact second Paige plopped down in an empty seat next to Reyna.

"What?" Paige shook her head and shrugged her shoulders at Reyna's gawking.

Reyna leaned in and whispered, "What's up with you? Girl, you look *good*. We have got to talk after this."

"Thanks. I think," Paige responded. "I didn't know I looked like a troll before."

Reyna playfully slapped her arm. "Come on now, girl. You know you needed some help."

Paige thought to offer a rebuttal, but Pastor Drake began talking, and after seeing the end results, Paige had to admit the divas had indeed helped her to "step her game up." Not only had Sergio-Xavier noticed—not that he mattered—but everywhere she'd gone today she'd received compliments on her hair and the red dress. She hadn't missed how Sergio-Xavier was checking out her legs in her office, either. She just hadn't addressed it, instead dancing around his admission of physical attraction, but she'd heard him loud and clear.

Pastor Drake's Bible study teaching was on the sacrifice that Christ had made to come down to Earth in human form to save mankind. He emphasized what the Son of God had given up to redeem people who had rejected him in life and would probably reject him in death. Yet He suffered so all who wanted freedom could freely have it. What Paige gleaned from the lesson was that as a Christian, she also needed to live a sacrificial life and place the needs of others above her own. She had to go above and beyond to help the less fortunate, namely, Seniyah. Before the benediction, Paige had formulated a plan for Seniyah to stay in school and raise her child.

Reyna instantly lit into Paige at the close of service. "What's his name, and when can I meet him?"

Paige moved her mouth to protest, but the prayer warriors attacked her before she could get a word in.

"Praise the Lord," Mother Scott hollered, calling more attention to Paige. Several members were already staring and commenting among themselves. "God sure does answer prayers."

"He sure does," First Lady Drake cosigned and then added a hallelujah praise.

"I was worried about you for a minute when you didn't come back to the second service on Sunday, until the Lord told me to let it go," Mother Scott explained. "I'm so glad I did, 'cause now look at you. Baby, you look good. Your husband can finally find you."

First Lady Drake patted Paige's forehead. "It won't be long now."

Paige hung her head in total embarrassment as the prayer warriors danced in the spirit and spoke in tongues in a circle around her.

"So who is it?" Reyna asked, pestering and shaking Paige. Then started naming old clients.

"I'm not seeing anyone," Paige said through gritted teeth. "Now, let's get out of here before they calm down."

It was too late. First Lady Drake recovered in record speed. "I'm so glad you've learned that you don't have to be in church every time the doors open to be saved. Now you have time for that doctor with the whole alphabet in his name."

Reyna gasped. "Dr. Simone? Paige, you're dating Sergio-Xavier?"

"No!" Paige screamed then lowered her voice when she continued. "We're just friends."

Reyna was too busy pressing buttons on her cell phone to hear the denial. "I can't wait to tell Tyson and Kevin. We were trying to hook y'all up at the christening, but you guys hated each other, so we left it alone. Wait until they find out our plan actually worked."

"What?" Paige shrieked. "How many times do I have to warn you about trying to fix me up?" Paige was livid. "I don't need help with my personal life!"

"Yes, you do," Reyna and the prayer warriors said in unison.

"No, I . . ." Paige's tirade was cut short when she noticed a brother staring at her legs. The deacon had always been cordial, and not once had she witnessed the lust she saw radiating from him at that moment. The man was actually licking his lips. "I have to get out of here." Paige grabbed her Bible and headed for the door.

"That's right. You go home and pray so the Lord can finish getting you ready," First Lady Drake advised.

Paige didn't verbally or physically acknowledge the woman's advice. She had to get out of the sanctuary before losing what little salvation she had left.

"Hold up," Reyna called, following behind her, but Paige didn't stop until she reached her car.

Paige spun around at the trunk. "Do y'all really think I can't get a man on my own? Am I so helpless, y'all started the Get Paige a Man campaign?"

"That's not it," Reyna said, catching her breath. "In the past, I was only trying to fix you up with Tyson, because I was too stubborn to admit I loved him. That's neither here nor there. We're happily married and insanely in love. So are Kevin and Marlissa and the Scotts. Don't knock us for wanting the same for you." Reyna's attempt at explaining fell on deaf ears.

"Sergio-Xavier showing up at my office was all a setup, wasn't it?" Paige charged.

"No, no! That was totally on the up-and-up. Kevin recommended you to Serg-X before Tyson and I met him," Reyna explained. "After we met him, Tyson and I thought you'd be great for each other. That's why we invited you both to the christening. We really didn't mean any harm."

Her former wayward employee was known for many things, but harmful was not one of them, at least not to others. What irked Paige most was that everyone from her mother to DWAP to what few friends and acquaintances she had seemed more in tune with her needs than she was. She no longer knew herself, and that frightened her.

"Whatever, Reyna." Paige waved her away, but Reyna wouldn't move.

"Come on, girl." Reyna nudged her. "You know the man is fine. You can thank us after he puts a ring on it."

Paige smirked. "Never. What I will do is call Dr. Jennings and Attorney Stokes and tell them off. For the most part, Dr. Simone is a good guy, but he's not *my* guy." Paige walked around to the driver's door, and Reyna followed, laughing.

"You know, I said the same thing about Tyson."

Paige got in the car, but before closing the door, she said, "I'll tell you what, Miss Matchmaker. If the good doctor does become my man and puts a ring on it, you'll be the first to know. In fact, I'll give you a year's worth of commissions as a finder's fee."

Reyna lips smacked. "You're saying that only because you don't believe it will happen, but I will hold you to it."

"Whatever, Reyna. Now, go home to that busybody husband of yours. He'll need you to nurse his wounds by the time you get home," Paige said, removing her cell phone from her waist clip.

Reyna pouted. "Go easy on him." She then leaned into the car and hugged Paige, although she resisted the affection. "You look good, girl. Keep me posted."

Jealousy threatened to overtake Paige as she watched Reyna walk away through the rearview mirror. She wasn't jealous of who Reyna had, but of what she had found. It wasn't just a baby, but the love and adoration of a good man meant more to Paige than she cared to admit. Still, she refused to accept what everyone else had suggested. Sergio-Xavier wasn't the man for her. This time the prayer warriors had gotten their lines crossed. The physical changes she'd made readily weren't for him at all.

She shook her head as if to clear it and then started the engine. Right now she had more pressing matters to deal with. Like how to save one child while raising another.

Chapter 16

Wednesday afternoon Paige found herself being elbowed and bumped up the stairs as she trudged into the school as students stampeded out. She'd planned to arrive well before the dismissal bell to avoid the foot traffic, but her appointment at the title company ran over. Now she had to race to catch Seniyah before she left the school. The other alternative was to drop by her house uninvited. She liked the first option. She pushed her way up onto the landing and into the building, then darted down the hall, toward the music room. Seniyah had choir last period.

"Seniyah," she yelled once she spotted her exiting the music room and going in the opposite direction.

Seniyah stopped and turned around. But Paige gained not only the girl's attention, but also the attention of several young men. Irritated but on a mission, Paige ignored the howls and whistles and proceeded to catch up with her star student.

"Seniyah, we need to talk," Paige said, nearly breathless. "I was hoping you could go for a ride with me." Paige took more than the usual glance at the girl. Sergio-Xavier was right; Seniyah's nose had spread. She was also wearing the wool coat, and it was snug around her tummy.

"Hi, Miss Paige. I know I missed another DWAP meeting, but something came up. I meant to call you." Seniyah nervously looked around, then back at Paige. "I have some errands to run for my mother, but we can talk outside for a few minutes."

That was not what Paige wanted to hear, but it was better than nothing. "Okay. We can talk in my car. I'm in the faculty parking lot."

Seniyah adjusted the backpack hanging off her shoulder. "I'll follow you."

"Fine." Paige started back down the hallway. If her nervous giggle was any indication, Paige would blow this conversation before it officially got started. Real estate negotiations, she could handle, but a pregnant teenager was out of her league.

"Miss Paige, you look different," Seniyah commented once they left the dimly lit building and stepped outside into the sunlight. "You look nice with your hair down and with make-up."

Paige half smiled at the compliment, then remembered that Seniyah's absence from the last session had all but sealed her fate with DWAP. Jasmine wouldn't hesitate to vote her out during the next meeting.

"Thank you. I have DWAP to thank for this, but I'll tell you about that later." Paige continued on toward the car.

"Can we stand out here and talk?" Seniyah asked once they reach the vehicle. "I have been sitting most of the day. I need to stretch my legs."

Paige inconspicuously attempted to inspect her lower legs. Even in sneakers, Seniyah's ankles appeared swollen. Paige had witnessed swollen ankles on her sister when she was late in her pregnancy, but she didn't think it normal for Seniyah's pregnancy stage.

"Sure." Paige waited until Seniyah leaned her back against the passenger door and stretched her legs before continuing. All the while she berated herself for not noticing the girl's condition sooner. Seniyah's belly bump had taken shape, and the coat was just as snug across her breasts.

"Seniyah, why didn't you tell me about the baby?" Paige's voice was so low, she doubted the girl had heard her. Judging by Seniyah's disconcerted expression, she hadn't. Paige was about to repeat the question when Seniyah finally answered.

"I was embarrassed, and you didn't ask. I thought you had figured it out when you brought me this coat after seeing me at the food bank." She picked several specks of lint off the coat. "It's a nice coat, but I don't think I'll be able to wear it during the whole pregnancy. I have already gained twenty pounds and still have four months to go." Seniyah conversed as if nothing was odd about her circumstances.

"I didn't know until the last DWAP meeting," Paige replied. "I didn't know you were sexually active. When we met last year, you said you were too focused on getting into college to even think about boys. How did this happen?"

"Would you believe me if I told you I swallowed a watermelon seed?" Seniyah laughed at her own joke, but Paige remained stone-faced. "There's nothing spectacular to tell," Seniyah continued after the car next to them pulled off. "I met a guy. He said I was cute. We had sex a few times, and now I'm having a baby."

Paige needed more information. "Are you and the father going to get married, or at least rear the child together?"

Seniyah's snickering caught Paige off guard. "It ain't that kind of party, Ms. Paige."

"What d-do you mean?" Paige stuttered.

"Please stop stuttering, before you start speaking in tongues." Paige expected this kind of taunting from Jasmine, but not from someone of Seniyah's caliber. "It's like this. We're not a couple. We were just hanging out. He already has two babies by his girlfriend. He lives with her to keep from paying child support." She patted her stomach. "He can't afford child support for this boy, either, since he can't get a job due to his felony record. Don't worry. I'm still going to Stanford. I've already signed up for state medical and cash assistance, and I am on the list for child care."

"Two kids? How old is this man?" Paige's voice rose two octaves, but she didn't care.

"Twenty-five."

Paige walked from one end of the car to the other, praying with each step that the ridiculous scenario that Seniyah had just painted wasn't real. The girl was an honor student. She had to possess more common sense than this. She stopped abruptly in front of Seniyah; something the girl said had registered.

"You said, 'Boy.' Are you having a boy?"

For the first time ever, Paige recognized serene pleasure on her face. "Yes. I had a sonogram two weeks ago."

A flood of past regret and hidden desire bombarded Paige's mind and erupted in a warped sense of reality and responsibility. She blinked back tears, thinking how she'd failed Seniyah. Her job was to mentor her, to make her life better, but despite all her efforts, Seniyah was in worse shape now than she had been when they initially met. Could this be why God hadn't blessed her with another chance at motherhood? She hadn't shown herself capable of caring for another life.

God had assigned her to guide Seniyah out of the hood, and she couldn't even do that without messing up the girl's life. If only she had paid closer attention to her and had spent more time with her, Seniyah wouldn't have given herself to a guy just because he labeled her cute. At any rate, God, with His infinite mercy, had just given Paige another chance to right her wrong for good, and this time she would not fail.

Chapter 17

For the first time ever, Paige worked from home for nearly a week. She still held to her rigorous daily schedule, rising at 5:00 a.m. and sitting, fully clothed, at her home computer by 7:00 a.m., checking e-mails. She arranged her appointments in the afternoon and late evening so she'd have to leave home only once and would not have to circle back before the church service and her ministry obligations. She didn't miss a client, a worship service, or a rehearsal and kept her volunteer time at the food bank. At the DWAP meeting, Paige didn't mind Jasmine taking over and directing the session, since it allowed her to sit in the back and work on her assignment. Since she'd talked with Seniyah, downtime for her was a thing of the past. Every free moment was spent preparing for her new addition.

She hadn't shared her complete plan with Seniyah yet, opting to wait until everything was in place. She had shared with Seniyah her commitment to helping her through the pregnancy and to assisting her in caring for her child once it was born, but she hadn't gone into any details. Instead Paige sprang into action.

With only about fourteen weeks left of the pregnancy, so much had to be done. One of the spare rooms needed cleaning out and had to be transformed into a nursery. Tomorrow the painter would arrive, and three days later, the decorator was scheduled to begin. In the past two days Paige had spent her last commission online, purchasing a crib, a mattress, bedding, a bassinet, a changing table, a swing, a car seat, a stroller, cloth and disposable diapers, and three different types of bottles. She wasn't familiar with current baby trends but based her purchases on research and ratings from other new parents. She'd even joined an online new parent group to stay informed about new products and concerns.

Although a search had yielded reliable child-care resources in her area, Paige determined she'd work from home most of the time and provide primary care for the child during the times Seniyah was away at school. She would also set up a playpen in her work office. Paige had everything covered, but she had yet to figure out how to tell her family and close friends she'd be co-parenting a child soon. Her sister and mother could offer good advice on child rearing, and so could Marlissa and Reyna, but Paige couldn't take a chance on them not understanding her decision to help Seniyah in this manner. She didn't talk to people, but she talked to the Lord every day and thanked Him for giving her another chance at mother-hood.

Before heading out to the storage unit she'd rented for the items she cleared from the spare bedroom, Paige checked her e-mail. Checking messages used to be a boring task, but now, after registering on multiple parenting Web sites, her mailbox was always loaded with special offers and exciting newsletters about her new adventure. After she skimmed through an e-mail filled with formula and diaper suggestions, an e-mail about Sergio-Xavier demanded her attention.

She hadn't spoken to him in days, since communicating that three of his offers had been accepted. Now the inspection reports were in. She scanned the reports for pertinent information and dialed his cell. With a child on the way, she needed those deals to close as soon as possible.

"Hey, Mr. Moneybags. I have some good news for you," she sang into the phone when he answered, then silently scolded herself for being excited about hearing his voice.

"Now is not a good time, Paige. I've had a rough morning."

The warm feeling turned into concern. "What's wrong? Are you sick? Do you need me to bring you anything? I can—"

He cut her off. "No, Paige. I just need to be left alone."

"Sergio!" she yelled into the phone, but it was useless. He'd already hung up. "What the heck is wrong with him?" she grumbled and pressed the REDIAL button. The call went to voice mail after the first ring, indicating he'd turned his phone off.

Paige paced the room, more worried than angry. The person on the phone wasn't the Sergio-Xavier she knew. Even when angry, he'd argue with her, but to dismiss her brashly when she hadn't said or done anything wrong wasn't normal. Something wasn't right, and he had been wrong in his earlier assessment of her character. She wasn't too self-absorbed to care.

She dialed Kevin's number in hopes of finding out what was going on. She didn't bother with a formal greeting.

"Kev, what's going on with Serg-X? I mean, Dr. Simone."

Kevin's chuckling reminded her that she'd forgotten to call and tell him off for trying to fix her up.

"So it's true, you guys are good friends. Reyna and I will split the finder's fee."

"Shut up and tell me what's going on with him. I just spoke to him, and he sounds really down."

He continued laughing. "This is hilarious. You're worried about your man. I can't wait to tell Tyson and the ladies."

What little patience she had ran out. "Kevin Hezekiah Jennings, if you don't tell me what I want to know, I'm going to come up to that hospital and steal your prosthetic leg," she yelled. "And he's not my man!"

"That was low, Paige." He whimpered, but Paige knew he was faking being offended. "After all I've done for you."

"Kevin!"

"All right. I haven't seen him or talked to him since this morning. We had breakfast in the hospital cafeteria. He did say he had a heavy case pending today. Maybe that has him in a funk?"

"Thanks." Paige had all the information she needed, and ended the call without bothering to say good-bye. She grabbed her purse and keys and raced out of the house. If she hurried, she'd beat the commuter traffic.

Thirty-five minutes later Paige pulled into the parking lot in Pacifica. Relief rushed through her when she spotted Sergio-Xavier's car parked in the next row over. She ran directly to the shoreline and then stopped, not knowing which way to go. The beach ran for miles. Sergio-Xavier could be anywhere. She bowed her head and did something she'd never done before. She prayed for her friend.

Along with the waves crashing against the rocks came more tears. Sergio-Xavier had been walking along the beach for at least an hour, and the cycle had remained the same: waves rolled in, and tears rolled down. The sleeves of his lab coat were so soaked, he no longer bothered to wipe his face. The liquid collected at his chin and formed a stain on his shirt. Sergio-Xavier loved God and his job, but on days like this, he didn't like either very much. He was so distraught, he'd forgotten to remove his dress shoes before trekking in the sand.

Usually on hard days he'd walk the beach and meditate and pray. Peace would overtake him and his strength would be renewed, but today the therapy wasn't working. His heart hadn't ceased to ache, and his disappointment remained. Just as he was about to abort his quest for comfort, a familiar voice calling his name reverberated over the waves. He turned to find what looked like an angel running toward him.

Paige, dressed in jeans and an oversize sweater, waved her hands frantically in the air. Her face was void of make-up, and her hair blew wildly in the wind.

"It's a good thing I used to run track," she said once she reached him. "Are you all right?"

Sergio-Xavier wanted to say he was more than all right now that she was there, but didn't. "How did you know I'd be here?"

"You told me you come here on hard days to clear your head. Kevin said you had a tough case today." She stepped in closer and used her sleeve to wipe his chin dry. "It must have been a very hard case. Do you want to talk about it?"

Sharing work issues with someone other than a colleague was foreign to Sergio-Xavier. What he was dealing with at the moment, some colleagues wouldn't fully comprehend. He didn't need Paige's off-the-wall comments, either, but she was there, and at the moment he desired human comfort.

"I may not get the technical terms, but I can listen. Come on, babe. Talk to me," she pleaded.

His chest muscles tightened at the sound of the endearing term, and he had to turn away before his true emotions for her poured out. He resumed walking.

"Today I was called in for a second opinion for a patient who'd been declared brain dead." He paused when Paige interlocked her arm with his.

She nodded for him to continue. "Go on. I'm listening."

"He was eleven years old and his mother's only child. He'd fallen off his bike and suffered a traumatic head injury. I pray before examining every patient. Today I prayed extra hard. I wanted so much to tell this mother that her only child would survive." He sniffled but didn't wipe his face. "I performed every test three times, but all I could do was confirm what the other doctor had told her. She thanked me and we prayed together, but my heart is broken." He stopped walking and dropped to his knees and looked up at Paige. "I know God is sovereign, but honestly, sometimes I don't understand Him. How could He take this woman's only child after she tried for ten years to conceive?"

He expected Paige to offer some off-base theological rhetoric, but instead she fell to her knees in front of him and embraced him. When she did open her mouth, the most beautiful sound filled his ears and afforded his soul the healing balm it needed. At the end of the a cappella rendition of "It Is Well with My Soul," he'd soaked her sweater and some of her hair with his tears.

"I'll get you another one," he offered while attempting to straighten the garment after they ended the embrace.

She afforded him a smile void of judgment and condemnation. "Don't worry about it. That's what friends are for. Next time I'll blow my nose on your monogrammed shirt."

"I'll be waiting." He stood and then assisted her to her feet.

On the walk back to the parking lot, Sergio-Xavier silently acknowledged that Paige's sudden appearance was more than a coincidence. Today she was divinely tuned in to his needs and was totally selfless in her response. He looked down at his left side and wondered if Paige even realized she was leaning against his body and rubbing his arm. The warmth of her body aided him in his decision not to bring it to her attention.

"Want to stop by my place for dinner?" Paige offered once they reached her car. "You look better, but you're not quite there yet."

He leaned against the car with folded arms. "Don't you have choir rehearsal tonight? Be careful, Ms. McDaniels. I might get the impression you like me."

Paige smirked. "Now who's talking stupid? I'm only fulfilling my Christian duty. I can miss one rehearsal for that." She removed his cell phone from his clip and pressed his keypad. "Before you ask, I'm typing my address into your GPS. Meet me there in an hour," she ordered, then placed the phone back at his waist and got into the car.

"Before I agree, can you even cook?"

She missed slamming his fingers in the door by a hair. "Of course I can cook. I may have to stop at the grocery store first, but I'm a very good cook."

"I'll be the judge of that." He reached into his wallet and tossed some bills in her lap. "Thank you." He turned and headed toward his car. Now that his burden had been lifted, Sergio-Xavier needed to pray for restraint before meeting Paige for dinner.

Chapter 18

The second she tumbled into the house with both arms loaded with grocery bags, Paige realized that inviting Sergio-Xavier over for dinner wasn't one of her brightest ideas. An hour wasn't enough time to shower and prepare a dinner that would make a good impression on him. Why did she care about impressing Sergio-Xavier, anyway? Her sprint to her bedroom slowed when her heart spoke the answer she refused to accept. "No," she said out loud and then continued on. Once inside the bedroom, she sent a text message telling him to give her an additional half hour. Fifteen minutes later Paige had showered and changed into leggings and a long Stanford sweatshirt, and since she hadn't had a chance to get a pedicure, she'd decided on casual flats instead of mules.

When the doorbell chimed, the skirt steak was marinating and she was in the middle of chopping onions, tomatoes, and cilantro for her homemade salsa. She answered the door with the knife in her hand.

"If you need more time, just say so. You don't have to cut me," he teased. "If you can't meet the challenge, I can always order Chinese." The smile she loved to hate had returned, and so had that smart mouth. He had traded in his slacks and dress shirt for black jeans and a cream mock turtleneck and carried a long, rectangular box.

"Get in here and close the door behind you. I'll be right back." She left him standing in the foyer while she went to start the indoor grill.

"An indoor charcoal grill . . . That's a cool amenity."

The voice from the archway leading into the kitchen startled her. Sergio-Xavier had followed her instead of waiting in the living room, like she'd requested.

"Thanks," she said over her shoulder but continued working. "On the other side of the brick wall is the fireplace for the formal dining room. Since you can't follow instructions, have a seat at the table. I'll be finished in about twenty minutes."

"If you show me where to put these, I can help you finish up."

"Huh?" Paige faced him and noticed the bouquet of yellow roses he'd removed from the box. "Oh. There's a vase up on that top shelf," she said, pointing. The yellow roses were a symbol of their friendship, but she'd rather have red ones.

"Are you moving?" he asked after arranging the flowers in the vase and placing them on the table. "Or do the boxes mean you haven't finished unpacking?"

In the rush to prepare dinner, Paige had forgotten about the boxes stacked in the living room, which contained items from the spare room. She had meant to take them to the storage unit that afternoon, but it had slipped her mind once she discovered Sergio-Xavier was in distress.

"Actually, I'm in the middle of redecorating." She hoped the evasive answer would be enough to squash any further questions. They were friends, and today the friendship had grown to a deeper level, but that didn't give him the right to know everything about her. Besides, she didn't want to hear any negative comments.

"Maybe you can give me a tour after dinner."

One sniff of the woodsy-scented cologne penetrating her nostrils and she knew, without even looking, that he was standing directly behind her. The firm hand on each shoulder confirmed it.

"Now, what do you need me to do?"

Although he asked the question in his normal voice, Sergio-Xavier leaned in against her ear, sending a warm, tingling sensation down the right side of her body. Her entire body stiffened. It had been years since her body had physically reacted to a man, but in an instant Paige's internal heat exceeded that of the coals on the grill. Her mouth was parched, and beads of sweat formed across her hairline. Good thing she wore a sweatshirt and not a T-shirt. She pivoted around, only to find a confused expression staring back at her. Had he sensed her unwelcomed desire? She moved her mouth to speak but couldn't think of what to say that wouldn't make her sound like a woman in heat or give him the false impression that she wanted him. To her relief, he took a step backward.

"My mother taught me how to cook. If you give me an apron, I'll prove it."

Relieved, Paige exhaled louder than normal. Sergio-Xavier was oblivious to her inner turmoil. She walked over to the utility closet and retrieved an apron. "Here." Instead of handing the garment to him, Paige tossed it across the room. "You can finish chopping that serrano pepper and mixing the salsa," she directed, pointing to the center island. "Once you finish that, sauté the shrimp."

"Aye, aye, Captain." He saluted her and then affixed the apron to his torso. "So what are we having? Ceviche?"

"Less talk and more work, Soldier." Without meaning to, Paige winked.

Hoping he didn't notice, she went back to the grill to check on the coals and then removed the steak from the refrigerator. While the meat cooked, Paige set the table and then placed the salsa, sour cream, cheese, and a pitcher of iced tea on it. By the time she had removed the steak from the grill and had sliced it, Sergio-Xavier had added the shrimp and warm tortillas to the table.

Before inviting him to the table, Paige started to turn on the sound system but then decided against it. Worship music seemed inappropriate for the occasion.

"It looks great," he said, complimenting her, once he was seated. "I love steak and shrimp fajitas."

"I figured you would, since it's part of your heritage. I hope you don't mind corn tortillas instead of flour."

"Corn is fine," he said, reaching for a tortilla. "I grew up on corn."

Paige cleared her throat. "Excuse me, Minister, but I know you're not about to eat without saying grace. You don't know what I put in this food."

"You're smiling, but knowing you . . ." He let the thought hang, and bowed his head.

While Paige listened to him say grace, another realization surfaced. Sergio-Xavier was the first non-related male in her home and the only man she had cooked dinner for, ever.

"This meat is seasoned perfectly, and it's so tender," he said after taking a bite.

"That will teach you not to doubt my abilities."

They ate in silence until Sergio-Xavier touched the subject she knew would come up one day.

"Why don't you date?"

She took a sip of iced tea before answering. "You mean other than the fact that I'm too self-absorbed and judgmental?" His opinion of her still hurt.

He raised his hands in surrender. "I take that back. You have grown. Today was a perfect example. You have a beautiful voice, by the way. I hope I don't have to be in a funk to hear it again."

She raised an eyebrow. "That depends." Did I just flirt with him? she wondered.

"So, why don't you date? Have you ever dated?"

The answer wasn't something Paige was proud of. In fact, it was rather embarrassing. She wasn't perfect, but neither was Sergio-Xavier.

"The sad truth is, I have never officially dated or had a real boyfriend."

"Somehow with your personality, that doesn't surprise me."

She didn't care for his chuckling but decided to lay it all out, anyway. He'd already shared his past, and hers wasn't any worse. "In my younger years I never had the time. I was too driven to finish college and become rich. I had a goal, and a boyfriend didn't fit. I had one male friend in college. We didn't date." She paused for a moment. "We just had sex periodically," she added and then took a bite of steak.

He shrugged. "A 'friend with benefits' kind of thing. It happens, but usually someone gets emotionally attached."

"Not us. We were the perfect match. He was more driven than I was to succeed. Sex for us was like an obligation. Something we did because that's what you do in college. Instead of multiple partners, we had an exclusive arrangement on our calendar. Thursday, from two to three, have sex. And that wasn't every week. "

She joined in with his laughter, having long ago acknowledged that the arrangement was crazy.

"I knew many guys in college who would have loved a deal like that," he said, reaching for another tortilla. "If I wasn't trying to live saved and later wasn't obsessed with Nicole, I would have been first in line. So after graduation you just parted ways?"

Her chewing ceased as Paige weighed how much she could divulge without revealing her most painful memory. "Actually, we never parted ways. I mean, we mutually removed sex from our calendars, but Tyson and I have remained friends."

His facial expression changed several times, but she couldn't read any of them. "Tyson? You and Tyson Stokes were sex partners? I never would have guessed that," he said after taking a sip of iced tea.

"Trust me. We were the perfect match back then. The easygoing, 'head over heels in love' guy you see today is not the same man I knew in college. We were both anal-retentive and totally emotionally constipated. We had different motives, but we were both driven by ambition. I think ambition gave us more fulfillment than sex."

"That's some ambition."

They shared more laughter, and then Paige sobered and stared at him.

"What's wrong?" he asked. His hand rested on top of hers, giving her the strength she needed.

"Sharing this with you has made me realize something for the first time. I was so wrong to judge Jasmine and the other ladies for having sex without a commitment. I did the same thing. They're in high school and I was in college, but I wasn't offered a ring or a commitment. All I garnered was an appointment slot. The kids today have sex because of peer pressure and their environment. I did the same thing back then. The sisters in the sorority I wanted to pledge made claims of sexual activity, so I thought I had to get my swerve on to fit in. I thought I needed their backing to fit in. I certainly can't knock Seniyah for getting pregnant." She hadn't meant to say the last sentence out loud.

"How is Seniyah doing? Have you had a chance to talk with her?"

Paige was not ready to divulge her plan, but she did share the details surrounding the conception.

"So what are you going to do?" he asked with that snide smile. "I know some plan is rolling around in that pretty head of yours. I know you've concocted some plan to *save* Seniyah and her baby."

She rolled her eyes, detesting how well the man knew her. "I'm working on something, but I'm not going to tell you what it is. At least not now."

"That's fine, but, Paige, promise me something," he pleaded, squeezing her hand.

"What's that?"

"Whatever you do, make sure you do it for the right reason. Make sure it's God's will and not merely a good idea birthed out of emotion."

That's why I can't tell you, she thought, choking back tears. *You won't understand.* "Sure," she said out loud.

"Now, open your mouth and do something for me right now."

"No thank you," she said when he stabbed a shrimp and waved it near her lips. "I'm never eating one of those things again."

"If you chew it thoroughly, nothing will happen."

The terror of that day at Kevin's house came rushing back. She'd almost died that day, and he wanted her to test fate again?

"No. I got the shrimp for you." In a surprise move, Sergio-Xavier got up from his chair and hunched down beside her chair. "You have to get over this fear. Trust me, nothing bad will happen," he assured her, placing an arm around her shoulder. "If you choke, I'm right here to save you, just like before."

"You're asking a lot," Paige said, referring more to the fact that she had never trusted a man, aside from Jesus, with her well-being than to the possibility of choking on a shrimp again.

"Come on, sweetheart. I may say things you don't like, but I would never purposely hurt you. Stand up. I'll put my arms around your waist, just in case," he offered.

Under no circumstances would he hold her tonight. The fire he'd created earlier hadn't been fully extinguished yet. If he touched her again, she might attack him and repent later.

"You stay right there," she ordered with her palm up. "I'll eat it." Instead of allowing him to feed her, Paige picked up the shrimp and cautiously placed it in her mouth. She remembered that in elementary school she learned to chew her food twenty-eight times. Tonight she chewed twice as long. When the shrimp finally slid down her throat, it felt like mush.

"Are you happy now?" she asked, reaching for another shrimp. "I might eat the rest of these."

"Go right ahead. I like seeing you happy."

"Then you'll be ecstatic."

They enjoyed the remainder of the meal, which included a question-and-answer session on their likes and dislikes. In the end, Paige finally knew the name of that intoxicating cologne she loved.

"Oh, I forgot the reason I called you earlier." She left him seated at the kitchen table while she went to her home office and printed the inspection reports. When she returned, he had finished eating and had loaded the dishwasher. "I don't need a housekeeper. I just need to have you over more often," she teased.

"That can be arranged." He laughed, but she had a feeling he was serious. She ignored the comment and got down to business.

"The inspection reports are in. I checked them over, and I didn't see anything major, but look them over and let me know your thoughts."

He accepted the documents but didn't read them. "I'm too emotionally drained to focus on these tonight." He tucked them underneath his arm. "I will look at them after rounds tomorrow and get back to you."

She followed him into the living room and then to the foyer. "Are you eating and running?" she asked.

"I'm afraid so, sweetheart," he said after turning to face her. "I have an early day tomorrow and clinic in the afternoon." He leaned down and kissed her cheek. "Dinner was wonderful, and the company even better. I'll call you tomorrow." Then he opened the front door, stepped outside, and gently closed the door behind him.

Paige stared at the front door until she heard his car pull off; then she locked the door and set the alarm system. The evening had ended too abruptly and somehow had been too "friendly" for her, but then again that's all they were—friends.

Chapter 19

Paige could hardly contain the joy bubbling through her as she stood in the middle of what would soon become the nursery. The painter's finished product far exceeded her expectations. Instead of one boring color, each wall was a different shade, forming a kaleidoscope of blue, sea green, yellow, and beige. She'd already selected the animal, number, and letter designs she wanted on the walls for the decorator to re-create. The stacked boxes in the living room had been transported to storage, only to be replaced with the delivered boxes from all the online shopping she'd been doing.

Normally, she would have found the clutter and disarray downright sinful. Cleanliness was godliness, or next to it. She was certain she'd read that somewhere in the Bible, or maybe it was an old saying of her grandmother. Whatever the case was, Paige believed a clean material house was an outward indication of a clean spiritual house. "Lord, you know my heart. Just a few more days and my life will finally be in order," she mumbled as she headed back through the living room to the kitchen. Another week had past, and she still hadn't discussed her plans with Seniyah, but she didn't think Seniyah would object once she saw the nursery and all the cute items Paige had spent a small fortune on.

Just as Paige had suspected, DWAP voted Seniyah out of the group at the last meeting. "It's not personal, just business," Jasmine had said after the vote. While watching her leave without staging a protest, for the first time Paige had wondered if Seniyah even cared about the DWAP project at all. To keep Jasmine from accusing her of favoritism, Paige hadn't gone after Seniyah right then, but she had called later that night to check on her. Today, after the food bank, Paige was picking her up for lunch and a trip to a discount retailer for maternity clothing.

Before heading out to perform her Christian duty, Paige picked up the phone to call her mother but decided against it after the first ring and hung up. She couldn't speak to her mother without sharing her good news, and she wasn't ready to do that yet. She sent her a text instead.

An hour later Sergio-Xavier's open arms welcomed her to the food bank's kitchen. "Hello, Paige. There's a beautiful young lady I'd like you to meet." He revealed this while he was still holding her, and she clearly heard the excitement in his voice.

Her body instantly stiffened, and she stepped back. Who was the woman, and why did he refer to her as beautiful? "Sure," she replied, trying to ignore his radiant smile. The woman undoubtedly held a special place in his heart.

As she watched him walk back to the storage area, Paige straightened her jeans and tunic, although they weren't wrinkled, and removed the hair clip that held her hair in place. She shook her hair out, allowing it to fall loosely down her back. She snuck a glance in the mirror above the sink. Her make-up was modest but classy. She wasn't at her best, but she wouldn't look like chopped liver next to Ms. Supermodel, either.

Sergio-Xavier emerged from the storage area with a woman on his arm who could easily be a stand-in double for Alicia Keys. True to Sergio-Xavier's description, the woman was drop-dead gorgeous.

"I am not jealous," Paige mumbled, but at the same time she wanted to slap the woman. By the time they covered the short distance to her, Paige had scrutinized the woman from head to toe, hoping to find an imperfection, but there were none.

"Paige," Sergio-Xavier said, looking down, "this is my niece, Alexis, the superstar I told you about."

Paige followed his eyes downward and for the first time noticed the little brown face with two puffy pigtails snuggled against Sergio-Xavier's leg, smiling up at her.

"Hello, Miss Paige. Do you want to hear me sing?"

"What did I tell you, Alexis? You're here to serve, not to perform."

The smile with a missing upper tooth disappeared. "Sorry, Uncle Sergio. I forgot again," the child said, dropping her head.

Sergio-Xavier immediately hunched down beside her and lifted her chin. "That's all right, sweetheart. Keep practicing. I can't wait to hear you next week at the party. I know you're going to sound absolutely perfect."

The snaggletoothed smile returned, and Alexis kissed his cheek. "I promise I will be for you."

Paige's jaw dropped. The stern six-foot-two-inch doctor had turned into mush right before her eyes and was blushing like a helpless puppy.

"Hello!" said the woman, who was now standing with her hands on her hips. "Aren't you going to introduce me to your girlfriend?"

The blushing ceased as Sergio-Xavier rose to his full height. "Didn't I tell you she is not my girlfriend?" he scolded and then went on to say something in Spanish that Paige couldn't understand.

The woman spat words right back, and then so did Sergio-Xavier.

Paige didn't remember enough from her high school conversational Spanish class to interpret the conversation, but from the woman's neck rolling and Sergio-Xavier's tone, she could tell the exchange was anything but friendly.

The two continued arguing back and forth, as if Paige and Alexis weren't there, until the woman yelled, "I'm telling Daddy!" in English.

So this is his sister. Thank goodness.

"Snitch! I'm glad you passed your detective exam. Now you can get paid for being nosy," he barked.

Her lips smacked. "Whatever. I only stick my nose into the business of people I care about. You fall into that category by default," she said after folding her arms.

Paige observed Sergio-Xavier huff and puff and glare, but the woman didn't back down. He was furious, and Paige was ecstatic to see that her friend had met his match.

"Don't worry," Alexis said, patting Paige's leg. "They do this all the time. They argue in Spanish so I can't understand, but my granny is going to teach me Spanish so I can argue to."

Paige couldn't help but laugh at Alexis, but then the other two adults started up again, only this time they spoke entirely in English.

"Once again, you're making me set a bad example for my niece," he charged.

"You do that just by waking up in the morning."

Paige bent over with laughter until she realized the arguing had stopped. She returned upright to find the pair and Alexis staring at her. Sobering quickly, Paige cleared her throat. "I'm sorry, but that was funny."

"So you're on her side?" Sergio-Xavier charged.

"Sergio-Xavier Winston Simone, stop stalling." The woman's demand saved Paige from having to come up with an answer.

Sergio-Xavier threw his hands up in surrender. "Fine. This is my broker and friend, Paige McDaniels." He then turned to Paige. "This is my eternal pest, otherwise known as my little sister, Tara."

Tara momentarily glared at her brother and then smiled at Paige. "Ignore him. We're only eighteen months apart, and he wasn't calling me a pest when I beat up those guys that tried to rob us."

Paige gasped. The thought of Sergio-Xavier being in danger scared her. "What happened? Are you okay?"

Tara smirked at her brother. "And she's not your girlfriend? Yeah, right. The idea of your rude behind being in danger has her petrified." She waved off Paige's concern. "That's another story for another day. Just know that *I* took care of them. He did stand over them after I got them in handcuffs."

Now Paige was really confused. "Handcuffs? Are you a security guard?"

Tara laughed. "Security guard? Girl, you're funny. A security guard doesn't carry one of these," Tara said, flipping her wallet open to reveal her law enforcement badge. "Or one of these." She lowered her jacket off of her shoulder, revealing her holster. "I'm a real detective. Enough about me. I want to hear all about you. It's not often my brother has a girlfriend. How long have you been dating?" Tara readjusted her jacket and folded her arms.

She wanted an answer, but Paige didn't have one to give her. At least not one she thought Tara would believe.

"Actually, we're just friends," Paige replied.

"I told you," Sergio-Xavier said, butting in.

Tara nodded. "Friends . . . That's a good place to start. Are you from the Bay Area? Do you have any kids? Do you have a criminal record? How's your credit? Do you know Jesus?" After bombarding her with personal questions,

Tara snapped Paige's picture with her iPhone. "I'm sending this to Mama."

"Uh . . . um . . ." Paige looked to Sergio-Xavier for help.

"That's enough, Tara," he said, reaching for Paige's hand. She eagerly accepted it. "We have work to do, and so do you. We'll meet you and Alexis back here after food distribution."

Paige had to skip to keep up with Sergio-Xavier's long strides. His grip was rough. "Nice meeting you, I think," Paige called over her shoulder to Tara, who was now texting. "See you later, Alexis." The girl smiled, but Sergio-Xavier steered Paige into the packing area before Paige could smile back.

In the midst of boxes, tables, and numerous volunteers, Sergio-Xavier found room to pace. "I'm sorry about that," he said once he finally stopped in front of her, throwing his hands up in the air. Then he went on a rant. "When I went to get Alexis, I didn't know the parasite would tag along. I hope you're not angry at me. Tara really is a good person. She just overdoes it sometimes when it comes to me and my brother. With that analytical mind of hers, she investigates everything. I bet she knows the answers to those questions she threw at you. She was testing your character. I know my cousins told her everything about you before they made it to the parking lot that Sunday after church."

Sergio-Xavier took a deep breath and exhaled so hard, his breath warmed Paige's cheek. "I'm so sorry. Please don't be mad at me for her behavior. I promise I haven't claimed you as my girlfriend. Trust me. I would never do that." Judging by his facial expression, it was clear that the idea petrified him.

Paige wasn't certain if she'd been insulted or not, so she let the subject drop. "Like you said, we have work to do." She reached for a plastic garment cover, but he removed it from the rack and wrapped it around her.

"So you're not mad at me?" His warm breath tickled her neck with each syllable.

"Of course not," she answered and then, after stepping away from him, finished tying the protective garment's belt. "Now, less talk and more work."

He nodded and went about unloading boxes on the assembly line.

For the next ninety minutes they worked side by side silently, as if the awkward fiasco hadn't happened. Paige welcomed the silence so she could mentally prepare for her outing with Seniyah. Today Paige planned to finally share with Seniyah what she believed the Lord had told her to do. If all went well, this time next year she'd hear the pitter-patter of little feet under her roof. She just didn't know if the feet would belong to a Jonathan or a J'quan. Her spirit soared at the thought of having a baby in the house. She began to hum the melody to "Lord You Are God" and bopped as she worked, as if headphones were on her ears.

"I've never seen you this happy before. What gives?"

Paige stopped bopping and spun around to find Sergio-Xavier grinning at her. "Shouldn't you be lifting a box or packing something instead of watching me?" She finally admitted to herself that she loved his smile, but she hadn't forgotten that petrified expression from earlier.

"Come on. Share the good news with me," he said, prodding her, but she wouldn't budge.

"You'll find out soon enough." As the words left her mouth, Paige made a decision: if Sergio-Xavier didn't agree with her plan, he could no longer be her friend. A sudden sadness washed over her, but she suppressed it and resumed sorting bags of pasta and jars of marinara sauce.

"Don't tell me the properties closed and you didn't tell me? I thought you said we had three more days. Did you cash that commission check already?"

"This joy I have neither the world nor that five-figure commission gave me. It's strictly from above. Only God can take what you mess up and turn it around for good. But you know that already, Preacher," she threw over her shoulder. "So I won't preach you a sermon. Just know that God has done something awesome in my life."

· "That's wonderful." His tone lacked its usual enthusiasm, but Paige didn't care to find out why and resumed humming and bopping. "How is Seniyah?" he asked after unloading a case of processed macaroni and cheese.

"She's great," Paige sang out. "And the baby is doing fine. In fact, we're hanging out together for the rest of the day. So do you have any big plans for this evening?" she asked after he didn't make any comment.

"Oh yeah, I have big, shiny plans. I'm hanging out with my chick on the side."

The cans of tuna fell from Paige's arms and rolled across the floor. "Chick on the s-side?" she stuttered.

"You sound like a scratched record. Hold that thought."

Paige couldn't think of a song to hum while watching him collect the cans. This chick on the side had better be another niece or cousin. He'd barely dumped the recovered cans on the table before she snapped, "So who is this chick on the side, Preacher?" with hands on her hips and her neck rolling.

He threw his hands in the air. "Whoa. Hold on. Take your mind out of the gutter. Lizzie is my saxophone. I need to practice the song my father wants me to play for my mother at their anniversary party."

Paige's neck stopped mid-roll. "Saxophone? You play the saxophone?"

"That's what most people do to the instrument." He pointed at his chest. "Me, I make the tenor sax *talk*."

Paige gasped. "I love horns, but I had no idea you played. Why didn't you tell me? Are you in a band? Can I come hear you play?"

"That groupie spirit is creeping back in," he teased. "To answer your questions, you didn't ask, no, I'm not in a band, and you can hear me play at my parents' thirty-sixth anniversary party next Saturday."

"Oh, I can't wait to—" Paige forbade the thought from forming. "What do you mean, I can you hear you at your parents' party? You're not taking me home to meet the family like I'm your woman. And what kind of party is it? Because you know I don't drink or smoke. Saturday night is the time I spend preparing to meet the Lord on Sunday. I can't be hanging out all hours of the night. I thought your family was saved. What are they doing partying in the first place?" She thought he'd understand, but the scowl on his face gave her a different reality.

"Paige, now would be a good time for you to sew your nose and lips together."

"Then I won't be able to breathe."

"My point exactly. And with any luck, it will be a long and agonizing death." He turned to walk away, but Tara blocked his path before he could complete two strides.

"Good. You're leaving. I can chat with Paige," she announced.

Sergio-Xavier retraced his steps, but the look he gave Paige was anything but friendly.

"Actually, I have an appointment. I really should b-be going," Paige stammered.

Tara's head bobbed from Paige to her brother. "So there's trouble in paradise, but y'all will be fine. I'll leave you guys alone to work it out. I'll see you at the party." She sneered at Sergio-Xavier. "You did invite her to the party, didn't you?"

Paige gave a silent thanks when he just nodded and didn't tell Tara she'd just insulted her family. The woman did carry a gun.

"Good. I'll see you then," Tara told her. She turned to her brother. "I'm still telling Daddy what you called me," she said through clenched teeth and then walked away.

Sergio-Xavier followed her lead but went in the opposite direction.

Paige checked her watch. She wanted to apologize but didn't have the time. Certainly, Sergio-Xavier would get over it.

Chapter 20

"How are you feeling? Are you tired? Do you need to sit down and rest? Want some more water?" Paige had asked Seniyah those questions at least five times since they arrived at the mall over two hours ago. From her sister and sister-in-law, Paige knew pregnant women tired easily and often needed rest. She was unfamiliar with the swollen face and hands but made a mental note to call and ask her sister about them. If she didn't have an answer, Paige would search Google.

"I'm about as fine as I was when you asked me three minutes ago." Seniyah smirked rather arrogantly, Paige thought, and then sipped from the water bottle.

"I'm just trying to take care of you and the baby. I don't want to tire you out."

Seniyah raised the shopping bag she carried and pointed at the ones Paige held. "Ms. Paige, we've been to two maternity shops and three baby stores, and now you don't want to tire me out?"

Paige joined in with Seniyah's laughter. "What can I say? I'm excited about the baby," she said. "And your future," she added after a pause.

"I could tell when you pulled up *Consumer Reports* on the mobile play set the salesperson attempted to sell you. You had him stuttering to answer your questions. You must have had one of those with your kids. By the way, how many kids do you have?"

Paige's steps slowed in front of the cell phone accessory marquee. She stretched her neck to give the impression that the designer phone cases interested her, while she gained the courage to admit that she had no children, and that the only reason she knew so much about baby furnishings was that she had plans for Seniyah's baby.

"Actually, I don't have any children." She faced Seniyah but didn't make eye contact, opting to focus on the sporting goods shoe display across the aisle. "But I do have one niece and two nephews. I spent a lot of time caring for them when they were infants." It was only a half lie. Paige had babysat on a few occasions.

"With your research skills and tenacity, you'll make a great mother. You and Dr. Simone should think about it," Seniyah threw out before taking another sip from the water bottle.

"Why would you say something like that?" Paige's loud voice garnered the attention of passing shoppers. She lowered her volume when several stopped to watch. "Dr. Simone and I are just friends. And friends shouldn't go around making babies unless they're married. At least not at my age," she said as hurt flashed on Seniyah's face.

Seniyah raised her hand and took a step backward. "Don't try to fix it. I know you look down on me for getting myself into what you consider a mess, but those are your high standards, not mine. I guess that's why you're mid-thirtyish, without a man, and childless." Her shoulders shrugged. "But, hey, if it works for you."

Sergio-Xavier's suggestion of sewing her nose and lips together rang loud and clear as Paige watch Seniyah waddle away without the shopping bags containing a small fortune from Paige's bank account. *Why can't I learn to be quiet?*

"Seniyah, wait!" Paige almost tripped twice while trying to run after Seniyah and carry the bags.

This was not how Paige wanted the day to end. She'd planned to take Seniyah to an early dinner and then present her fabulous plan. Three stores down, Paige's strides slowed as realization of what had happened set in. Seniyah had insulted her, and now Paige was running after her to force her to accept her gifts. She'd heard stories from her mother and sister, but now she had witnessed it with her own eyes. Pregnancy really did alter a person's personality. The introverted and insecure teenager she'd met over a year ago would have never spoken to her like that.

As Seniyah exited the mall, Paige came to a complete stop and plopped down on an empty bench with the bags stacked at her feet. Ignoring the stares and murmuring around her, Paige lowered her head and cried. Her retribution and future were slipping through her fingers. If she wasn't careful, she'd condemn herself to a life of sorrow.

"Ms. Paige, is that you? Are you all right?"

Paige's jerked her head upward to find Jasmine and the divas staring down at her. She couldn't think of an adjective to describe adequately how low she felt. It was one thing to cry in the presence of absentminded shoppers, but for her mentees to witness the meltdown was beyond humiliating.

Paige quickly dried her face and acted as if all was right with the world. "Hey, divas. I didn't expect to see you today. What's up?"

As usual, Jasmine spoke for the group. "You tell us. Why are you sitting in a crowded mall, bawling? What happened to all that poise and sophistication?" She moved in closer. "Did Dr. Simone do something to you? 'Cause if he did, we'll go down to that hospital and put him in check. My cousin works up there, and she'll take us right to him. I don't care how fine he is. He can't be disrespecting you like this."

The other divas echoed Jasmine's sentiment.

Paige jumped to her feet, waving open-palmed hands. "Whoa. Hold on. This has nothing to do with Dr. Simone. I just got some bad news, that's all," she lied.

"Oh." Jasmine backed down. "Well, I'm just saying, if you need us to handle something for you, we got yo' back."

"Thanks. I appreciate that," Paige said, knowing full well she'd never take them up on the offer. However well-meaning their intentions might be, forming an alliance with her mentees was something she would never do.

"So, do you want to talk about it?" one of the girls asked.

Paige looked down at the pile around her feet. "No. I think I'd better get home. It's been a long day."

Jasmine's face twisted as if she was contemplating a serious decision. "Change of plans, divas. Let's help Miss Paige take this stuff to her car, and then we're taking her to the nail shop with us," she finally announced. "We're getting pedicures today," she told Paige.

By the time Paige formulated an excuse, the divas had picked up her bags and were waiting for her to lead the way.

"Okay. I guess it won't hurt," Paige said, yielding, and then started walking toward the exit.

"Miss Paige, are you trying to tell us something?" Jasmine asked, walking beside her. "From the looks of the stuff you bought, you and Dr. Simone have been gettin' busy." Jasmine burst out laughing. "I ain't mad at you. Even saved professionals have needs."

Paige glared so hard at Jasmine, she walked into the glass exit door. This time onlookers didn't stare; they laughed in her face.

Chapter 21

For the second time Paige examined her make-up, frowned, and then wiped her face clean. Over the past few weeks, Paige had gotten good at mixing the color palette and applying make-up, but tonight her novice efforts were useless. Twice she applied too much liquid eyeliner, and the eye shadow combinations reminded her of a raccoon.

"I can't do this," she mumbled, then stomped from the bathroom and fell backward on the bed. "I can't meet his family," she kept mumbling, trying to hide the fact that she really wanted to meet the Simones, and she wanted to spend time with Sergio-Xavier. She missed him.

They hadn't talked much since the signing at the title company four days ago, where she apologized for her outburst at the food bank and accepted his invitation to his parents' party. As always, all was forgiven, but Sergio-Xavier had warned her against losing control of her tongue around his family. "Please try not to be yourself," he'd teased. "You might want to meditate on Psalm one-forty-one, three."

"Set a watch, O Lord, before my mouth; keep the door of my lips." Paige lost count of how many times she'd recited the scripture over the past four days. So far the ritual had worked. She hadn't verbally offended anyone, but she'd been to the office only once and she'd left Bible study immediately after the benediction to avoid speaking to anyone. Tonight would be different. If the previous interactions with the Simones were any indication, Paige would be bombarded with questions and assumptions about her and Sergio-Xavier's nonexistent relationship.

She sat up and wrapped her arms around her body. She needed to go tonight. She needed something to counteract the depression threatening to overtake her. After dropping by the high school twice, Paige had yet to make contact with Seniyah. If the girl didn't respond to the messages she'd left with the school counselor soon, Paige would be forced to drop by her home uninvited.

A smile escaped as she fingered the lime-green dress with purple trim lying on the bed. It was beautiful and looked fabulous on her. She was sure Sergio-Xavier would love the way the cut accented her figure and the way the length provided an ample display of her legs. She hadn't forgotten his preoccupation with her legs; she'd just never called him on it.

New determination fueled her steps back to the bathroom. "I am going to this party," she told her reflection, then once again reached for the make-up bag.

Thirty-five minutes later, Sergio-Xavier rang her doorbell. "Hey, you look handsome. Come in," Paige greeted. "I just need to grab my purse and coat, and we can head out."

She was halfway down the hall before she realized he hadn't returned the greeting. He hadn't said anything. She retraced her steps to find a grave expression veiling his face. "Is everything all right?"

His rapid blinking coincided with the sideways movement of his head. "I'm good. Just a little anxious, that's all."

"Hasn't your family heard you play the sax before?"

"Of course."

"Then why are you anxious?" She had an idea but wanted him to confirm it.

Instead, he looked down at his watch. "It's a thirty-minute drive. We should be going, just in case we run into traffic."

"Sure. Give me a minute." She accepted his response for the avoidance tactic it was, and went to retrieve her purse, suppressing the disappointment she felt over the fact that he had not complimented her. "I don't need his approval," she grumbled once inside her bedroom. "I know I look good."

When she returned, his grave expression had been replaced by the smile she'd come to adore. His arms held her coat wide open for her to step into.

Paige appreciated the gesture but wanted more. "Thank you," she said before turning her back to him.

"You look absolutely stunning," he whispered in her ear. His lips were so close to her neck, the hairs in his mustache tickled her skin, causing her to jump. She stepped away from him with one arm hanging outside the sleeve.

"Thank you. I'm glad you like it," she said once the coat was securely fastened. She looked up and found his eyes fixed on her lips.

"Oh, I more than like it, but we can discuss that later." In lightning speed, sheer pleasure disappeared and anxiety returned. "Let's go."

"Lead the way." She locked the door and followed him to a car she hadn't seen before. "I didn't know you had one of these," she said in reference to the black Bentley coupe. She climbed in the passenger seat.

"Paige, there are many things you don't know about me, but I have a feeling that might change soon," he said before closing the passenger door.

Paige didn't guess what he meant while watching him walk around the front of the vehicle and get in on the driver's side. She didn't care. She'd gotten her thrill for the evening.

Chapter 22

Awestruck, Paige surveyed the Windsor estate home. She had seen homes like this before but had never had the privilege of listing one. From her estimation, the European-style custom home was at least ten thousand square feet and sat on five acres of land. On the mile drive from the private road turnoff to the parking stalls, she'd admired the beautiful landscaping, the pond, and the rows of fruit trees that framed the perimeter of the property.

"Wow, this is beautiful. I would love to see this place in the daylight," Paige said.

"Good. Next time we'll come and hang out for the day. Maybe go horseback riding and then have a picnic or take a swim. You can swim, can't you?"

"Huh?" Paige turned to find him staring at her. She hadn't realized she'd uttered the words out loud.

"Can you swim?" he asked again.

"Yeah, sure." The rows of high-end luxury vehicles with personalized plates distracted her. So did the armed security officers roaming the grounds. Theoretically, Paige understood Sergio-Xavier was from a wealthy family, but how deep the wealth ran had eluded her until now. Tonight she'd be surrounded not only by doctors and lawyers, but also by CEOs of multimillion-dollar companies.

He opened the passenger door after retrieving Lizzie from the trunk and extended his hand to Paige. "Shall we?"

Paige hesitated, suddenly feeling insecure. "Not yet."

Sergio-Xavier misinterpreted her apprehension. "Sweetheart, don't worry. My family won't bite. They will ask a ton of questions, though."

"What if I don't fit in? I'm not exactly on their level."

He reached in and took her hand. "You're doing it again—judging people before you meet them. Not all wealthy people are arrogant snobs. We're saved, remember? If you weren't on my level, you wouldn't be here. Just remember Psalm one-forty-one, three, and you'll be fine."

"Okay," she said and stepped from the car. "Set a watch, O Lord, before my mouth; keep the door of my lips," she whispered when Sergio-Xavier placed his right index finger on an electronic screen and then entered the home.

They stopped in a foyer that was larger than her living room. After setting Lizzie against the wall, Sergio-Xavier helped Paige remove her coat. Paige admired the marble flooring and crown molding while he hugged and greeted the housekeeper, who collected their coats.

Sergio-Xavier's firm hand resting on the small of her back and urging her forward cut short her admiration of the home's interior. "Come on. I'll show you around."

Paige latched on to his arm and walked through what seemed like a maze of rooms and then into a room, one she didn't know whether to call a great room or a ballroom. Vaulted ceilings and soft natural colors gave the room an expansive look. The room contained a grand piano, two fireplaces, a bar, two sixty-inch, wall-mounted TVs, and a dance floor, along with leather furnishings. The buffet took up an entire wall.

The people milling about the room were a true representation of California's diversity. The Simones came in all shapes, sizes, and colors. The African American heritage dominated, but Caucasians were also prevalent. In terms of ethnicity, the French and the Latinos were well represented. From a quick scan of the crowd, Paige learned that while the Simones lived well and drove well, they didn't wear their money on their backs. The majority of the people in the room had on simple clothing with little or no flashy jewelry.

Paige recognized Pastors Reggie and Julia; her idol, Marcus, and his family; and Sergio-Xavier's cousins from church, but she didn't recognize the plump, fair-skinned woman with long, dark, curly hair rushing toward them with open arms. The man trailing behind her was an older version of Sergio-Xavier.

"My baby!" The woman exclaimed and wrapped her arms around Sergio-Xavier's neck.

"Hey, son!" The man joined them in a group hug.

Paige stood back, admiring the affection Sergio-Xavier and his parents shared. It reminded her of her own family, except Sergio-Xavier kissed both his mother and father on the cheek.

His mother faced Paige, practically beaming, and elbowed her son in the side. His father stood beside his wife, wearing the same grin Paige had come to love. Paige chuckled at the not-so-subtle hint.

Sergio-Xavier chuckled too. "Mom, Dad, this is my broker and friend, Paige McDaniels. Paige, these are my parents, Stephan and Teresa Simone."

"Happy anniversary. It's nice to meet you." Paige extended her hand, but Teresa knocked it away and gave her a bear hug. His father did likewise.

"Welcome to our family," Teresa said in English. Then she turned to her son and said in Spanish, *"Hijo, ella es muy hermosa. Ya era hora que encontraras a una persona digna de tu amor y respeto."*

Paige cringed, remembering what Sergio-Xavier had told her about what his mother had said about the last woman he brought home.

"Ma!" Sergio-Xavier exclaimed.

Teresa waved off her son's concern and took Paige by the arm. "Come on. Let me introduce you to everyone." She steered Paige away before she could telepathically plead with Sergio-Xavier for help.

"You'll be fine," Paige heard him call after her.

With each step, Paige silently recited Psalm 141:3 and at the same time wondered what Teresa had said about her.

Teresa finally came to a stop in the eat-in kitchen, which was the size of Paige's living room, kitchen, and formal dining room combined. "Everyone, this is Paige, Serg-X's girlfriend," Teresa announced to the room filled with women.

"I don't like him like that," Paige said, trying to correct her, but Teresa talked over her and went around the room, making introductions. Within seconds Paige had met over thirty women, including the Simone matriarch, Grandma Ana. Halfway through the introductions Paige realized everyone was hugging her and ignoring her extended hand.

"You catch on quick," Teresa said once Paige stopped offering her hand.

"Have a seat, baby." Grandma Ana patted the empty chair beside her.

Paige thought Grandma Ana looked pleasant enough. Even in old age the woman's ebony skin glowed and her smile was welcoming. Paige let her guard down and sat in the chair. Before she could scoot the chair in, she realized she'd grossly underestimated Grandma Ana.

"What I want to know first is, do you really know Jesus, or do you just attend church?" Grandma Ana began.

"My grandson is a minister, and he can't be tied down to a woman who doesn't know Jesus. In fact, this whole family believes in the Jesus, born of the Virgin Mary, who was crucified on the cross, buried, and was resurrected on the third day, and is now seated at the right hand of God. Now, we don't judge nobody's spiritual beliefs, but if you don't believe in Jesus, let us know now so we can pray the devil out of you, or pray you away before you officially join the family."

"I love the Lord. I know Jesus very well. Probably better than most of—" She left out the rest of what she was going to say as the scripture she'd been silently reciting raced through her head. "You don't have to worry about me, because I don't like Sergio-Xavier like that. We're just friends."

"Uh-huh" echoed throughout the room.

"So, how did you meet my son?" Teresa asked from behind her. "Was it at the food bank? What attracted you to him? It was that dimple, huh?"

Paige turned to find not only Teresa waiting on the edge of her seat for the answers, but also everyone else.

"Sergio-Xavier was referred to me by a mutual friend for real estate services. While he does have a cute dimple and an adorable smile, I'm not interested in Sergio-Xavier outside of business," Paige informed them.

"We don't need to ask about your real estate business, but we would like to know about your family," an aunt stated. "Where are you from? Do you have children? Do you want children? What are your views on divorce? Because we don't advocate divorce in this family. We believe in sticking together and taking care of our own, but we need to know who you are first."

"Where do you stand with giving back to the community?" another aunt added. "You're not a snob, are you?"

Paige sighed and lowered her head and rubbed her temples, hoping to send the message that their questions were too much and unnecessary. Her plan failed. When she raised her head, all eyes were focused on her.

To keep her voice from trembling, Paige slowly shared her family dynamics and then went on to answer every question. However, she wasn't so sure if she was lying or not when she declared she wasn't a snob.

"So how much longer do you think the two of you will date?" Teresa asked. "We have a big family, and we need time to plan the wedding. Along with your parents, of course."

Paige stood from the table but didn't raise her voice. "Just in case I wasn't clear before, I'll say it again. I don't like Sergio-Xavier that way. We're just friends."

"Girl, sit down," Tara said as she barged into the kitchen with Staci and Lashay in tow. "If you say that long enough, you might believe it. If you didn't *like* him, you wouldn't have been mean mugging me at the food bank until you found out I was his sister."

The women laughed.

Paige gasped and slumped back into the chair. She hadn't meant to be so transparent.

"You're a bit uptight," Tara continued, "but we'll work the kinks out before the wedding. I will love you like a sister and will treat you as one, but if you mess over my brother, I'll pistol-whip you with my gun and then repent." Tara patted her shoulder. "So how many children do you and my brother plan on having?" she asked as if she hadn't just threatened the woman.

"I told you . . . ," Paige began.

"You don't like him like that!" the crowd exclaimed in unison, finishing her thought. Then they laughed in Paige's face.

"Is everything all right in here?"

Sergio-Xavier's interruption was the distraction Paige needed, but the reprieve was short-lived.

"Boy, get out of this kitchen and go on back in there with the men," Grandma Ana ordered. "We got Ms. Paige covered. Tell your grandpa and your daddy to get you straight."

Obviously, he was used to this craziness, because Sergio-Xavier left without saying a word.

Paige continued fielding questions from newly arrived cousins and aunts until Teresa announced it was time for the entertainment. Before heading back into the great room, Paige made a vow to apologize to Mother Scott and First Lady Drake. They were nowhere near as nosy as the Simone women.

"How are you holding up?" Sergio-Xavier whispered in her ear from behind while she visited the buffet table.

Paige started to sneer at him but then relaxed. "Honestly, I get where your family is coming from, but they have the wrong impression about us."

"And what impression is that?" he asked, reaching for a strawberry.

"They think we're a couple. Oh, before I forget . . . What did your mother say in Spanish about me?"

He ate the strawberry before answering, and Paige knew he was stalling. "You don't want to know," he said finally.

"Yes, I do."

"I'll tell you later, I promise. Now eat."

Watching his back retreat, Paige wondered if he had set her up to be the laughingstock of the party. She didn't have time to dwell on it; Teresa called her name and waved her over.

"Sit next to me," Teresa ordered. "You're going to enjoy this. Alexis can really sing, and Serg-X isn't bad, either."

Denying Teresa's request would be useless, so Paige sat down. She'd indulge her now, but she was never coming back to any address where the Simones took up residence.

By the time she finished feasting, it was time for Alexis to sing. Paige had to admit the six-year-old performed "Because You Loved Me" remarkably well. Paige doubted if most of the adults knew all the words to the song. Alexis received a standing ovation, and her father, uncle, and grandfather all gave her roses.

"That is one spoiled child," Teresa remarked. "The man who gets her will have a lot to live up to."

"I'll be right back," Paige said when Sergio-Xavier approached the microphone with Lizzie in hand. In record speed she tossed her trash and relaxed in the seat before he began playing.

"This song is dedicated to my mother, from my father. Happy anniversary, Mom and Dad." Sergio-Xavier said before he began playing.

"You better play, boy," someone yelled out.

The first note Sergio-Xavier played of "When a Man Loves a Woman" sent Paige sliding to the edge of her seat, with her hand over her heart and her mouth agape. Sergio-Xavier told the truth. He made that tenor saxophone talk. She tuned out everything and everyone around her and concentrated on the fine man producing the magnificent sound. Every note sent Paige either moving from side to side or sliding forward, as if she were on a simulated ride. The first notes of the last stanza were so powerful, Paige slid off the chair and landed on her butt. She jumped up, hoping no one had noticed, but the snickers behind her were a clear indication she hadn't moved fast enough.

"It's a good thing you don't like my son. If you did, you might have fallen through the floor," Teresa teased once Paige was seated again.

Paige listened to the rest of the song with her hands gripping the sides of the chair.

"Well, what did you think?" Sergio-Xavier asked when he joined her later with bottled water in hand. "Can I play or what? Before you conjure up a lie, I heard about your butt kissing the floor."

His smiled warmed her, and Paige couldn't help but giggle. "I can't stand you, and yes, babe, you can play. I loved you before, but tonight I fell in love with you *and* Lizzie." Her giggles ceased when Sergio-Xavier choked on his water. That was when she realized what she'd said. *Me and my big mouth,* she thought, wanting to scream, but instead she turned away.

Sergio-Xavier recovered and grabbed her hand. "Come on. Let's dance."

Maybe he hadn't heard the declaration, or maybe he didn't care. Either way, Paige had to regain control of the situation.

"I'm saved. You know I don't dance," she said, snatching her hand away. "I thought you were saved too."

He released her hand. "I'm not going to address you questioning my salvation. What's wrong with dancing? We dance at every family gathering."

"That's what heathens do," she snapped.

"For your information, everyone on the dance floor is a Christ follower, including your idol, Marcus."

Paige's jaw fell when she spotted Marcus doing the Cupid Shuffle.

"You fall out in high praise every time you turn on his CD. Would you call him a heathen?"

Paige didn't answer.

"You said Pastor Reggie was a powerful teacher. He's out there moving to the left, along with everyone else. Would God give him great revelations if he were a heathen?"

Paige still didn't answer.

"No one is bumping or grinding, and the music isn't sexual or vulgar. Every man is dancing with his wife or significant other. Just because *you* can't dance and keep it holy, don't condemn those of us who can." He looked down at his watch. "It's eighty thirty right now. Don't talk until nine thirty. Maybe by that time you'll learn how to bring your mouth and brain in sync. Unbelievable," he mumbled and stormed away.

Paige didn't mind the argument. She'd do whatever it took to keep herself from having to deal with her slip of the tongue. However, she did mind the young woman who soon followed Sergio-Xavier to the dance floor. At first Paige assumed she was a relative, but something about the way the woman smiled at him didn't set right with her. Halfway through the song, Tara confirmed her suspicions.

"I see Angela found him," Tara stated from beside her. "She can spot my brother anywhere."

"Is she another cousin?"

Tara smirked. "Don't throw that wild child into my family. We have enough of them already. Angela is a friend of my cousin Leah. She comes to all the family gatherings. She's been chasing my brother for at least three years. Since you don't like my brother, her presence shouldn't bother you."

"You're right." Paige nodded but didn't miss the snide smile on Tara's face.

After finishing her punch, Tara leaned against her. "My mother and grandmother gave me some good advice a long time ago. Since I like you, I'll share it with you."

"Why, thank you, Officer Tara." Now it was Paige's turn at sarcasm.

"Anytime, sis." She looked directly into Paige's eyes. "They told me that if I voluntarily give up my place, don't get mad at the person behind me for stepping up." Tara patted her shoulder and left Paige alone in her turmoil.

What was she supposed to do? Go snatch Sergio-Xavier off the dance floor? Or worse, beat Angela down? Paige couldn't do either without declaring publicly that Sergio-Xavier belonged to her. The reality was he didn't belong to her and he could dance with whomever he wanted. True, she'd let her feelings slip, but he obviously didn't feel the same, or else he would have said so.

She stewed and paced back and forth, but she refused to go to him. That is, until the music changed to a slow love song and Angela latched on to Sergio-Xavier's neck. By the time he'd set Angela away from him, Paige was beside him, waiting to squeeze into the gap.

Angela appeared surprised, but Sergio-Xavier didn't. "Excuse me, Angela, but I slow dance only with my lady," he said and then gathered Paige in his arms, keeping the two women at a safe distance from each other.

Thoroughly confused, Paige fell into rhythm with him without bothering to see if Angela left or not.

"This is our first dance. Please don't open your mouth and ruin the moment," he whispered in her ear.

Paige closed her eyes; she couldn't speak if she wanted to. What had just happened? Did he refer to her as *my lady?* Maybe he just did that to get Angela to back off. Whatever the case, that didn't explain her public show of possession, especially after she'd spent half the evening denying she liked the man. Paige opened her eyes to find several Simone women, including Grandma Ana and Teresa, pointing and laughing at her. Tara offered her a thumbs-up.

Paige closed her eyes again and leaned her head against his shoulder and allowed herself to relax and enjoy the dance. If she were truthful, she'd admit she enjoyed dancing and had missed it. She'd given it up only as a condition of her salvation. She didn't think dancing fell into the chaste category.

Sergio-Xavier smelled good and felt good . . . but then the lyrics of the song registered. Her head snapped up just as Etta James sang the last line of "At Last." There was something in Sergio-Xavier's eyes that she hadn't seen before or had just failed to recognize, and she had to turn away. Oddly enough, Paige thought of his mother.

"Translate what your mother said about me," she whispered in his ear. This time he didn't stall, and she wished he had.

"She said that you're beautiful, and that it's about time I found someone worthy of my love and respect,'" he whispered back in her ear.

"Oh." She nodded against his shirt and somberly left the dance floor. She didn't have to look over her shoulder to know he was following her, as his heat permeated her senses. For the rest of the evening, the only time he left her side was to dance with his mother.

Chapter 23

Except for the horns of Dave Koz and Gerald Albright, the ride back to Paige's home was quiet. Sergio-Xavier wanted it that way. That was why he turned on the sound system before securing his seat belt. He needed to clear his head and weigh his options before taking this next crucial step. Once he crossed this line, there would be no turning back and no more straddling the fence. His heart wanted it all, but his head reminded him how his heart had steered him wrong before and had blinded him to obvious truths. Now his logical thinking was blocking him from allowing what God had planted in his heart to flourish. He'd learned years ago not to place God in a box, but did his heart's desire have to come in such an unconventional package?

He glanced over at Paige, who was practically hugging the passenger door and was faking sleep. He knew she was faking, because he'd caught her peeking at the highway signs several times. Paige didn't want to address the evening's events, either. Her actions proved it. He'd heard her declaration of love and recognized that their argument was the smoke screen she'd used to cover it up. He'd gone along to keep her from losing control in front of everyone, but before the night was over, their time of reckoning would come.

He released a low chuckle when Paige added snoring sound effects to the act. The woman was hilarious, especially when she fell from that chair while he was playing Lizzie. Her body hadn't got the memo to respond only to gospel music. He'd bet his trust fund that Paige didn't know how truly entertaining and comical she was. She'd invested too much energy into being a starchy Christian to relax and enjoy a fulfilled life, the way God intended. That was his purpose—to help her discover life.

Am I ready for this? he pondered while turning off the interstate. Paige was more than a handful with her preconceived ideas. She had a good heart; God had shown him that. Yet somehow Paige failed to recognize that goodness. She seemed to be on some sort of quest to prove her worthiness. Her devotion to God didn't help her comprehend that she was good and worthy simply because of what Christ did on Calvary.

He pulled into Paige's driveway, and Sleeping Beauty lurched forward and opened the car door.

"Drive safely. See you later." Paige spat the words with lightning speed and jumped from the Bentley before Sergio-Xavier got his door open.

In an instant the peace he'd been seeking enveloped him, extracting boisterous laughter from a place in his heart he didn't know existed. "Oh, yeah, I am more than ready for this," he said aloud while watching Paige struggle to run up the walkway in heels and feel around in her purse at the same time.

He climbed out of the car and headed up the walkway. "Need some help with that?" he offered upon reaching the front door. He had to think of something deadly serious to keep from laughing in her face. In her effort to avoid him, she'd dropped her house key three times.

"No, I'm g-good," she stuttered. "It's late, and you have church in the morning."

"I attend the late service, remember?"

Sergio-Xavier stooped and caught the falling keys before they hit the ground. "Allow me, please." He unlocked and opened the door with ease, then stepped aside for her to enter.

He followed behind her, knowing she wouldn't invite him in. If the terror etched on her face was any indication, she'd rather be stranded in the desert without water than be there with him.

His hands rested on her shoulders. "Let me hang up your coat."

She stilled long enough to slide the wool down her shoulders.

He couldn't resist the urge to make her sweat, so instead of just removing the coat from her arms, Sergio-Xavier allowed his palms to travel slowly across her shoulders and down her arms to her elbows.

"I need something to drink." Paige shook him and the coat loose and then ran into the kitchen.

Payback is sweet, he thought while hanging up her coat and removing his own. She'd been torturing him with those lethal legs for days. It was time she got a dose of her own medicine.

The victory was meaningless once he rounded the corner and entered the kitchen. Paige was bent over the double sink, crying, with the water running full blast. Her hands cupped her mouth to help muffle the sound. He prayed for discernment, and then the source of Paige's tears was clearly revealed—this was her first time loving anyone and she didn't feel worthy of having that love returned. Why she felt unworthy remained hidden.

From behind her, Sergio-Xavier turned off the faucet and placed the paper towel he'd gotten from the counter against her chest. After she accepted it, he wrapped his arms around her waist and embraced her from behind, with his chin resting on her head, until her body stopped trembling. Once certain the storm had passed, he scooped her up and carried her into the living room and placed her beside him on the sofa.

She didn't resist when he held her hand with one hand and lifted her chin with the other, forcing her to make eye contact.

"You're not in this alone, sweetheart. I stopped lying to myself some time ago. It's time for us to stop lying to one another and face the truth, which is crystal clear to those around us. God's knows I didn't mean to love you. In fact, I fought hard not to, but the more I resisted, the more my heart created a spot that only you can occupy. I call it Paige's Place."

"Aw," she whimpered. "I didn't know you had game like that."

"Baby, please don't open your mouth and ruin the moment. Save it for our next argument, which I'm sure will be soon."

She started to pout, but then her face settled into the kind of smile he'd give away half his fortune for.

"Tell me again," he said, then released her hand and pointed at her chest. "Tell me what's in here, like you did earlier. Only this time, don't let the words slip out and then give me that regretful look, like what you feel for me is bad. Take your time and tell me how you feel with the same confidence you had when you booted Angela off the dance floor. Just like I didn't leave you hanging then, I won't leave you hanging now."

He expected her to put up a protest or at least stall, but she disappointed him in the best way.

"All right. I love you. I don't know how it happened, but I do. I tried to pray it away, but that only endeared me to you more. I'm stuck and not sure what to do about it, if anything. Your presence is precious to me, and I don't want to share you, but I don't know how to keep you, either."

"Sweetheart, I'm not going anywhere, unless you want me to. And even then, I won't go far. I love you." Sergio-Xavier leaned in and treated himself to something he'd been craving for weeks. He gently massaged her lips with his own but then pulled back when Paige's lips parted.

"Is that it?" she said. The frown was back.

He released her chin. "What? You don't want me to kiss you?"

"Of course I do, but not like that. You have no idea how many fantasies I've had about kissing those full lips. There are too many to count, but not one of them started and ended with a peck," she explained. "You're a doctor. You do know the tongue is used for more than tasting food."

"I was trying to be romantic."

"Well, can you add some passion and not kiss me like I'm a child? I take that back. You gave Alexis more energy than that grandpa smack."

He patted her hand, hoping to make her understand. "We're not naive teenagers, Paige. It's my job to protect you and not lead us into temptation. If I unleashed the passion I feel right now, we'd both have to lie under the altar tomorrow."

The neck rolling started the second she jumped up. "Speak for yourself. I can handle my flesh. Not one time have you caught me staring at your rear end or those oversize pectorals that keep blocking my vision. You have no idea how your hot breath against my neck affects me. I almost fell down on my kitchen floor, but I didn't. So don't tell me I can't handle my flesh."

He rose and stepped into her personal space with his palm raised. "I do know. Why do you think I keep brushing up against you like that? And because I'm a doctor, I can tell you exactly how much your pulse and respiration increase the second you sniff my cologne."

Paige gasped. "Well, why do you think I keep wearing dresses around you? I love watching you drool over my legs."

"It's not my fault you have the sexiest legs I've ever seen!" Sergio-Xavier threw his hand up and stomped to the coat closet. What should have been a compliment came out as an angry yell. "This is insane. You're insane," he called over his shoulder after snatching his coat off the hanger.

She ran and blocked the front door so he couldn't leave. "Wait!" she ordered. "I just have one question for you."

Physically and emotionally frustrated, Sergio-Xavier emptied out his lungs and ran his sweaty palms through his hair, wondering why he couldn't have a normal girlfriend. Any other church girl would have appreciated his control and consideration, but not Miss Saved and Sanctified to the Bone.

"What more could you possibly have to say, Miss McDaniels?"

"If I'm insane and you love me, what does that make you? Maybe you're a little insane as well."

The innocence with which she asked the question shattered his resolve. The woman was just too adorable with those pouty lips.

Laughter poured from them both as he reached for her. "Come here, woman. I can't believe your big mouth ruined our first kiss," he said, taking her into his arms.

She hadn't learned her lesson yet. "Don't blame me. If you'd done it right, my mouth would have been too occupied to talk."

Experience is the best teacher, he decided and then lifted her chin and gave her what she *thought* she wanted. Sergio-Xavier didn't end the kiss until Paige started sliding down the door, gasping for air.

"That will teach you to stop running your mouth," he said with a satisfied grin after he steadied her and pulled her away from the door.

"You should go now." Her alto voice had dropped to bass tenor, and beads of sweat outlined her forehead.

He opened the door but had to get one more dig in. "Good night, beautiful. Sleep well."

If her heated glare was any indication of Paige's internal burning, she wouldn't be able to sleep until summer.

Chapter 24

Eight hours after finally confessing her love to Sergio-Xavier, Paige stood behind the stage at Restoration Ministries, praying for the strength to lead the church into high worship and praise for the eleven o'clock service. She had learned only minutes earlier that the scheduled worship leader for the second service had called in sick. As the assigned backup, Paige had to fill in. Any other Sunday, Paige would have been ecstatic about singing for the Lord, but today her spirit was too uneasy to act out the joy she'd become accustomed to faking. Today claiming something she didn't possess seemed pointless, and so did speaking manufactured church lingo.

When the usher asked how she was doing this fine Sunday morning, Paige responded, "Tired and sleepy," instead of the usual "Blessed and highly favored." She wasn't mad or angry. She wouldn't say she was happy, but she was content. Something inside her had changed, but unable to identify what, Paige attributed it to fatigue.

After taking a cold shower last night and praying, she had called Sergio-Xavier and they had talked half the night about everything, anything, and nothing. When they started arguing over who should hang up the phone first, Paige realized she'd never slowed down long enough to have a boyfriend or to be courted. She wanted that experience with Sergio-Xavier, but she hadn't reconciled how he fit into her plans for Seniyah and the baby.

The first chords of the overture played by the band redirected her focus to the task at hand. After entreating the Lord to anoint her voice once more, Paige walked to the center of the platform and removed the microphone, and after a brief exhortation, she closed her eyes and offered the one thing she knew God accepted from her—worship.

"Girl, the Lord anointed you today," Reyna said when Paige slipped into the seat she'd saved for her on the second row after praise and worship.

"To God, be the glory." Paige looked down the row and greeted with a wave the Jenningses and the Scotts, who were seated next to Reyna and Tyson. They returned the greeting, then directed their attention back to the screen displaying upcoming events.

"Is there enough room for me?"

Paige's head jerk created a domino effect. As if on cue, seven heads, including baby Destiny's, turned sideways, and everyone gaped at Sergio-Xavier, who was standing at the end of the row.

Elation didn't begin to describe how Paige felt. He'd called her this morning just to say, "Good morning, love. Have a peaceful and blessed day." Then he'd hung up. Now he stood within inches of her, looking fine as ever with that defined dimple.

"There's always room for you." She offered him a smile and then sneered at her friends down the row. "Move over," she ordered.

Kevin and Tyson chuckled and exchanged high fives before waving at Sergio-Xavier and scooting down the row. Reyna was too busy giggling to move her stuff fast enough. Paige pushed the baby's diaper bag out of the way.

"Thanks, sweetheart," Sergio-Xavier whispered in her ear.

"What are you doing here?" She was the reason he was there, but she wanted to hear him say it. He didn't disappoint her.

"I wanted to hear you sing."

"Oh," she said, pouting. "Praise and worship just ended."

"I know. I've been here since the beginning of the service. I didn't know where you were sitting, so I stayed in the back until you were done, and then followed you to your seat." He squeezed her hand. "You really blessed me today."

"How did you know I'd be the lead today? I wasn't scheduled."

He shrugged. "An unction, I guess."

Paige blushed and turned away, only to find the attention of everyone in the row glued on her instead of on the big-screen announcements. Thanks to their nosiness, her friends wouldn't know anything that was going on at church.

"Mind your business," she mouthed and then rested against Sergio-Xavier's arm.

Unlike the previous time they attended a church service together, this time felt normal. They shared Bibles and took notes, even commented briefly on key points. It felt as if they were one, like a missing part of her had suddenly been reconnected. During the prayer after the sermon, they held hands, but instead of praying for strength and healing like Pastor Drake had instructed, Paige tried to envision Sergio-Xavier's role in the life of the child she planned to raise.

Mother Scott and First Lady Drake made a beeline to her immediately after the benediction. This time Paige didn't attempt to run away. She opened her arms and embraced them both. After the Simone interrogation, she'd gained a new appreciation for the bossy pair.

"God sure is working in your life!" First Lady Drake exclaimed. "I've never seen you look this good. You're not there yet, but you are well on the way."

"On the way to what?" Paige asked, but the prayer warriors carried on the conversation as if Paige weren't there.

"About three more all-night prayer sessions ought to do it," Mother Scott concurred. "She'll be good and ready by then, and tired of faking too." She then turned to Sergio-Xavier. "Just a few more kinks and you'll be ready too. Now that you've stopped lying to yourself and everybody else."

"I appreciate your prayers." Sergio-Xavier leaned in and kissed both women on the cheek. "One can't help but get right and stay right with the two of you on the job."

"That's what we're here for." Mother Scott interlocked her arm with Sergio-Xavier's. "Since you're practically family now, I have a question for you."

"Mother Scott, don't!" Paige reached for Mother Scott's hand to keep her from saying something that would embarrass her. As always, her effort was in vain.

"Calm down, girl. We claimed your snobbish, rude, judgmental, and full-of-attitude self as a daughter a long time ago. If we can accept you, we can accept him too. Besides, he's cute," Mother Scott declared.

"Yes, Lord," First Lady Drake agreed in a soft tone. "You hit the jackpot and don't even know it."

Paige wanted to hit Mother Scott for dissecting her character perfectly and Sergio-Xavier for laughing.

Mother Scott cleared her throat and continued speaking to Sergio-Xavier. "Like I was saying, you're one of those brain doctors, aren't you?"

"Yes, I'm a neurologist."

"I've been having these headaches. What do you think it could be?"

"I don't believe this. The prayer warrior seeking free medical advice," Paige grumbled and turned to leave. Unfortunately, her friends were lying in wait.

Reyna attacked first with an uncharacteristic bear hug. "I'm so happy for you."

Marlissa joined in, making it a group hug. "You two look so good together. And you're glowing."

"No, I'm not," Paige snapped with less fire than normal.

"Yes, you are," Tyson said, giving her a hug. "Congratulations," he said out loud and then whispered in her ear, "I told you it would happen."

For once, pangs of envy over Tyson's happiness didn't attack her. "Thank you."

"I'll collect my finder's fee in the form of free real estate services for a lifetime," Kevin teased before embracing her.

She stepped back, and with one hand on her hip and a finger wagging in their faces, Paige prepared to tell her friends exactly what she thought of their little matchmaking scheme. "That reminds me. The next time you feel the urge to butt into my love life, or lack thereof, don't! I don't need your help," she scolded.

"That's because she has me now," Sergio-Xavier said, butting in, having completed Mother Scott's free consultation. "And I'll make sure she never lacks anything."

The wink that accompanied his promise crushed Paige's emotional protective wall. She had to regain control before she turned into mush before her friends. "What you need to remember is, I'm an independent woman. I'm not some needy and helpless woman who needs a rescuer. I can take care of myself," she asserted.

Sergio-Xavier turned to Kevin. "Man, I don't know if I should thank you for connecting me to this woman or punch you in the face."

Paige's gasp was overshadowed by the group's laughter.

"I love this woman," Sergio-Xavier declared, placing his arm around her, "but I'd pay good money to tame that mouth."

At that moment, it was *his* mouth that Paige wanted to tame. Sergio-Xavier had just publicly declared his love for her, and if the relationship didn't work out, everyone would believe it was her fault.

"Would you like to join us for dinner?" Reyna offered between giggles. "There's more than enough food."

"Thank you," Sergio-Xavier answered before Paige could. "But we'll have to take a rain check. Our plane leaves in an hour."

Paige had no idea what he was talking about, but she played along. "Yeah, we'd better get going." She tugged his sleeve. "Come on, honey. We don't want to be late." They started walking down the aisle. "See you busybodies next week," Paige called over her shoulder.

"Why did you lie in church, Minister Simone?" she asked him as they neared the door.

"I didn't lie, sweetheart. I booked reservations at my favorite seafood restaurant in Los Angeles. The family plane is waiting at Oakland International." Her steps slowed. "I hope you don't mind," he added. "The place has a spectacular view of the coastline. I know you're going to love it."

"It's not that I mind. I just forgot you have it like that."

"Being my lady has many privileges," he said once they were in the confines of his car. "I hope you're ready for the ride."

Paige tried her hand at flirting. "I'm yours. Take me anywhere."

He chuckled and kissed her cheek. "In time, sweetheart, in time."

Paige relaxed in the leather seat and for once enjoyed the moment. She didn't remember she'd signed up to visit the sick and the shut-in with the home care ministry until the plane landed at LAX. Although she felt bad for breaking a commitment, she didn't have an ounce of regret for spending quality time with the man she loved.

Chapter 25

"What?" Paige stopped singing long enough to ask this question when she walked into the office Monday morning with just minutes to spare before the weekly staff meeting. The receptionist and the agents roaming about had stopped mid-stride and stared.

"Nothing. I assumed you were already in your office." The receptionist looked down at her watch. "You're usually the first one here. It's almost nine thirty. And you're singing?" She leaned over the desk. "And you're wearing bright orange? Are you ill?"

Paige set the pastry box she'd been carrying down on the desk. "I'm great," she sang with a giddiness she couldn't control, and spun around. "Isn't this gorgeous? I never thought I would look good in this color."

"You look good in it, but if you don't hurry, you'll be late starting the meeting."

Everyone at Highpoint Real Estate was well aware of Paige's obsession with punctuality. Most agents arrive thirty minutes early for the weekly meetings to avoid tardiness. This morning Paige couldn't care less about time or the meeting, but since she made the meetings mandatory, she'd decided to make an appearance.

She patted the box. "Take these to the conference room. I'll be in there soon."

Paige strolled down the hall, wishing Sergio-Xavier was beside her and they were strolling down Rodeo Drive, like they were doing fifteen hours ago. After a succulent lobster meal, Sergio-Xavier had treated her to a mini shopping spree on the famous strip. Her bounty included two dresses, a designer purse, and a pair of stilettos with the exclusive red bottom. While Sergio-Xavier had been getting measured for a tailored suit, Paige had sneaked out and purchased a red leather miniskirt for when the "in time" that her man had promised came.

She should have been tired after the long, physically and emotionally draining weekend, but she wasn't. This morning, following mediation and a brief phone prayer with Sergio-Xavier, Paige had put the finishing touches on the nursery, and then she'd gone for a run around the track at the local high school. She'd forgotten how much she loved running until the wind stroked her cheeks and her ponytail bounced rhythmically, in sync with her strides. As she rounded the sixth lap, Paige vowed to incorporate running back into her daily routine. The real estate office wouldn't fold if she came to work at 9:00 a.m. instead of 7:00 a.m. The time she'd spent working from home and creating the nursery had proven that.

Upon entering her office, Paige set her briefcase on the floor against her desk, and after booting her computer, she printed copies of the agenda for the meeting. She turned to leave the office, and just as she reached the door, her cell phone chimed.

"Hey, you," she said and giggled into the phone after checking the caller ID.

"How's your morning?" Sergio-Xavier asked, as if they hadn't talked already this morning.

"Better now." Paige leaned against the door and chatted like she didn't have a roomful of people waiting for her.

"Promise me that you'll go straight home after DWAP and get some rest."

Paige hesitated before answering. She had plans to stop by Seniyah's house after the meeting. "I will go straight home when I'm done," she answered evasively.

"I'm serious, sweetheart. You had a long weekend, and you have a busy week ahead. I don't want you to wear yourself out."

Being in an exclusive relationship had its advantages, but she wasn't sure if Sergio-Xavier's protectiveness was normal. "So, are you my daddy now?"

"No, but as your man, it's my job to look out for your well-being. It's one of the benefits."

Her breath caught. No one but her father had said that to her or even implied it. She swallowed a shallow response and spoke from her heart. "I like your benefits package. Thanks for looking out. You were a good friend, but you're an outstanding boyfriend." A knock on the door reminded her of the time. "Babe, I have to go, but I'll talk with you later. Get some rest. That 'looking out' rule works both ways."

"I love you, too. Talk to you later. I have to contact the construction company."

Paige stuffed the phone in her pocket and darted to the conference room. She was halfway through the productivity report when Sergio-Xavier's statement registered. He was ready to build his home.

"I am so proud of you!" Paige hollered. With only three weeks left in the program, DWAP had not only reached its goal of five thousand necklaces sold, but had also exceeded it by 20 percent. They had enough capital to purchase five hundred blankets at wholesale for the shelter.

"Are you really proud of us?" Jasmine asked. "Or are you just saying that? We worked really hard and did everything you said."

For once, Paige recognized Jasmine's need for her approval. She used the pronoun *us,* but judging by the expectancy dancing in her eyes, she had really meant *me.*

Paige patted her shoulder. "Of course, I mean it. You're going to do well in junior college."

"Well, actually, we've been thinking that our grades aren't that bad. Maybe we should . . . ," Jasmine began. "Never mind. Thank you."

Paige overlooked the longing that covered the girls' faces. She couldn't identify the source of it, and at the moment she didn't have time to inquire about it. If the session ran over, it would be too late to stop by Seniyah's house to present her proposal.

"Since we have only three sessions left, we should start planning our last session. Each of you will receive a certificate of completion signed by the regional program director, and I will issue special recognition awards. We'll also have refreshments. I can reserve the performing arts room. It should be large enough to accommodate your family and friends."

Her statement was met by silence.

"Well?" Paige asked when no one offered any input.

For once Jasmine turned away and allowed someone else to answer. "Ms. Paige, we don't need that much room. Our families don't usually attend things like that," the girl explained. "Between the seven of us, we might get twelve people to come, and five of them will be kids, and the other seven, our boyfriends. Our mamas who aren't on drugs are too busy with man problems to care. At least Jasmine has her brother. That's why we stick together. We're all we got."

"Well, I . . ." Paige searched for an answer and couldn't find one. In theory, she knew their family dynamics presented challenges, but the reality of those challenges had never set in until now. Had she been too consumed with Seniyah to notice? She shook the thought away. Seniyah needed her help.

"If that's the case, why don't we hold the celebration off campus?" said a male voice.

Simultaneously all heads turned toward the voice. Paige hadn't seen Sergio-Xavier standing in the doorway, and she was sure the divas hadn't, either.

He stepped completely inside the room. "I know of the perfect beachfront restaurant that would give us a private room. A buddy of mine owns a limousine service, and I'm sure I can get him to donate us a vehicle for the evening."

With renewed excitement, the divas surrounded him.

"For real? Dr. Simone, you wouldn't play us, would you?" Jasmine asked.

"Never. If Ms. McDaniels agrees, I'll make the arrangements."

I love this man, but why is he here? Paige thought, but she said, "I don't think it will be a problem moving the celebration off-site as long as we have parental consent."

"Give us the form and we'll sign it. I mean, we'll take it home and bring it back signed," Jasmine said, correcting herself.

The divas started the celebration right then, and there with high fives and dancing.

"This will make up for two proms I missed," one of the girls stated.

While the divas made plans for the big event, Paige pulled Sergio-Xavier aside. "What did you just do, and why?" she demanded more than asked.

"Sweetheart, don't let your mouth blow it for these young ladies," he warned with a smile. "I simply gave them something to look forward to. You heard for yourself. All they have is each other. You just finished raving about the outstanding job they've done. Their families aren't there for them. Somebody has to celebrate their accomplishments to keep them feeling encouraged. Didn't you hear what she said? She missed both of her proms."

She smiled back. "I get it, but why do you have to be the one?"

"Why do you have to be the one for Seniyah?"

Her smile fell, but she didn't offer an answer.

"I admire those young ladies for trying. They could have given in to the elements and become a statistic, but they didn't. For that alone, they deserve a standing ovation. A night on the town for them isn't going hurt me one bit. It's as simple as making a phone call. You'd be surprise how many people are willing to help those who help themselves. In fact, if they set their goal beyond junior college, I'd be more than willing to make sure they reach it."

"Ms. Paige," Jasmine called out, interrupting them, "you wear long gowns to formal events, right?"

"That's right," Paige answered through a manufactured smile.

"Good. We decided we want to go formal. To make sure we don't look like hoochies, can you help us pick out patterns? My cousin Porsche can make our dresses, but she doesn't have any class. She can sew, but she dresses like a . . ." Jasmine paused. "You get my point."

"Sure. Of course, I will," Paige answered, trying not to laugh.

"See, sweetheart? Not only do these ladies need your help, but they also *want* your help," Sergio-Xavier whispered in her ear.

His statement held a dual message that Paige wasn't ready to receive. She'd gone too far to turn back. "Why are you here?" She had to change the subject.

"I came here to make sure you went straight home. I'm not nearly as slow as I look. I caught that evasive response over the phone. You're done after this session. Don't worry about dinner. It's in the car."

Paige rolled her eyes and stomped away. Maybe having Sergio-Xavier as her man wasn't so great, after all. They needed to have a talk soon. He needed to understand his place in her life. He was mistaken if he thought her love for him was enough to make her abort her plan.

After Sergio-Xavier followed her home, Paige ate, showered, and then stretched out in her bed and watched a Lifetime movie. Halfway through the romantic comedy, she admitted that Sergio-Xavier had been right. She did need some rest. She also needed to call her mother and tell her the good news.

Her mother answered on the second ring. "Hey, baby. I'm enjoying this caller ID. I've been avoiding them telemarketers like the plague. What's going on with you?"

Paige went straight to the point. "I have a boyfriend, man, significant other ,whatever the politically correct term is. I got one."

"What? Is it serious?" her mother screamed into the phone.

"We're in love, if that's what you mean."

"Thank you, Jesus!" her mother yelled into the phone. Then Paige heard her tell her father, "Our prayers have been answered."

For once Paige wished she could freely express her excitement.

"Tell me about him," her mother ordered.

Paige leaned back, stroking the pillow. "Let's see. He's two years older than me. He's African American, Latino, and French and over six feet tall. He's a minister and a neurologist."

"Hallelujah!" her mother screamed into the phone. "He's the one!"

Paige shook her head, as if her mother could see her. "Ma, you don't even know his name."

"He's a minister and a doctor. I don't care what his name is. It could be Donald Duck, for all I care. I'll be the proud mother of Mrs. Reverend Doctor Donald Duck."

Paige laughed along with her mother, but that wasn't the only news she wanted to share. "Mom, how do you feel about another addition to the family, say, a baby?"

"You know you ain't supposed to be giving the goodies away before he puts a ring on it, but the Lord can forgive you for that too. When is the baby due?"

"Oh, no, Ma, I'm not pregnant. We're not having sex. I was just asking because—"

Her mother cut her off. "Good, because I don't want you to make the same mistake I made with your daddy, but if you do, I got your back. Now, tell me how y'all met, and don't leave anything out."

What had started out as a pleasant evening transformed into despair within seconds. Paige thought that she could confide in her mother and that her mother understand her plan, but that wasn't the case. Everyone seemed to be against her. First, Sergio-Xavier had ruined her evening by showing up and foiling her plan to visit Seniyah, and now her mother was ready to marry her off to a man who might not fit into the grand scheme of things. After indulging her mother, Paige cried herself to sleep for what she vowed would be the last time.

Chapter 26

"Coming!" Paige yelled the second time the doorbell chimed, and then continued brushing her hair. She could take an hour and her visitor wouldn't leave. Since officially stepping into the role of the man in her life, Sergio-Xavier was always present in one form or another and was always in her business. He made sure Paige took care of herself before running out to save the world. If they weren't talking on the phone, they were exchanging mushy text messages. The bouquet of long-stem red roses and a mini chocolate cake with the photo of them he'd taken with his iPhone were so cute that it took her two days to eat the cake. And Lizzie . . . When the man serenaded her with that saxophone, Paige wanted to fall down and kiss his feet. If she'd known the man had this much game, she would have come out of denial a long time ago. Paige loved the attention and bottled up every memory.

After tonight, memories and dry rose petals might be all that was left of the whirlwind romance. The choice was Sergio-Xavier's. She'd lay out the facts, then give him the option of remaining in her life on her terms, but under no circumstance would she compromise.

"Five more seconds and I'm going home," he warned just as she twisted the knob.

Leaning against the door, she struck a pose that emphasized her bare legs. "You want me to look my best, don't you? It takes time to look this good."

"You're just as evil as you are sweet." He shook his head as he passed her en route to the kitchen. "I hope you have a taste for Thai."

A sudden sense of sadness, almost like mourning, hit her. She lingered in the foyer until she was able to suck back the tears threatening to fall. She had to move forward. When she finally reached the kitchen, Sergio-Xavier had already fixed their plates and was pouring pear cider into wineglasses.

He set the bottle on the table and reached for her. "Come here, you little vixen. Don't I at least merit a kiss for all the suffering you're putting me through with that dress?"

Paige obliged him with a lingering kiss, which she prayed wouldn't be their last. Just as she deepened the kiss, he pulled back.

"Let's eat. I promise you're going to love this pumpkin curry," he said, and they both took a seat at the table.

Something wasn't right. Sergio-Xavier didn't just physically withdraw from her. Emotionally something had shifted, but she couldn't identify what. He normally asked about the office or the divas' latest antics and then relayed messages from his mother. Tonight he didn't do any of that, but his lips appeared to move.

"This curry is good," Paige said in an effort to break the silence.

His lips stopped moving long enough for him to say, "I'm glad you like it," and then the movement of his lips resumed. That was when Paige realized he was too busy praying to carry on a conversation. She left him to his private thoughts and finished the meal in silence.

Once they were finished, Sergio-Xavier helped load the dishwasher and then, without warning, took her by the hand and led her into the living room. Instead of sitting beside her on the sofa, he hunched down in front of her.

"Sweetheart, what's wrong?" he asked while gripping her hand. "Don't say, 'Nothing,' because that's a lie. You're fretting about something. I felt the anxiety in your kiss. Did the comment I made a while back about contacting my contractor scare you? Are we going too fast?"

The man knew her too well and cared too much to allow her to stew in agony. She stroked his cheek with the back of her hand. "I love you, really I do, but I have to tell you something."

"I'm listening."

"We're not moving too fast, but as much as I want it to, this still may not turn into happily ever after."

"That only happens in fairy tales." He kissed her hand. "I'm looking for a real life commitment, one with the peaks and valleys of this thing called life."

Paige closed her eyes and said a prayer of her own. "I need to share a part of my life with you, and then you can determine if I'm the person you want to pursue or not."

He nodded contemplatively. "Go on."

"I, um, well . . ." Paige snatched her hand from his grip and jumped up. "Why don't I just show you? That way you'll understand how serious I am."

"Okay." He rose to his full height.

She led him to the back of the house, to the room next to the master bedroom suite. Before opening the door, she started to pray he'd understand, but then determined she didn't care.

She turned to him with her back against the door. "This will explain everything." She opened the door, stepped aside, and allowed him to enter the fully furnished nursery.

She observed Sergio-Xavier's every move and facial expression as he walked around the room, touching the furniture and examining the wall decor. Finally, she was able to read his thoughts, but what she perceived crushed her spirit.

"You're having a baby," he stated more than asked.

"Yes, well, not exactly. I figured out a way to help Seniyah take care of her baby and stay in school. This is how I'm going to help her."

"Please explain this to me like I'm a two-year-old, because I don't get it." If his labored breathing was any indication of his inner turmoil, Sergio-Xavier would explode at any second.

Paige presented the explanation that sound logical in her heart. She had never told anyone this before.

"Just because Seniyah made a mistake by getting pregnant shouldn't mean she has to abort her college dreams. I have the room, and I can rearrange my schedule to help her. If she grants me temporary guardianship, I can raise the baby while she's in school. On the weekends and breaks she can stay here with us. This way she won't lose her scholarship, and she can focus on school without worrying about the baby." She paused. "It's a win-win for all," she added when his piercing glare remained. "It's really the best solution."

"I can't believe Seniyah has agreed to allow to you to take her baby."

"I'm not taking her baby," she snapped. "I'm helping her, and I'm fulfilling my Christian duty. Besides, she hasn't agreed to anything. I haven't presented the idea to her yet."

"What!" Sergio-Xavier stepped toward her, then backed away. "Woman, are you insane? You have a fully decorated nursery, complete with diapers and formula, and you haven't even spoken to the girl about this crazy idea? If you want a baby that badly, I'll give you one. I'll meet you at the courthouse first thing in the morning. You'll be pregnant by sundown. You don't have to take someone else's baby and justify it as your Christian duty."

She couldn't prevent her finger from wagging in his face or stop her lips from moving. His words hurt, and he had to pay for that. "I knew you wouldn't understand and would pass judgment on me. That's why I didn't tell you sooner. I don't care what you think, because I don't need your approval."

"My approval is not the issue here," he countered. "I would think you'd respect me enough to discuss something that will have a bearing on our relationship. Raising someone else's child is a major decision. That's not something I have considered."

"You don't get it, do you?" she said, shaking her head. "I'm not asking you to do anything." She stepped as close as possible to him, wanting him to feel every blow. "I don't need your help having or raising a child. I don't care if you walk out that door and never come back. I'm doing this for me." Her lips curved into a satisfied grin as she watched his skin turn a shade of red. The victory was short-lived.

"That's good, because I wouldn't want to be held accountable for creating a self-centered replica of you. This is not about helping Seniyah. It's about you satisfying some sick desire and feeding your ego. You haven't even talked to her. Seniyah may not want or need your kind of help."

His words stung, and she began shaking. She felt herself losing control, but she was helpless to stop the eruption.

He went on. "You're so self-absorbed, you don't care about anyone but yourself and what you want. It's a good thing you don't have any children, because you don't deserve to reproduce."

Thirteen years of guilt and suffering rushed to the surface and gushed out in a shrill that filled the room and probably the entire house, but Paige didn't care.

Sergio-Xavier had no idea how much she had endured, but he was about to find out.

She lunged forward and slapped him, then started punching him. "How dare you say that to me! You don't know what I've been through. I've been paying for my mistake for thirteen years. I know I was wrong, but you don't have the right to judge me. Everything I do is to make up for my mistake. You don't know how many tears I've cried. How many times I've apologized." The punching continued until Sergio-Xavier pinned her against the wall, with her arms above her head. Then the yelling turned into sobs.

Her descent down the wall was almost in slow motion. He released her arms and held her stationary. Her head buried in his chest, Paige felt suspended between love and hate as her feet dangled just above the floor.

"It's okay, sweetheart. Calm down." She heard the words whispered in her ear, but didn't receive them. How could he be so loving after the horrible things he'd just said about her?

He set her on her feet but still held on to her. "Please tell me what this is really about," he pleaded, but instead of talking, Paige pushed free and stumbled out of the nursery and into her bedroom.

"You have no idea how much I hurt," she wailed. She rambled on as she rummaged through the nightstand drawer. Papers flew until she found the faded envelope. Without any preliminary, she thrust it in his face. "Look at it!" she screamed.

"Whose baby is this?" he asked after pulling out the sonographic image. "I know it's not Seniyah's from the date."

She fell on the bed and bawled with her head in her hands. "It's mine."

He sat beside her and attempted to embrace her. "Did you have a miscarriage?"

She yanked herself away from him. "No, you idiot. Tyson and I didn't want any kids, so we killed our baby," she cried. When his stare continued to penetrate her, she went on. "I was so selfish back then. We both were. We found out I was pregnant, and went to the clinic the next day to make the arrangements. Not once did we discuss what was best for the baby. It was all about what we wanted, what we had to do. We didn't love each other, but we could have raised the child if we hadn't been so self-centered. Money wasn't the issue. I just didn't want to be bothered."

The breath Sergio-Xavier exhaled sounded as if a weight had been lifted. "Now you're trying to make up for aborting the baby," he mused and then returned the sonographic image to the envelope and placed the envelope on the nightstand.

"I have been trying for thirteen years to make retribution for my mistake. Why do you think I practically live at church and spend all my free time serving others? I have to show God that I've changed. I have to prove that I'm not selfish anymore. I have to show that I can sacrifice my time and comfort for the sake of others. That's why I have to help Seniyah. It's my one chance to prove I can sacrifice my wants for the life of a child."

He walked into the bathroom and returned with a wad of tissue and handed it to her. "Did you repent to God for aborting your baby?"

"Of course I did," she snapped between wipes.

"Then, Paige, it's over. God has already forgiven you. Working yourself into the ground and rearing Seniyah's child isn't going to make you any more forgiven. You have to let this go."

She smirked. "That's the perfect theological answer. Have you ever been so ashamed of what you've done that you couldn't look yourself in the mirror? Do you even know what it's like to feel so unworthy that not even God could love you? That you've gone so far that His arm can't reach you? Until you've been there, don't tell me to 'let this go.'"

"I've been there and back. Remember, I'm the one who denounced my call to the ministry for sex with a lesbian. That's not any worse than the choice you made." He took her hand once again. "You have to do the same thing I had to do. You need to forgive yourself for making a bad choice and move on. Seniyah's baby is not your atonement. The blood Jesus shed on Calvary is."

For a moment, Paige considered his words. They actually made sense.

"You're letting one bad past decision cloud your present judgments. You don't trust your own decision-making process anymore. That's why you keep everyone in a box and have to maintain control all the time. Your guilt has made you blind to what God wants you to do. Seniyah's situation has blinded you to those who really need your help. Raising that baby will not erase what's going on inside your heart. You can't replace your child with hers. When all is said and done, your child will still be dead. With or without me, you need to live, and you won't be able to live the way God intended until you forgive yourself."

Instead of comfort, his words unleashed a rage in her, one so potent, it scared her. She heard the foul language pouring from her mouth but couldn't identify the source, nor could she stop the words from flowing. Even when Sergio-Xavier stood and started for the door, she couldn't slow down. It was like an out-of-body experience. "I hate you!" were the last words she screamed before the front door slammed in her face.

Finally, her mouth had run him off and had restored the control she needed to complete her mission. Sergio-Xavier was wrong. She was on her way to living again, and Seniyah's baby was the vehicle that would lead her to that abundant life everyone kept talking about.

"You are so wrong," she smirked when his tires screeched in her driveway.

Chapter 27

Paige's sweaty palms slid down the sides of the leather steering wheel in her Lexus for the third time. She'd been sitting outside of Seniyah's subsidized housing complex for ten minutes, trying to summon the courage to get out of the vehicle and knock on the door. The development was surprisingly clean for a low-income community. Except for the sporadically placed candle and T-shirt memorials in honor of lost lives, the streets were free of litter. However, from the confines of her locked vehicle, Paige had already witnessed two drug transactions and a young pimp on a bicycle chastising one of his girls.

She was having second thoughts, had been since she'd calmed down after running Sergio-Xavier off last night. She still couldn't remember everything she'd said to him, but what she did recall left her too embarrassed to look in the mirror. They didn't have to end like that, but he didn't have to say what he said, either. He could have kept his opinion to himself and supported her, but no, he had to psychoanalyze her and call into question her motive for every decision she'd made. Forgiveness, she would never grant him, but she would prove him wrong and gloat. Despite what he'd said, it was her divine purpose to help Seniyah.

She stepped from the car and checked her attire, hoping the jeans and Nikes made her look less conspicuous. She reached into the backseat and retrieved the items she'd purchased for Seniyah on that disastrous shopping trip.

She hadn't brought her purse, instead opting to slip her phone and keys into her front jean pocket after setting the power locks in her car.

"Don't go in there."

Paige stopped before stepping onto the sidewalk and looked around for the source of the voice. She saw no one and stepped over the grass.

"Let it go."

The soft voice spoke again, but this time with more urgency. Paige looked down both sides of the street. No one was there. "I must be losing my mind," she mumbled, then continued up the walkway and pressed the doorbell.

Paige had met Seniyah's mother twice before, but on those occasions she didn't look like the fashion queen who was standing before her now. The baggy fleece sweatpants and shirt had been replaced with designer jeans and a silk blouse. The head that was once home to matted cornrows was now covered with long, curly honey-blond locks. Her fingertips were covered with designer acrylic nails, and her face gave the impression that she'd just stepped from the M•A•C counter at Macy's.

"Ms. King?" Paige asked to be sure this was the same woman. "How are you?"

"Seniyah didn't tell me you were coming by." The woman didn't bother returning the greeting and didn't invite Paige in, either.

Thrown off by her abrasiveness, Paige rushed her response. "She didn't know I was coming. Since she left the junior entrepreneur group, I haven't seen her much, and I was worried about her." When the woman continued glaring at her, Paige held the bags out. "I brought some things for her."

Ms. King's facial expression softened. "Well, come on in." She stepped aside to let Paige enter. "Seniyah!" she called up the stairs and then led Paige into the living room.

Paige had assumed Seniyah lived with meager provisions. After all, the girl visited the food bank on a regular basis. The leather furniture and mounted big-screen television were a surprise. So was the floor-to-ceiling, three-piece oak multimedia unit. Paige sat down and tried to make sense of her surroundings. How could someone in Ms. King's position afford all this stuff?

The woman must be a drug dealer. I have to get Seniyah and the baby out of here, Paige thought.

"Yes, Mama?" Seniyah entered the living room in sweats and a T-shirt. She was barefoot, and her feet had swelled to the point where they looked like someone had injected a liter of fluid into each foot. Her hands and face hadn't fared much better.

"You have a visitor," Ms. King announced, sitting back in the leather recliner.

"Ms. McDaniels, what are you doing here?" Seniyah asked.

Paige forced her eyes from Seniyah's protruding stomach and made eye contact with the girl who carried her redemption. "How have you been? You haven't returned any of the messages I left with your counselor."

"I've been busy," Seniyah, answered while shrugging her shoulders. "Is there something you want?"

Paige uncrossed and recrossed her legs. "I wanted to drop these off." She pointed to the bags she'd placed on the floor. "You forgot these when we went shopping."

"Oh yeah. Thanks."

Paige's heart constricted at the dry and unappreciative response, but she pressed forward, anyway. "I also wanted to talk to you about the baby."

Seniyah sat on the love seat adjacent to Paige and rubbed her stomach. "What about my baby?"

Paige rubbed her sweaty palms against her jeans. She wished they could have this conversation without Ms.

King around, but that wasn't going to happen. Ms. King was leaning back, reading a magazine. "I was serious when I said I was going to help you take care of the baby while you attend college."

"What do you plan to do? Pay for child care until my name comes up on the list? Or buy me a car so I won't have to take public transportation?" Seniyah leaned forward expectantly. "Since you're in real estate, maybe you can put me up in an apartment."

Paige shook her head as if to clear it. Where was Seniyah getting these outrageous ideas from? "Actually, I was thinking of something more stable and reasonable."

"Like what?"

Paige measured her words to keep from stuttering. "I have the room, and I am willing to keep the baby for you so you can focus totally on school. All you have to do is grant me temporary guardianship, and I'll make sure all his health needs are met. You won't have to worry about food or clothing. I'll take care of everything. I have a spare bedroom you can stay in on weekends and during school breaks." Paige took a long breath, but she didn't feel the relief she'd expected. Quite the contrary, as fear gripped her. She was about to lose something, but she didn't know what.

"Woman, have you lost your mind?" Ms. King threw down the magazine and jumped to her feet.

It took Seniyah longer to stand, but she wanted to know the same thing. "Are you crazy? You want me to *give* you my baby?"

"No, that's not what I'm saying," Paige responded, defending herself. "I want to help you take care of your baby, that's all," she added, although she wasn't so sure anymore.

Ms. King stood over Paige and pointed an acrylic nail in her face. "I told Seniyah when you made it your mission to get her that scholarship that we could use you for a few things. I was thinking a car, but I didn't know you were crazy enough to try to take her baby."

Paige's face stung, as if she'd been physically slapped. "What do you mean, *use* me?"

Ms. King broke it down for her. "Look around, Ms. Do-gooder. We don't need you or your money. We know how to work the system quite well to get what we need. For what the system doesn't provide, there are dumb church folks like you willing to make up the difference."

Paige felt herself shrinking as Seniyah and her mother took turns pointing out her stupidity.

"You took one look at me and assumed I needed you to rescue me," Seniyah pointed out. "I didn't *need* you to help me get into Stanford. I started that process long before I met you. You brought me that wool coat because you thought I didn't have one. You never asked me what I needed. For your information, I have a closet full of designer clothes and coats. I just don't wear them to school or around you. I don't need you to take care of my baby. His daddy will provide everything he needs and a car for me to drive."

Paige's head snapped up. "How can he if he doesn't have a job?"

Seniyah shook her head. "You are really dumber than you look. Do you really think I'm dumb enough to get pregnant by a man without a job? My mama taught me better than that."

The image of mother and daughter exchanging high fives nearly made Paige gag.

"I fed you that ridiculous story to see what I could get from you. My baby daddy is a forty-year-old, married business owner who will do anything to keep his wife from finding out about his love child. I'll have an apartment and a car before I leave for school, and I'll get a monthly allowance."

For the second time in less than twenty-four hours Paige had an out-of-body experience, but this time she wasn't the one in control. They were. She wouldn't win this battle.

"Why?" she whispered. "Why did you do this to me?"

Seniyah smirked. "Don't blame us because you judged a book by its cover."

"You're a church lady, right?" Ms. King asked.

Paige nodded her response.

"Then you should try praying before casting your pearls before swine next time." Ms. King laughed. "And doesn't the Bible say something about testing the spirits to see if they are godly or not?"

Sinister laughter pounded Paige's head as mother and daughter continued mocking her and her faith. The invisible weight bearing down on her chest and the imaginary chains encasing her legs made it nearly impossible to move. She didn't pray for strength; instead, Paige relied on herself and ran out of the apartment. When she tripped and fell down the steps and landed on her face, the image of Seniyah and her mother pointing and making fun of her was fuel enough for her to get up and hop to the car without asking for help.

Her body shook uncontrollably and she dropped her keys twice before stilling her hand enough to deactivate the alarm and unlock the door. When she pulled into her driveway twenty minutes late, Paige didn't know how she'd made it home. One thing was certain. She was never leaving there again.

Chapter 28

"Hey, lady. Can you push me?"

Paige let the bags fall from her arms and ran to grant the little boy his wish. She'd walked through the neighborhood park on numerous occasions, but she'd never seen this brown- skinned kid with hazel eyes before. He was too adorable in his jeans and Disney Cars T-shirt with the matching shoes.

"Of course I will." Paige scanned the playground. "Where are you parents?" she asked before giving the swing a light push.

"My father is around."

Paige looked around again in every direction. "Where? I don't see him."

On the backswing the little boy held his head back and revealed the cutest smile. "I know. Nobody can, but he's always around, watching me."

"If you say so." Paige wasn't convinced. Her neighborhood was relatively safe, but not to the extent that she'd leave a child unattended in broad daylight.

"You can go higher. I'm not afraid," the boy called out several backswings later.

"You're a brave young man. How old are you?"

"I don't know. My father told me not to worry about my age."

Paige smirked, thinking the boy's father must be some sort of psycho. She guessed from his size he was around five. She lost track of time as she pushed him and listened to him pretend to be a superhero flying though the clear blue sky. His giggles soothed her heart and lifted her spirit.

"Okay, you can stop now." The boy stilled his legs and looked up at Paige.

Paige grabbed the chains and brought the swing to a complete stop. "Is anything wrong? I'm not in a hurry. I can push you as long as you want."

"No, that's okay," he answered, shaking his head. "It's time for me to go now."

Paige surveyed the park for the third time to see if the child's father had shown up. The park was completely empty. "Where are you going?"

The boy jumped off the swing and took off running through the sandbox and across the grass.

"Wait!" Paige called before she took off running after him.

"Let me go!" the boy screamed when she grabbed him from behind. "Let me go!"

"Honey, calm down. I don't want you to run out into the street and hurt yourself." Paige's efforts at soothing him failed.

"No! Let me go!" The tighter she squeezed, the louder he screamed and the wilder his arms flailed. "You have to let me go!"

Violent tremors sent Paige thrashing around the bed, but unlike the two previous times she'd had the dream, she didn't acquire any new wounds. The first time she tried to escape the dream, she bruised her left elbow on the nightstand. The second time had her running for cover and twisting her right ankle, just as she'd done during her escape from Seniyah's house. Her foot had given way, causing her right knee to crash onto the hardwood floor. Her cries of agony had gone unheard and unanswered as she crawled back into bed.

Her whole body ached. The down comforter she loved so much and the six-hundred-thread-count sheets were soaked with a mixture of sweat, water from the melted ice she'd used to numb her ankle, and urine. She couldn't remember exactly how many times, but at least twice she had tried to slide off the bed and hop to the bathroom and had failed. For once she didn't care how she looked or smelled. She didn't care about anything; she'd completely surrendered to depression.

Her stomach stirred. It seemed like the second consciousness set in, her stomach churned. She forced her eyes open, only to be greeted by the sunlight peeking through the drapes. She'd seen sunlight at least three times since returning home and collapsing on the bed after Seniyah's betrayal, but she wasn't sure if it was the same sunlight or a different day.

"Oh no," she groaned while clawing her way through the mangled bedcovering. Not only was her stomach awake, but her bladder had also decided to join the party. Too weak to stand and hop, Paige maneuvered her way to the floor and attempted to crawl across the hardwood to the bathroom. When she was less than halfway there, a sharp pain shot through her right ankle, causing her to wail and lose the battle with her stomach and bladder. Figuring the end had to be near, Paige lay in the mess and wept until another deep sleep overtook her.

Sergio-Xavier checked his watch, just in case the clock on the wall was wrong. Unfortunately for him, the Rolex confirmed what he feared—it was only 10:30 a.m. Another ninety minutes to kill. Tuesday mornings were his downtime, when he caught up on dictation, returned patient e-mails, or read medical journals. The last several Tuesday mornings he'd spent the majority of this time courting Paige.

For a split second he considered calling her but quickly dismissed the thought. He was done. She'd crossed the line. He didn't expect the woman who could potentially wear his name to be perfect, but he did expect her to respect him as a man. Paige had proved she had more regard for a dog, and because of that, whatever plans he had for their future had been canceled. He would honor his promise to DWAP, but after that Paige McDaniels would be completely erased from his agenda. Just like with Nicole, he hurt, but he would survive.

His intercom sounded just as he opened a medical journal. "Dr. Simone, there are some people here to see you," the secretary announced.

He wasn't expecting anyone and checked the schedule on his iPhone before responding. "Is it a patient?"

He heard a smirk. "I doubt it, but from the looks of things, you may have to treat one or two of them in the near future."

He had lost his tolerance for drama four days ago, when he walked out on Paige. Whoever was there to see him had better have a clear purpose and not waste his time.

"Send them in."

Sergio-Xavier reached for his lab coat. He'd gotten one arm in when the divas—all seven of them—rushed into his office, with hair color to match the green, yellow, blue, and pink knockoff designer purses on their arms. From the determined looks on their faces, the divas definitely had a purpose and wouldn't leave the building until the mission was accomplished.

"What are you doing here? Shouldn't you ladies be in school?" he began, but Jasmine cut to the chase.

"We signed in before we cut . . . I mean, before we sort of got permission to leave. Have you seen Ms. Paige?"

"Excuse me?" he said.

Jasmine's loud tone matched her bright yellow hair. "I said, have you seen . . ." She let the thought hang, as if she had remembered something, and then continued. "We don't mean to barge in and interrupt your schedule, Dr. Simone, but we're looking for Ms. Paige. She didn't show up for DWAP last night," she explained in a normal tone. "We tried calling her last night and this morning, but she's not answering her cell phone. We don't have her home number, but I'm sure you do. We just want to make sure she's all right."

Just what he didn't want or need—more Paige drama. "Maybe she was just tired and decided to stay home last night," he suggested, more to ease their worry, because at the moment he didn't care where she was.

"She never cancels on us, and she's not at work today, either. We stopped by her office first," the girl with pink hair added. "Ms. Paige never misses work. She told us she even has a home office so she can work from home."

"That's true," he said contemplatively.

"Have you talked to her?" Jasmine asked. "Can you call her?"

The seven pairs of worried eyes staring at him made him angry all over again with Paige. These young ladies genuinely cared about her well-being, and she didn't show them the slightest regard. She was too busy forcing her hopes and dreams on Seniyah to notice they needed her.

"Have you checked with Seniyah?" he offered. "I'm sure she's heard from her."

This time the one with green hair spoke up. "That's what we thought too, so we checked with her first. We went to her complex before school, but she wasn't there."

"Maybe they're together?" he offered.

"No, they're not," Jasmine went on to explain. "Seniyah's in the hospital. She lost her baby over the weekend.

She had pre-clampses, and her baby came early and is dead."

"Preeclampsia," he said, correcting her.

"Well, you know what I mean. Seniyah's mother said they had been at the hospital for two days and hadn't seen Ms. Paige since she dropped some stuff off on Saturday."

The new information made him more than a little concerned. *How will Paige handle the loss of Seniyah's baby?* he wondered. He hadn't seriously considered her a mental case, but the woman did have a furnished nursery and had, as Tara would say, "flipped the script" on him.

"I haven't talked to her in few days," he admitted and then picked up the phone. "But I'll call her office. I'm sure she's there by now."

The divas huddled around him in expectation, only to groan in disappointment when he told them Paige still hadn't made it in and probably wouldn't, since she'd been working at home lately. He thought that was the end, but the ladies had more in mind.

"Call her at home," Jasmine stated more than asked.

For their sake, he obliged. Once again they huddled around as he dialed Paige's home number. After eight rings, he disconnected.

"Come on, Dr. Simone. Since we don't know where she lives, we'll follow you. I have my brother's car," Jasmine announced, and the divas headed for the door. "What are you waiting for?" she asked when Sergio-Xavier didn't follow suit.

"Hold on, ladies. She's probably at an appointment," Sergio-Xavier said, with less certainty than before. "Let me make one more call."

The girls huddled back around him as he dialed his colleague. "Hey, man," he said when Kevin answered the line. "Did Paige lead praise and worship yesterday?" He maintained his smile, although Kevin's response gave him cause for more concern than he wanted to have for Paige. "All right. Thanks, man." The line went dead, but Sergio-Xavier continued talking. "Really? That's great. I'll give her a call later."

He prayed he sounded convincing. If he told them Paige had missed her scheduled praise and worship time, they'd panic, like he was about to.

"There's nothing to worry about," he assured them. He prayed he wasn't lying. "Ladies, relax and go back to school. I promise to make sure she calls you later today." He intended to keep that promise, even if he had to pin Paige down and press the phone to her ear.

Jasmine wasn't convinced. "Are you sure she's all right? Because it's just not like her to leave us hanging."

"Trust me on this. You'll hear from her today. Give me your cell number, and I'll make sure of it."

"All right," Jasmine said, relenting. "But you better. I mean, please call me."

"I promise, as long as you all promise to go back to school."

Jasmine conceded, "That's fair."

"What is it, Jasmine?" Sergio-Xavier asked after he entered her number into his iPhone, and she continued staring, like there was something she wanted say but didn't know how. "What's up?"

Jasmine looked back at the girls, and they nodded, as if giving their consent. All of them had the same unsure and vulnerable facial expression.

"About school. We know we're not four-point-oh students, and our attendance isn't the best. We need to work on our communications skills and get a better grip on the English language. And we may need to tone down our wardrobe, but just a little." Jasmine paused and took a deep breath. "We need some work, and it may take a miracle, but we've been thinking that maybe we shouldn't settle for junior college. Maybe we should try our luck at a regular university or a state college."

Sergio-Xavier imagined his grin resembled that of a proud father. "That's great. Are you serious?"

"Well, yeah. I mean yes," Jasmine continued with more confidence. "I picked junior college because that's what my brother did. That's what everybody we know does. We didn't think we were capable of more until DWAP. We figured since we did such a great job running our small business, with some knowledge from the university, we could start our own corporation. We're talking logos and franchises."

Sergio-Xavier chuckled as the girls exchanged high fives.

"We know it's going to take a miracle for us to get in, but we're thinking about giving it a shot," Jasmine said. "What do you think? Do you think we can do it?"

"Yeah, do you really think we can?" the others chimed in.

Fourteen fearful and expectant eyes, hanging on his every word, tugged at his heartstrings. These young ladies were truly remarkable. Why couldn't Paige see that? The mere fact that they considered stepping out of the box and not settling had earned them his respect.

"I believe you can do anything you set your mind to," he answered honestly.

"Thank you, Dr. Simone!" Jasmine exclaimed.

Sergio-Xavier had to lean against his desk to keep from falling over from the force of the group hug they lavished on him.

"Okay, Doc. You go check on Ms. Paige, and we're going back to school and to talk to a counselor. And don't forget to call me," Jasmine reminded him as they trotted out the door.

As excited as he was for the ladies, Sergio-Xavier couldn't savor the moment. He had to go and find Paige. Sure, he was angry and hurt, but he knew her well enough to know she wouldn't miss two days of work without calling, unless she couldn't call.

He hung his lab coat on the rack, and then, while calling a colleague to cover his afternoon clinic, he changed from a white dress shirt into a mock turtleneck sweater. While jogging down the stairwell to his car, Sergio-Xavier acknowledged something else but refused to admit what his heart already knew.

Chapter 29

The second he pulled in front of Paige's house, Sergio-Xavier's chest started pounding. The Lexus parked in the driveway confirmed his fears. Paige normally parked inside the garage. He turned off his vehicle and sprinted to the front door, terrified of what he might find inside. The doorbell chime made him aware that his body was shaking. He abandoned the doorbell and pounded on the door. "Paige!" he yelled.

When no response came after what seemed like hours of pounding, he turned the doorknob, and to both his horror and surprise, the door opened. Apparently, Paige hadn't locked the door when she returned home, or someone leaving hadn't bothered securing the residence. Sergio-Xavier's first thought was to pray, but his feet carried him inside before he could form words.

"Paige!" he called once inside the foyer. An uneasy silence greeted him as he continued down the hall and into the living room. He called her name again once inside the kitchen. Still no answer. To his relief, nothing appeared out of place except the cell phone lying on the counter. He went to check her bedroom, and just before reaching the door, the stench of human waste stopped him dead in his tracks. The one-name, one-word prayer he'd come to depend on filled his head, but Paige's name flowed from his lips. His breath caught, and temporary paralysis handicapped him. Finding Paige on the floor, lying on her back, with her head turned toward the door, soaking in her urine and vomit, chilled him to the bone. He held his breath until his trained eye scanned her neck and torso and identified respiration and a pulse. Before he inhaled again, Sergio-Xavier was on his knees beside her, shaking her.

"Paige, wake up!" He shook more vigorously after the heat from her forehead singed him. "Baby, please wake up."

She moaned his name and then began coughing.

With a careful, but firm grip, he lifted her upper body and positioned her back against his leg and her arms around her. He attempted to pull her disheveled hair from her face and discovered too late the yellow streaks were dried vomit. He took a closer look and saw that the front of her top was covered with the substance, and her jeans from the hem up were stained with old urine and with the fresh puddle on the floor, which was now lubricating his slacks.

For the moment his anger dissipated, and the pain of having loved and lost this woman lifted. "What happened to you?" he asked, choking back tears, once she stopped coughing.

She opened her eyes, and her head darted from side to side, like she was trying to get her bearings.

He braced her back with one arm and cupped her chin with his free hand, forcing her to look at him. For once Sergio-Xavier wished she'd use that vicious mouth of hers. "Talk to me, baby. Are you sick? Did you take any medication? Have you been drinking?"

"No," she mouthed.

"Tell me what's wrong. I'm listening," he said after wiping the single tear from her right cheek.

"I can't walk. It hurts," she finally answered. "I fell and twisted my ankle today."

He glanced downward at her bare feet. The right one was twice the size of the left one and discolored. "Why didn't you call someone?"

Paige pointed toward the far corner, where the cordless phone base had been disconnected from the wall jack. "I couldn't get to the phone, and I don't remember where I threw my cell phone."

"It's in the kitchen," he said, distracted. Paige wasn't making sense. The condition of her foot and her hygiene didn't correlate. "When did this happen?"

She hesitated and sniffled before answering, "Today, when I was leaving Seniyah's house."

Now Sergio-Xavier knew something wasn't right. "Did you also hit your head when you fell?"

"No, but I wished I had," she whimpered.

More concerned about her having a traumatic brain injury, Sergio-Xavier ignored the remark. "Paige, what day is it?"

"Saturday."

"What did you do today?"

"I went to Seniyah's house to talk to her about the baby, but it didn't go so well. As I was leaving, I tripped down the stairs. I came straight home and went to sleep after I disconnected the phone."

He knew there was more to the story by the way her head hung, but he wasn't going to push her. The time for him to know her business had passed. "Sweetheart, it is Tuesday afternoon. You've been in this room for four days."

Confusion covered her face.

"When was the last time you ate?"

She turned away. "The night we broke up."

"That's explains a lot." He stood and carried her to the bed. "Let's get cleaned up. You need to get to the hospital for tests to make sure you don't have a head injury. You're dehydrated, and you need an X-ray of that ankle. From the looks of it and your fever, you may have broken it and it may also be infected."

"I'm not going to the hospital," she announced while shaking her head. "I'd rather stay here and die by myself."

"You don't mean that," he said, setting her down on the bed.

"Yes, I do," she said just above a whisper. "I don't have anything to live for."

He hunched back down and tried to reason with her. "Paige, I know the death of Seniyah's baby has hit you hard, but you have to pick yourself up and keep living. You did the best you could for Seniyah. Now you have to move on."

Her shocked expression surprised him. "The baby died?"

"Didn't you know that?"

She shook her head from side to side but didn't shed any tears.

"Didn't you go to her house . . . ?" He let the statement hang. Maybe the time would come for him to hear the whole story, maybe not. Right now he needed to get her to the hospital. He stood again. "Look, either you allow me to help you get cleaned up and to take you in my car to the hospital, or I can call an ambulance and you can go as you are."

"Do whatever you want to do," she said defiantly. "I'm not going anywhere."

"Fine." Without another word, Sergio-Xavier stood and walked away.

"What are you doing?" she inquired when he starting searching her drawers.

"Looking for your underwear," he said, as if it was a normal occurrence.

"Why?"

"So I can put them on you after I bathe you." He held up a black pair and a bra. "How about these?"

She leaned up on her elbows. "No, you will not, and those will do just fine." Her voice was weak, but he heard her.

"Good. Now let's find something to wear." When he held up the black leggings and gray sweatshirt, she just nodded.

After placing the set of clean clothes and a pair of slippers in the bathroom, Sergio-Xavier realized the magnitude of his predicament, but it was too late to turn back now.

"Look, Paige, you need a bath, but I can't allow you to take one unattended. You're too weak, and you might have a head injury. Also, I'm sure you can't get those pants over your foot or get in and out of the bathtub without assistance. So help me out here."

Her expression changed from horror to relief. "I have some plastic chairs in the garage. I can sit on one in the shower. That way I can wash my hair too."

"Okay, but promise you won't try to stand."

"Promise you won't look." She lay her head on the pillow but then frowned and sat back up.

"I'll be right back. Don't move."

After setting the Keurig to brew some chamomile tea, Sergio-Xavier ran out to his car and removed the travel bag he kept a change of clothing in from his trunk. His steps were lighter now that he knew Paige wasn't in harm's way, but resentment wasn't far behind. Just days ago the woman had treated him like a dog after all he did was try to love her. Now he had to take the high road and be the one to help her. When she recovered, he was going to send her the bill for ruining his slacks.

He placed his travel bag in the foyer and then went into the garage to retrieve a plastic chair. He left the chair outside the bedroom, then grabbed his travel bag from the foyer, entered the kitchen, and took a garbage bag from a drawer and the brewed cup of tea from the Keurig. With his travel bag, the garbage bag, and the teacup in hand, he hurried back to Paige's bedroom.

"Here. Sip on this," he said, setting the cup on the nightstand. "You need some fluid, but take small, slow sips."

"Whatever you say, Dr. Simone."

He waited with his arms folded to make sure she complied, and to make sure she had enough strength to hold the cup. After she took a few sips, he continued the preparations for the big event. She'd sipped half the tea by the time he had the chair stationed in the shower, his travel bag and the garbage bag on the floor in front of the sink, and towels in close proximity for Paige's use.

He took the cup from her shaky hands, then carried her into the bathroom without preliminaries. "Let's get this show on the road. I mean, let's get you cleaned up," he said, editing himself after Paige soft nudged his abdomen.

He placed her in the chair, and they began what at times resembled a game of Twister, as he had to strip her while she was seated with the drawn shower curtain between them. For added privacy, Sergio-Xavier slammed his eyes shut and felt his way. As he tugged the soiled pants down her legs, he shook his head at the irony of it all. He'd had many fantasies of stripping Paige, but they had all included satin and lace. Not urine and vomit.

"I'm ready," she groaned after tossing the last piece of clothing out of the shower stall.

"I'll be right in here at the sink, washing up and changing my clothes. If you need help, call me. Don't try to get up. When I call your name, please answer, or else I'm coming in there, and I won't have my eyes closed," he warned.

"Whatever you say, babe."

His heart ached at the hopelessness in her voice, but he also remembered the venom that was capable of flowing from those same lips, and stepped away.

He collected her soiled clothing and put it in the garbage bag, then removed his own clothing and added it to hers. Every so often, he stood by the shower and called her name. With each answer, her voice grew stronger. He washed up in the sink and changed into the sweat suit in his travel bag with a watchful eye on the shower. He'd just finished tying his Reeboks when the water stopped. He rushed to the shower in time to hand Paige a dry towel.

"How are you coming along?" he asked as he rested against the wall closest to the shower, waiting for her to finish drying off so they could start tussling with her clothing again.

"Besides the throbbing in my foot, I actually feel a little better. I think the hot water did me some good." She threw the towel out, and one item at a time, he passed her clothing to her. "I'm ready," she announced, pulling the shower curtain back.

In one swift motion, Sergio-Xavier lifted her from the chair. "Let's go," he said and started for the bedroom once she had secured the underwear and leggings over her bottom.

When it was clear that he had every intention of carrying her out to his car, she said, "No, wait. I can't leave yet."

He continued walking. "We're not going to argue about this. You're going to the hospital, and that's final."

"I need to blow-dry my hair and brush my teeth first."

He thought she was stalling again, until he stopped and looked up at her head. Drops of water had already moistened the shoulders of her sweatshirt, and her breath reeked. He retraced his steps and went back into the bathroom, but this time he sat her on the toilet seat.

"Where's the blow-dryer?" She pointed to the cabinet below the sink.

"Will you do it for me?" she asked when he handed the plugged-in dryer to her.

While looking into those desperate and helpless eyes, he prayed one day soon his heart would no longer belong to her. "Of course, sweetheart. Relax, and I'll have you dry in no time."

She rested her forehead against the vanity and remained motionless while he dried her long tresses in less than eight minutes. "How did you learn to do that so fast?"

"I used to wear my hair long." He unplugged the dryer and, after positioning her over the sink, held her hair in place until she'd brushed her teeth and rinsed her mouth.

"Thank you." She reached for a tissue and dabbed her eyes. She was crying.

He scooped her up once again, but this time he didn't stop until he'd secured her in the passenger seat of his car. He ran back inside and discarded the garbage bag, grabbed her purse, and locked the house. Then he jumped behind the wheel, and they sped toward the highway.

Arriving at the emergency room in the arms of a lead staff physician worked in Paige's favor. She was whizzed through the registration and triage process and received an X-ray within thirty minutes of her arrival. Dr. Simone didn't identify Paige as his girlfriend to the hospital staff, but he was certain the constant physical contact between them implied it. Addressing her as "sweetheart" didn't help, either, but he couldn't stop himself. Seeing her so vulnerable had touched the part of him that still loved her.

He brushed her hair away from her face and kissed her forehead, then stood to leave when the nurse left the room after starting the IV fluid. "You're in good hands.

I'm going to take off now. Your ankle isn't broken, but you have a bad sprain. A couple of bags of fluid, and you'll be good to go, but follow the discharge instructions and stay off of that ankle."

"You're not going to stay and take me home?"

He pressed past her expression of shock. "No. The staff notified your mother, since you listed her as your emergency contact. She'll be here soon."

"Wait a minute," she pleaded before he could step away. "What made you come looking for me today?"

He knew this woman too well. She wanted an answer he could no longer give. "The DWAP ladies barged into my office today. They were worried about you because you missed their session last night and you weren't at the office this morning." He sat back down and pulled out his cell phone. "That reminds me. I promised Jasmine you'd call her." He dialed the number and placed the phone against her ear. "Be nice. They're really concerned about you."

He waited patiently while Paige assured Jasmine she was fine but would be confined to the house for a while. Her voice was upbeat, but he noticed the water in the corners of her eyes and looked away.

"Thanks." She pulled her head away from the phone, and he ended the call. He clipped the phone to his belt and went to stand, but she grabbed his hand. "I need to tell you about what happened at Seniyah's house."

Sergio-Xavier needed to put some distance between them, but her trembling lower lip indicated Paige needed to talk. "Were you with her when she lost the baby?" he asked and at the same time reached for her hand.

"I didn't know about that until you told me." Her hand rested on his as she then related the events at Seniyah's house.

Although he remained composed, Sergio-Xavier's heart broke for her. Despite her many faults, Paige had a good heart and didn't deserve that type of treatment. He'd tried to warn her, but she'd refused to listen. Now he couldn't help her.

"I'm sorry to hear that," he said, placing the tissue box within her reach.

"I didn't mean what I said to you the other night," she admitted after blowing her nose and wiping her face. "Honestly, I don't remember everything I said, but what I do remember, I didn't mean. It wasn't from my heart. I was just angry because I didn't like what you said. You were trying to tell me the truth, but I didn't want to hear it, so I lashed out, but I didn't mean it. Really, I didn't." More tears flowed as she declared, "I love you."

Relief washed over Sergio-Xavier, for he now knew for certain that the things Paige had said weren't from the heart, but that was as far as it went.

"I know you didn't mean it," he said, standing up. "But that's the problem with words—they have the power to take you places you never intended to go, and to make you stay longer than you want. If Seniyah's betrayal had never happened, you wouldn't be admitting your mouth got you into trouble. I believe you care about me, but you need something I can't give you, and until you find it, you're not good for me. You're not even good for yourself." He started backing away from the bed. "I'll call and check on you from time to time, and I will keep my promise to DWAP, but beyond that, we're done."

He practically ran from the room to keep from yielding to his emotions and losing his resolve. Paige needed to rely on the faith she sang and bragged about to find her way. He loved her, but he wasn't her savior.

Chapter 30

"Paige, baby, can you please explain to me again why you have a furnished nursery and you don't have a baby? According to you, you're not even doing what it takes to get a baby," Paige's mother said from the doorway of her bedroom. She'd been staying with Paige since Sergio-Xavier phoned her from the hospital three days ago.

"Mama, I told you. It's complicated." Paige hugged her pillow, hoping her mother would drop the subject. She wasn't ready to explain the humiliating circumstances surrounding her ordeal. Paige was having a hard enough time accepting the facts herself.

Her mother stepped into the room and sat on the bed. "It can't be any more complicated than me and your dad having to swap out your mattress and scrub vomit off the floor."

"I appreciate everything you've done, and I'll pay Dad for the mattress. Please, Mom, just let it go." Her mother's tender touch as she rubbed her back soothed Paige, as it had done when she was a child and was suffering from a cold. Paige could enjoy the soft strokes forever, if only her mother wouldn't ask questions.

"Don't worry about the mattress. Dr. Simone had that delivered."

Paige's head shot up.

"He's the one, isn't he?" When Paige nodded, she continued, "I knew it when he called from the hospital. He was too concerned about you. Also, an emergency room doctor wouldn't know the condition of your bedroom or the size of your mattress. He also wouldn't call me every day to check on you. That man cares deeply for you, and you say you love him. What I don't understand is why you aren't talking to each other."

A soft smile rested on Paige's face. She'd no idea that Sergio-Xavier was checking up on her. When he walked out of that hospital room, she thought he no longer cared. That was the first time she needed his strength and comfort and he didn't freely offer himself to her. Paige didn't have the chance to tell him how grateful she was to him for coming to look for her. Paige had honestly wanted to die, but when she heard Sergio-Xavier's voice calling her name throughout the house, her desire to live had been sparked.

"Come on. You better talk to me before I call those prayer warriors from your church back over here," her mother said, rousing Paige from her reverie.

Last night Reyna and Marlissa had brought Mother Scott, First Lady Drake, and the entire intercessory prayer team by the house. They had anointed Paige with oil and then had prayed, sung, spoken in an unknown language, and beaten the tambourine until Paige lay flat on her back with her hands in the air, surrendering to the Lord. "That ought to do it," Mother Scott had declared before she left. "She's gon' be all right now."

Paige appreciated those bossy women now more than ever, because honestly she didn't have the strength to pray for herself. She couldn't even remember the words to her favorite worship songs.

Paige turned onto her back and maneuvered into an upright position with her back against the pillows. "Mom, I messed up," she began. "I messed up a long time ago and haven't been right since," Paige admitted for the first time.

"You haven't known Dr. Simone that long, so this has to be deeper than him." Her mother pulled the covers back and sat in the bed beside her. "I'm listening. I can't wait to hear how Dr. Simone, the nursery, and that sprained ankle all fit together."

Paige leaned her head against her mother's shoulder and exposed thirteen years of heartache. She'd never shared with her mother about the abortion and the torment she'd endured on a daily basis. It took what seemed like hours to get from the old, discolored photo in her nightstand to why Sergio-Xavier would express his concern for her over the telephone only through a third party.

"Mama, I hate myself for what I did. I have been trying so hard to clean up my mess. I do love the Lord, but I don't attend church so much because I love being there. I go to church so much because I'm trying to show God how sorry I am. I wanted to prove that I'm not selfish. That's why I volunteer so much and give so much away. That's why I dressed like a nun. I wanted to prove that I was humble and not high-minded anymore. In the process, I started judging and condemning everyone around me, because that's how I felt about myself. I don't know who I am anymore. I was so busy seeking a second chance and salvation in Seniyah's baby, I was blinded to the fact that she was using me. I didn't pray about helping her. I just jumped in, and honestly, I did have plans to take and raise her baby.

"I think I started falling for Sergio-Xavier the first time I laid eyes on him. He challenged my misguided beliefs and corrected my ill-formed judgments. I didn't like him for it, but I needed him to help open up my understanding. I can honestly say I am a better person because of him, but I chased him away because he called me on my mess. He loved me beyond my issues. He was even going to build me a house some day."

Paige's mother rubbed her back and allowed the tears, sobs, and subsequent tremors to flow without urging her to stop. When the purging ended, Paige felt as if a weight had been lifted. Her heart still ached, but for the first time ever she sensed that a real healing was possible for her.

"Are you finished? Did you get it all out?" her mother asked after a period of time.

Paige started to nod but then uttered the answer instead. "Yes."

"I knew you were driven by something, but I could never figure out what. Okay, so you had an abortion. So what? Millions of other women have done the same thing and been forgiven and have gone on to enjoy a wonderful life. Seems to me, the problem you have is with forgiving yourself for making a selfish decision. You're not the same person you were back then. You've grown. That's the way life is. We live and we learn from our mistakes. Trust me, you've learned your lesson. Now I have a question for you."

"I'm listening," Paige mumbled against her mother's chest.

"I know it's crazy for you to have a fully furnished nursery and to belong to several online parent groups when you don't have any children, but did the thought ever occur to you that perhaps God is preparing you for your own family? God never intended for Seniyah's baby to occupy that nursery. That's evident by the fact that the baby no longer exists. You just said that you're a better person because of Sergio-Xavier and that the man was ready to build you a house. It could be you decorated the right room, but in the wrong house."

Paige's head jolted forward. She stared at her mother, speechless. Those ideas had never crossed her mind. Sergio-Xavier had told her he'd called his contractor, but she'd been too consumed with her own plans to put much stock in it. He wanted children, and he wanted them with her. He'd said as much in his own way the night they broke up.

"I prayed. How did I miss all that?" Paige posed the question more to herself than to her mother.

"You were praying, but you weren't praying for the right thing, and you weren't waiting for God to answer," her mother explained.

Paige smirked. "And I thought *you* were the baby Christian. It doesn't matter now, because my man is gone. I ran him off."

"You didn't run my son-in-law off. You may have backed him into a corner, but he's long from gone. Don't worry about him. Just work on you."

Paige's head fell on her mother's chest again. She wasn't crying. Instead she was thinking that Sergio-Xavier wasn't the only person she owed an apology to.

Trying to exhibit some level of independence, Paige balanced her body on the crutches and started toward the front door. The rapid chimes from the doorbell meant the divas had arrived. Sergio-Xavier wasn't the only one making daily checks on Paige. Jasmine and the ladies called every day, and sometimes twice a day, to update Paige on DWAP's outreach efforts and the liquidation of their company. Not one call ended without them offering to lend her a hand around the house or to run an errand at the store. When the ladies had called in a panic this morning, Paige had suggested they all come over to the house for dinner.

"You go sit down in the living room. I'll get the door," her mother said as Paige maneuvered past the kitchen.

Before obeying, Paige admired the soul food meal, complete with German chocolate cake, spread out on the center island. "Thanks so much, Mama. You really outdid yourself with this spread. You made my favorites—fried chicken and catfish."

A smile of complete contentment spread over her mother's face. "No need to thank me. The good Reverend Doctor Simone ordered this when I talked to him this afternoon and told him those girls from the high school were coming over. The delivery came while you were in the shower. He said after tending to you all day, I didn't need to be slaving over a hot stove."

Paige stood there, speechless, until the doorbell chimed again. *I love that man,* she thought as she sat down in a wingback chair in the living room and tried to get comfortable. Somehow, they had to find their way back to each other.

"Hey, Ms. Paige!" the divas chorused when they appeared in the living room.

Paige was used to their loud voices, but the hugs the divas showered on her caught her by surprise. All seven of her mentees were practically glowing from being in her presence.

"Hi, ladies. It's good to see you. I've missed you." That was the truth. Teaching the junior entrepreneur class was one of the few activities Paige felt passionate about.

Although there was an empty sofa and love seat available, the girls chose to hunch down and sit around Paige's chair.

"Thank you for allowing us to come over. We just can't figure out what to do." As always, Jasmine spoke for the group. "We only have ten days to pull this off, and we want to do this right." She placed an open portfolio on Paige's lap.

The intensity with which the young ladies had selected dresses for the recognition dinner made Paige laugh. One would have thought the girls were planning a wedding.

"We've narrowed it down to these five." Jasmine turned to the folded pages.

"What do you think?"

"They're beautiful," Paige answered honestly. The dresses the girls had chosen were beautiful and appropriate for the occasion. Two were short and three were long, but they all were classy.

"Are you sure? We don't want to embarrass you, and we don't want to look cheap and ghetto, either," Jasmine told her.

Paige realized the ladies were dead serious. The seven pairs of eyes staring at her told her the girls desperately needed her approval and wanted to make her proud. Flashes of past conversations ran through her mind, causing her heart to ache. The seven beautiful young women huddled around her had been seeking her acceptance from the beginning, but she hadn't been able to see it or hadn't cared.

"Ladies," she finally responded after swallowing the lump in her throat, "the dresses are lovely. I would wear any one of them."

The girls let out a collective sigh and relaxed.

"Okay, good. My cousin will start on them tomorrow. We already have shoes picked out," Jasmine added.

"You guys have put a lot of thought into this. I'm impressed," Paige admitted. She noticed the girls were exchanging nervous glances. "What is it?"

Jasmine cleared her throat. "We've been thinking about other things too. Like skipping junior college and going straight to the university. We already started filling out applications. Our counselors say we don't have the grades for a scholarship, but if we get in, we'll be eligible for financial aid. We can get part-time jobs to help cover some of the cost."

"Dinner is ready," Paige's mother called from the archway leading to the kitchen. "Come eat this good food Dr. Simone sent over before it gets cold."

"You don't have to tell me twice," one of the girls said and pulled out a bottle of antibacterial gel and passed it around.

Paige giggled to keep from crying while watching the girls get cleaned up for dinner. As each one trotted off to the kitchen, a unique characteristic was revealed to her. Something special that she'd overlooked before.

Jasmine stayed behind. "Do you need some help, Ms. Paige?" she offered, holding out her hand.

Paige smiled and prayed her sadness didn't show through. "I'm fine. I'll be in there soon. Eat all you want, but save me a chicken wing and a piece of catfish. Oh, and don't y'all dare cut that cake until I get in there."

"I got your back, Ms. Paige." Jasmine giggled and then walked out of the living room and joined the rest of the gang.

Once alone, Paige buried her face in her hands and cried, "Oh, God, what have I done?"

The power of Jasmine's words had shattered the remaining disillusions she had about the young women, whom she'd considered ghetto and hopeless. From day one, they had had her back, but she hadn't been able to see it, because of her obsession with Seniyah. They had genuinely cared for her and had proved it on several occasions. It was because of their aggressive, unpolished behavior that Sergio-Xavier had come to her rescue. It was they who had reminded her that she didn't have to hide behind her clothes. When she was sad, they had taken it upon themselves to cheer her up.

Unlike Seniyah, these ladies hadn't set out to use her under false pretenses. They had wanted only her knowledge, in hopes of making a better life for themselves. They had valued her opinion and had hung on her every word. The power of success and failure for those girls lay in her hands, and so far Paige hadn't invested in their success.

Father, forgive me for mishandling your children.

For the remainder of the visit, Paige chatted and laughed with the girls, but inwardly she prayed for a way to invest in them and help them accomplish their goals. She had an idea, but after the Seniyah fiasco, she had learned that Proverbs 3:5–6 was an actual verse to live by, and not just a nice saying to quote.

Confirmation came just as she settled into bed; she had to talk to Sergio-Xavier. If anyone could help her pull off her plan with such short notice, it was him. Plus, she missed him and wanted to hear his voice. Without any more thought on the matter, she dialed his cell phone.

He answered on the second ring. "Hello, Mrs. McDaniels. Is everything all right with Paige?"

Paige covered her mouth and giggled. Obviously, Sergio-Xavier had checked the caller ID and had thought it was her mother calling.

"Paige is doing great at the moment." When she heard his breathing accelerate, she released the one she'd been holding.

"Paige," he finally answered in a subdued tone. "You sound great. How are you?"

If he wanted to play games, so could she. "I would tell you, but my man might get jealous."

"What man?" he yelled into the phone.

"The one who bought me a new mattress, who calls my mother every day to check on me, and who sent that fabulous dinner over. He might have a problem with me conversing with my ex." The line was silent for so long, Paige thought he'd hung up. "Sergio-Xavier, are you there?"

"Of course. I'm always here for you. I was trying to come up with an excuse for my actions, but there isn't one, other than the obvious."

She grinned at the phone. Her mother was right; her man was not gone. He had just needed some space and time to heal. "I love you to, and thank you for everything, but that's not why I called. I need your help."

"Anything for you, sweetheart. Just say the word and I'll move mountains for you, or at least try to."

Even through the sarcasm, she heard the sentiments his heart would never acknowledge again. "Oh, that's so sweet. If you were here, I'd kiss you."

"Ms. McDaniels." His public voice had surfaced. "Stay focused and get to the point."

Once Paige poured out her plan, a sense of peace overwhelmed her and she had to stop talking and shed silent tears.

"Wow, babe. That's wonderful," Sergio-Xavier said after a long silence. "I am so proud of you for even considering such a thing. I think you're on the way to identifying your purpose. You're growing. Now stop crying. We have a lot of work to do in ten days."

"Do you think we can pull it off?"

"Ms. McDaniels, we don't have to be a couple to work together on a worthy project. We can accomplish anything together as long as you keep your mouth shut."

Chapter 31

Paige ended the weekly staff meeting, which she conducted remotely through Skype, and limped into her kitchen for a cup of tea. Her ankle had healed enough for her to hang up the crutches, but the limp would remain for a few days. Thanks to Skype, Paige had been able to keep an active office presence. Despite her physical absence, new listings had been pouring in steadily, and thanks to record low interest rates, more qualified buyers were dropping in. The real estate office seemed to be taking care of itself, which had freed Paige to focus on her new project.

In the three days since embracing what God had placed in her heart, she'd had minimal sleep. She'd worked on the computer throughout the night, electronically submitting letters and requests and filling out forms. During the day, Paige had made so many phone calls, her mouth had run dry, but she'd never complained.

"Sergio-Xavier's mother will be here any minute," Paige told her mother, who was busy arranging refreshments.

"I know. You've told me three times," her mother teased. "I don't know why you're so nervous. You've already met your future mother-in-law once."

Paige stopped short of rolling her eyes. "Ma, this is business, not personal, and she's not the only one coming."

Sergio-Xavier had suggested that Paige and Teresa work together on the project for the girls. Paige was hesitant until she learned that Teresa Simone practiced business law as a profession. So far the information Teresa provided had proved invaluable and had cut the red tape to almost nil.

Tyson's mother was also coming to the planning session. As a socialite and the wife of a judge, Beverly Stokes had mastered raising money. Pastor Drake would provide spiritual advice and would represent the faith community. The president of the local board of Realtors had also been invited. In all, Paige had selected seven people to help bring her vision to fruition. What was amazing to her, and definitely God's doing, was that no one had declined her invitation. Even the prayer warriors were on board.

Sergio-Xavier had also been invited, but she doubted he'd come. He'd said he preferred to work behind the scenes, without an official role, to avoid a conflict of interest later. For once, Paige clearly heard him and accepted it without jumping to conclusions.

So that she could focus solely on administrative matters, Paige had designated Reyna and Marlissa the program coordinators. Paige had complete confidence they would plan an event the ladies would remember forever.

"Don't worry, baby. This new venture is going to be everything you want it to be and more," her mother assured her just as the doorbell chimed.

As she walked to the front door to answer it, an excitement Paige hadn't experienced in years settled in her spirit. Ten minutes later, when Teresa Simone and Beverly Stokes handed her the contributions they'd collected in just three days, Paige cried like a baby.

"When God gives a vision, He always gives provision," Teresa reminded Paige while rubbing her back.

Paige frantically searched the neighborhood park for the little boy with hazel eyes. She'd been worried sick about him since he ran away from her. She had to find him and apologize for scaring him the other day. She searched the slide and the jungle gym and the sandbox. Nothing. Giving up, Paige slumped in one of the swings and cried.

"Hey, lady. Stop crying."

Paige's head snapped up at the soft pat on her arm. It was the little boy, but this time he wore a black SpongeBob shirt.

"Hey, baby. Where have you been? I was worried about you."

The boy smiled, and Paige noticed he was now missing a tooth.

"Don't worry about me, I was with my father. He takes very good care of me."

Paige scanned the play area and didn't see a man or woman standing around. "Well, I'm just glad you're okay. Would you like for me to push you on the swing again?" She started to stand but sat back down on the swing when the boy started shaking his head from side to side.

"My father is waiting. I can't stay long. I want to tell you something."

"Okay." Paige nodded, trying to hide her disappoint-ment. She needed to spend time with the little boy to take her mind off of her problems.

"I'm not mad at you for sending me away to my father. I like living with my father. I'm happy."

"I don't understand."

"Look at me." The boy's voice dropped an octave. "Look at me real good."

The longer Paige stared at the boy, the more she saw herself and Tyson. His high, rounded forehead mirrored hers, but the circular face belonged to his father. The long, narrow nose with the mole on the left side belonged

*to her, and so did the rounded ears. The child's small
hazel eyes sparkled brighter than Tyson's, but the long
eyelashes belonged to her. Paige covered her mouth and
began weeping.*

*Little arms wrapped around her neck and squeezed.
"Don't cry." The child's voice returned to normal. "I
forgive you. Let me go so your other babies can come."*

*Her cries grew louder, and Paige felt larger, stronger
hands squeezing her.*

*"Good-bye. I forgive you," the child said, and he
repeated those words until his voice faded away.*

"Good-bye." More words flowed from Paige's lips in
a steady stream long after she was fully awake from the
dream. She lay flat on her back, staring up at the ceiling,
waiting for the tears to fall. None came. She turned onto
her left side and squeezed her pillow. Still nothing. Finally, she sat up and removed the old, faded sonographic
image from the nightstand drawer. The tears flowed
heavily then, and so did the giggles.

For the first time since that fateful day, Paige didn't
feel guilt and condemnation. Instead, joy and laughter
overwhelmed her. Without any consideration of her
recovering ankle, Paige got out of bed and went forth in a
personal praise and worship service.

Chapter 32

"Ms. Paige, you've got to hold your head up straight, or else your twist is going to be lopsided," Jasmine warned. At the last minute, Paige had decided to change things up and wear a French twist for the big event.

Paige was trying to keep still, but the anticipation was too much to contain. Her future and the future of the seven giddy young ladies roaming around her house, getting dressed, depended on this evening's success. This was a genesis for them all. In ten days, with the help of her newly established board, she had doubled her original goal, and the checks were still coming.

"I'm trying," Paige whined, "but I'm just too excited."

"It's not like you haven't been to a fancy dinner before," one of the girls commented.

"You're right," Paige readily agreed before she let it slip that tonight wasn't just a fancy dinner with her and Sergio-Xavier. She changed the subject. "I'm so glad you guys suggested getting dressed over here. Y'all know I needed some help deciding on a dress that would look good with flats." With her ankle still being a little sore, Paige didn't want to risk reinjuring it by wearing heels.

"That emerald-green, strapless dress is bangin'," Jasmine hollered. "Dr. Simone is going to love that. Even in those flats your legs look good."

"Whatever, ladies," Paige said, brushing off their teasing, because she agreed. She'd Sergio-Xavier in mind when she express ordered the knee-length dress online.

Although they talked on the phone daily about the project, not once had she and Sergio-Xavier discussed their status, and she hadn't seen him since he walked out on her at the hospital. Instead of dwelling on his physical absence, Paige rested on the comfort that Teresa had given her before leaving after the board meeting. "He wouldn't have sent me here if his heart wasn't with you," Teresa had said on her way out the door.

Paige felt like a proud mother as she visually inspected the young women around her. Jasmine was right; her cousin could sew. The dresses were masterfully tailored to accent each girl's figure. The young ladies looked fabulous, but something was missing. *That's it!* Paige thought after further visual inspection of their hair. For the first time since she'd met them, the divas were all wearing their natural hair color. A few tracks and hairpieces had been attached here and there, but all of these matched their natural color.

Paige giggled at the irony of it all. Tonight she'd planned on asking Jasmine to spray some green in her hair to match her dress.

"You're not losing your mind, are you, Ms. Paige?" Jasmine teased when the doorbell sounded.

"He's here," one of the ladies announced and then headed for the front door. The remaining girls squeezed in front of the full-length mirror for one last dress and hair check, and then followed suit.

Paige retrieved a little plastic Baggie from the nightstand and grabbed her purse before joining them. When she reached the living room, the ladies were admiring the wrist corsages Sergio-Xavier had presented to them.

"Dr. Simone, you think of everything. If things don't work out with you and Ms. Paige, we'll take you," one of the girls teased.

Paige cleared her throat to alert the divas to her presence before she'd have to beat one of them down for flirting with her man, even if they weren't officially together. "Good evening."

The divas rushed over to Paige and showed her the floral box. She only half listened to them rant and rave about the corsages; her eyes were glued on the fine man in the black tuxedo, with the dimple.

"Oh, hi, Paige," Sergio-Xavier responded casually, but the rapidly pulsating vein in his neck betrayed him.

"Ms. Paige, I think this one must be for you." Jasmine had to say it twice before Paige heard her and looked down at the beautiful red rose corsage. "Let me pin it on for you."

Jasmine's body blocked Paige's unobstructed view of Sergio-Xavier, but she still managed to maintain eye contact with him while Jasmine had pinned on the flowers.

"What do you think, Dr. Simone? Did I do it right?" Jasmine asked over her shoulder.

"It's lovely, simply perfect," he answered, never breaking eye contact with Paige.

Paige blushed. "Can Dr. Simone and I have a moment alone, please?"

The girls left the room, but not before warning Sergio-Xavier not to try anything frisky.

"Those ladies are too much—," Paige began, but Sergio-Xavier cut her off with a soft kiss on the lips. "Have you forgiven me?" she asked after returning the kiss.

His arms rested around her waist. "Any lingering harsh feelings were dissolved the second I saw you in this dress. You're absolutely stunning. I am so grateful this house is full of people right now."

Her heart knew the truth, but Paige needed to hear him say it. "That's just physical."

"You can't begin to imagine how much I've missed being near you," he admitted, drawing her closer. "To answer your question, yes, I love you. I never stopped. I needed to give you some space to resolve your issues and release the guilt and condemnation you'd been carrying. As much as I love you, I can't heal you. Only God can do that. I had to move out of the way so I wouldn't be an obstacle, but I was never far away. I also needed time to nurse my wounds and to make sure my heart was in the right place and attached to the right person. "

She stepped from his embrace and reached for his hand. "I have something to show you." She placed the Baggie in his hand.

He held it up and saw that there were ashes inside it. "What's this?"

"I burned it," she answered without emotion. "I burned the old ultrasound picture. I let it go." She didn't have the chance to read his facial expression before he collected her in his arms.

"I am so proud of you," he whispered repeatedly in her ear.

"Hate to break this up, but shouldn't we be leaving? I don't want to be late for my first fancy dinner. We still need to take pictures," Jasmine announced.

Paige and Sergio-Xavier broke their embrace to find that the divas had clutch purses and camera phones in hand, ready to take pictures.

"Ladies, put those away," Sergio-Xavier said between chuckles. "I promise there'll be plenty of opportunities to take pictures at the restaurant."

"Oh, okay," they said, almost in unison. In a nearly synchronized motion, the ladies stuffed the phones inside their purses. "We're ready," they chorused.

Sergio-Xavier walked to the front door and held it open for them, but the divas didn't move. Instead, they looked back at Paige and waited for her to lead the way. Paige thanked Sergio-Xavier for holding the door open; the divas did likewise as they exited the house.

Outside at the limo, all eyes were on Paige again. The ladies appeared to concentrate on how Paige first sat on the seat and then lifted her legs into the limo. Each one did the exact same thing and then thanked the chauffeur, as Paige had done.

"They're imitating you," Sergio-Xavier whispered in Paige's ear.

"I know," she said, reaching inside his jacket for his handkerchief. "I hope I don't let them down."

"You won't."

Near the end of the thirty-minute ride, Jasmine pulled out a sheet of paper and the girls huddled around her.

"What's that?" Paige wanted to know.

"It's the table place setting I pulled from online. We're just reviewing it so we won't come across as not having any class. You know, using the dinner fork on the salad."

Paige couldn't wait to see how they'd react when they found out the true purpose behind the evening.

Chapter 33

"Wow!"

"OMG! We're right on the beach!"

"This is incredible."

Paige's chest swelled with pride as she listened to the girls' approval as they rode the elevator to the second level of the beachfront restaurant. Due to the incredible response, the entire upper level had been reserved for the newly formed nonprofit organization Divas with a Purpose. Paige's vision for the organization extended beyond a high school business and entrepreneurship class. Her goals included mentoring at-risk young ladies in business and in life skills and community outreach. She wanted to go beyond college preparedness and offer the girls financial assistance to further their education. Each year the organization would select seven young ladies and train them in everything from personal hygiene to public speaking and career planning.

"Look at that!" one the girls exclaimed, pointing at the banner hanging over the sign-in table. "That has our name on it."

While the ladies admired the logo that Paige's brother had created, Paige checked in at the contribution table. She reached into Sergio-Xavier's jacket again for his handkerchief when Teresa showed her the check from the Simone Family Community Fund and Beverly Stokes announced the total sum she'd collected from the superior court judges. As Paige was standing there, people, some of whom she'd never seen before, stopped at the table and placed checks in the contribution box.

Sergio-Xavier rubbed her back. "Come on, sweetheart. Let's look around."

The ladies accosted Paige before she took a single step. "Ms. Paige, what's going on?" one of them asked. "Why are you crying? Is something wrong?"

"Everything is perfect," Paige told them, then wiped her face and interlocked her arms with two of the girls. "Come on. I have a surprise for you."

Paige entered the banquet room and stood there in complete awe. Reyna and Marlissa had done an outstanding job of decorating the room in vibrant colors that matched the printed programs on the tables. The banner hanging above the head table read DWAP FIRST ANNUAL SCHOLARSHIP BANQUET. The room was filled nearly to capacity with agents from her office. Both Kevin and Tyson had filled tables with people from the hospital and Tyson's law practice. Pastor Drake and Restoration Ministries occupied two tables, and Pastors Reggie and Julia from Sergio-Xavier's church had filled two more tables. Members of the Simone family took up at least four tables. Paige's musical idol, Marcus, had even brought his family out for the occasion.

Paige walked past the "prestigious" people and the live band and continued on to the most important tables in the room.

"Ms. Paige, what are all these people doing here?" Jasmine asked as she and the other girls followed closely behind. "Who are these people?"

Paige stopped in her tracks. "They're here because they're investing in your future," Paige answered, knowing the girls wouldn't understand. Then she continued on. She heard a loud collective gasp behind her when she finally arrived at the most important tables.

"Mama, what are you doing here?" one of the girls asked.

"Grandma, is that you?" another asked.

"How did my brother get here?" Jasmine wanted to know.

"Daddy?"

Paige stood back and watched each diva's reaction to seeing her parent or guardian and family members seated near the head table. She'd assigned Mother Scott and First Lady Drake the task of going out onto the highway and into the hedges to compel the families to come. Paige could only imagine what the prayer warriors had done and said to get the families on the bus the church had sent for them. It didn't matter to Paige that they wore jeans and miniskirts, had tattoos and body piercings, and smelled like smoke. The important thing was that they were there to support their children.

After hugs, kisses, and a few tears, Paige shook hands with everyone and personally thanked them for coming. She paused at the end of the table and gave Mother Scott and First Lady Drake a high five. The prayer warriors had the Bible open and a bottle of anointing oil on the table.

"So, my baby is really going to college?" a mother asked.

"Of course," Paige answered and hastily excused herself. It wasn't time for that yet. "Come on, ladies. There are some people you need to meet."

Strategically, Paige led the girls around the room, introducing them to major contributors and then community leaders, and finally, to her parents and some of the people from her church. Paige was impressed with how well the ladies followed her lead and greeted everyone and held eye contact.

"Ms. Paige," Jasmine asked, once they were heading to their seats, "how did you get all these people to come out for us? I mean, the way people are smiling and taking pictures, it's like we're celebrities."

"Welcome to the life of a true diva," Paige teased. "Now, have a seat, and I'll be right back." Paige didn't consider herself a groupie, but her favorite artist was in the building, and he was a contributor. It would be rude for her not to thank him personally and ask for a photo. She beckoned the photographer and made a beeline to Marcus's table.

"How's your ankle holding up?" Sergio-Xavier had snuck up from behind while she was telling Marcus how much she enjoyed his music.

"Fine, and you're jealous," she answered back, only to have the two cousins double-team her.

"My little cousin has nothing to be jealous of, seeing how he and Lizzie had you sliding all over the floor," Marcus teased.

"Babe, make sure you hold on to your seat tonight," Sergio-Xavier added. "I wouldn't want you to reinjure that ankle."

Paige pouted and looked to Shannon for help.

"Sorry. I can't help you. Everyone in this family is fair game," Shannon explained.

Paige realized then Sergio-Xavier's arms were resting around her waist. He was making a public statement that she was his. "Come on. It's time you met my parents," she told him. She stepped away, but he didn't budge.

"I already did. In fact, your dad and I played golf together three days ago."

Paige's jaw dropped at the exact second Reyna announced that it was time for the program to begin.

Paige barely touched the four-course meal. Between the butterflies floating around inside her stomach and the

incessant questions from the ladies about why their pictures, along with brief bios, were printed in the program,
she couldn't eat. Sergio-Xavier's fingertips stroking her
calf underneath the table didn't help, either.

Paige uncrossed her legs and, ignoring Sergio-Xavier's
protest, reviewed her speech for the umpteenth time.

"Are you nervous?" Sergio-Xavier directed the question
to Paige, but the ladies were so tuned in to their mentor,
they became part of the conversation.

A chorus of "Yes," and "Of course" floated around the
table.

"I'm *so* nervous," Jasmine said, weighing in. "When
the waiter offered me a shrimp cocktail, I said, 'No thank
you. I'm too young to drink.'"

"And I ate my salad with the dinner fork," another girl
added. "Now I don't know what to do."

"Stop fretting," Paige said between giggles. "You're
doing fine, but I would advise you to have some tissues on
hand for later." She took a sip of water without explaining
and resumed reading her speech.

Reyna returned to the microphone and announced that
it was time for some entertainment.

"That's my cue! Hold on to your seat, sweetheart."
Sergio-Xavier pointed at the ladies. "One of you might
need to sit in her lap to keep her from falling off her seat."
He winked, and Paige rolled her eyes at him as he walked
away.

"What's Dr. Simone talking about?" one of the girls
asked, and then they all laughed in Paige's face once
she told them about Lizzie and the floor. The laughter
stopped once Sergio-Xavier began playing Lizzie with
precision. By the time he finished "The Greatest Love of
All," Paige and the divas were leaning to one side.

Tara recited the spoken word, and representatives
from the community gave congratulatory remarks and

well wishes to Paige and the DWAP board. When Beverly Stokes introduced Paige to make the presentations, Paige changed the setup at the last minute. Instead of standing at the podium alone, she brought the divas onto the raised platform with her. Ignoring their nervous comments, Paige positioned them on both sides and stood in the middle, at the mounted microphone.

She reached over and handed Sergio-Xavier her index cards, deciding to speak from the heart. "Before I present to them what they believe is a simple recognition certificate for their successful completion of the junior entrepreneur program . . . ," Paige said, then stopped and chuckled along with the audience. A moment later she continued. "There's something I'd like to say about these awesome young ladies you've so generously invested in."

Paige took a deep breath and then let the words flow. "When I first met you seven young ladies, honestly, I didn't like you. I had a misconception about what a diva is. I thought the term meant a sassy mouth, disrespectful, loud hair, long nails, spiked heels, tacky clothes, and an attitude of entitlement. For a long time I didn't allow myself to see you in any other light. I am ashamed to say, I didn't envision much of a future for you. I expected you to become another statistic. Your disposition made you difficult to handle, so I basically ignored you and went down the path of least resistance. For that I am so sorry." Paige's heart ached at the disappointment on their faces, but she wanted them to get the complete picture.

"Somehow, while riding on my high horse with my head in the clouds, things changed. I ceased being the mentor and became the mentee. I was no longer the instructor, but a student. I learned more from you than I was capable of teaching. Sure, I can teach you about numbers and balancing books, but the seven of you taught me about purpose—my purpose.

"From you I learned that a true diva is not just a mere woman who looks good on the outside, but a woman who is true to herself on the inside. She's a woman who may not have the best of everything but always makes the best of every situation. She doesn't lament that she doesn't have something, but multiplies what she's given and shares with others. She takes the lead and makes things happen, instead of waiting for a handout. A diva is that ride-or-die chick who will not hesitate to break rules and will go looking for a friend who's missing in action. Most importantly, a diva is not ashamed or afraid to ask for help, and she admits when she doesn't have it all together."

Paige paused and placed her arms on the shoulders of the two girls closest to her. "I'm almost twice your age, but I learned all that from you seven beautiful young ladies. Through you, I have learned my purpose, which is to mentor genuinely and to nurture more ladies like you. I have also rediscovered who I am. The first day we met was the beginning of my journey of finding my way back to me. For that, you're my hero."

Paige nodded toward the band, and piano notes filled the air. She proceeded to serenade the divas from her heart with Mariah Carey's "Hero." At the conclusion of the song, Paige didn't see the standing ovation she received. The divas nearly toppled her in a group hug. Sergio-Xavier had to brace her from behind to keep her from falling.

The divas were still shedding tears when Paige announced their names one by one and presented them each with a plaque and a certificate from DWAP for a full scholarship to the college or higher-learning institution of their choice. When she finished, Paige sat down before the girls could topple her. Sergio-Xavier's arms were no match for the stampede of hugs and kisses from the divas and their family members.

The scene left Paige both emotionally and physically spent, and she had to step outside on the balcony for some air. She smelled Sergio-Xavier's scent before she felt his arms around her waist.

"Since tonight is all about the divas, I won't propose formally to you this evening." He kissed her exposed neck. "Let this serve as an official notice that your days of being Ms. McDaniels are numbered."

"Oh, really?" She leaned to give him better access.

"Really. It'll take my contractor ten months to build the house."

She turned around, filled with a sense of naughtiness. "You know," she said, fingering his lips, "it's not like we're homeless. I mean, we don't have to wait for the house to have a place to live. I have a house. You have a loft."

He smiled that wicked grin she loved. "We don't have to have a big wedding, unless you want one."

"I hear small weddings and big receptions later are in."

"Yeah?"

"Yeah."

"There's only one major problem with this plan. Who's going to tell our mothers?"

"Oh yeah," Paige said, pouting, and then thought for a moment. Her mother would kill her if she eloped, and she was sure Teresa wanted a big wedding. "Let's send them a text on the way to the airport."

Hearty laughter erupted from Sergio-Xavier before he cupped her face and kissed her. "I love you, and I'm very proud of you. Now, let's go make some babies before all your eggs dry up."

She slapped his arm. "That's why I don't like you. Your mouth is always ruining the moment."

"If you'd been kissing me, my mouth would have been too occupied to ruin the moment."

Instead of a devising a comeback, Paige accepted the dose of her own medicine and gave the doctor what he wanted.

Discussion Questions

1. Paige's "unforgivable" sin was an abortion. Have you ever done something so horrible, you doubted God's ability to forgive you? Did you live in a state of self-condemnation and guilt? How did you learn to accept God's forgiveness?
2. Paige attended church regularly and led the congregation in worship. Yet she struggled with depression. Have you ever had to function in the church while feeling internally broken?
3. Paige prayed daily and mediated, yet her understanding of the Word was misguided. She prayed but failed to listen for the answer to her problems. Do you think this is common for Christians?
4. Paige found it easy to judge those who lived and worshipped differently from her. Is this common within the Christian community?
5. What are your thoughts on Sergio-Xavier's view of Christians vs. Christ followers?
6. Paige gravitated to Seniyah because Jasmine and the other divas were difficult to deal with. Have you ever settled on the "easy path" because you were afraid of difficulties? Do you feel that Christians assume the "easy road" is God and the road paved with complications is the devil?
7. Jasmine and the divas were anxious to learn and rise above the hood, but they didn't know how to. What do you feel is the faith community's responsibility for or obligation to at-risk youth?

8. Sergio-Xavier acknowledged that although he loved Paige, he wasn't her savior: she needed a healing he couldn't give her, and therefore he stepped back. In relationships, do you feel more people should adopt this view?

9. Did the real Seniyah surprise you?

10. What are your thoughts on Ms. King's comment about church folks being dumb and easy to take advantage of?

11. Paige included people from all walks of life to establish and fund her nonprofit organization, and she included the divas' families. Does this give credence to the saying "It takes a village and everyone can contribute something"?

About the Author

Wanda B. Campbell is an extraordinary and talented writer who brings creativity, a new sense of hope, and restoration through the healing power of God to the Kingdom by way of Christian fiction. She uses real-life, every-day issues to exhort, motivate, and give comfort. *Back to Me* is Wanda's ninth published title.

Wanda is a graduate of Castlemont High School in Oakland, California (Go, Knights!), Western Career College, and Boston Reed College. In addition to building a career in health care, she completed Christian ministry studies at the Leadership Institute at Allen Temple and is currently pursuing her bachelor's degree in biblical studies.

Wanda is a mother of three, currently resides in the San Francisco Bay Area with her family, and enjoys spending time with her grandson. Her hobbies include writing and reading, traveling, watching basketball and baseball, and collecting magnets from around the world.

To learn more about the characters in *Back to Me*, be sure to pick up copies of the novels *Silver Lining, Doin' Me,* and *Unresolved Issues.*

UC HIS GLORY BOOK CLUB!

www.uchisglorybookclub.net

UC His Glory Book Club is the spirit-inspired brain-child of Joylynn Ross, an author and the acquisitions editor at Urban Christian, and Kendra Norman-Bellamy, an author for Urban Christian. It is an online book club that hosts authors of Urban Christian. We welcome as members all men and women who have a passion for reading Christian-based fiction.

UC His Glory Book Club pledges its commitment to providing support, positive feedback, encouragement, and a forum whereby members can openly discuss and review the literary works of Urban Christian authors.

There is no membership fee associated with UC His Glory Book Club; however, we do ask that you support the authors by purchasing their works, encouraging them, providing book reviews, and, of course, offering your prayers. We also ask that you respect our beliefs and follow the guidelines of the book club. We hope to receive your valuable input, opinions, and reviews that build up, rather than tear down, our authors.

What We Believe:

—We believe that Jesus is the Christ, Son of the Living God.

—We believe that the Bible is the true, living Word of God.

—We believe that all Urban Christian authors should use their God-given writing ability to honor God and to share the message of the written word that God has given to each of them uniquely.

—We believe in supporting Urban Christian authors in their literary endeavors by reading their titles, purchasing them, and sharing them with our online community.

—We believe that everything we do in our literary arena should be done in a manner that will lead to God being glorified and honored.

We look forward to online fellowship with you.

Please visit us often at *www.uchisglorybookclub.net*

Many Blessings to You!

Shelia E. Lipsey,
President, UC His Glory Book Club